All material contained herein is Copyrighted © Payne & Taylor Publishing 2018. All rights reserved.

This is a work of fiction. Names, characters, businesses, places, events, locales, and incidents are either the products of the author's imagination or used in a fictitious manner. Any resemblance to actual persons, living or dead, or actual events is purely coincidental.

http://www.viviennesavage.com

XANDER

THE NOVA FORCE: BOOK 1

VIVIENNE SAVAGE

CHAPTER ONE

After serving a standard galactic year at a tiny naval base, Doctor Xander Vargas looked forward to his new assignment aboard the HMS *Jemison*. Fuck, every day of that sentence had been hell, each day confined to a small military clinic where he'd been lucky to receive a cybernetics patient once a week to occupy his time.

Then again, for what he'd done, maybe the punishment hadn't been severe enough. If not for a couple close friends, he'd still be there pushing a digital pencil through medical records.

Or in prison.

Before passing through decontamination, Xander double-checked the shine on his dress shoes and smoothed the front of his uniform. A combination of sterilizing lights and germicidal gases cleared him to board the space vessel. Like all other models developed by the Lexar—humankind's new alien overlords—it beat the technology developed by the scientists of Old Earth. But he also suspected a gerbil in a hamster ball could have improved the ships developed by their Terran ancestors.

This ship, though? It was a work of art, a real beauty, and his mounting excitement grew in leaping increments, since he'd never served on a Lexar ship. They'd only started rolling out the new ones to the human military branch within the last five years.

After a moment of waiting inside the airlock, the chamber opened to reveal his new commanding officer, Ethan Bishop's stocky frame lit by the blue overhead lights of the quarterdeck. "Welcome to the *Jemison*, Xander."

Xander saluted. "Commodore."

Chuckling, Ethan stepped forward and embraced him in a bear hug. "Forget the formality. It isn't every day that a man's closest friend comes to serve aboard his ship."

The uneasiness faded and tension drained from Xander's body. Home. He was finally home again, and with that in mind, he embraced Ethan in return. "Thank you. Words can't describe how much I appreciate this opportunity. You saved my ass by pulling me off desk duty."

As Ethan guided him inside, the airlock sealed behind them. "Once you see your new caseload, you won't be thanking anyone." The whirrs and noises of the ship's electronic interface were joined by a low hum, reminding Xander of how simultaneously noisy and quiet military ships could be.

"Trust me, you could work me through thirty-six-hour shifts and I'd still be thankful."

Ethan laughed. "Come on, I'll show you to Medical. But first, let me introduce you to Jem."

"Greetings, Doctor Vargas. I am Jem, the artificial intelligence personality of the HMS *Jemison*," a sensual female voice announced from the nearest audio aperture.

"Hello, Jem." Xander glanced at Ethan. "A custom voice instead of the default synthesized robot personality?"

"The Lexar weren't too amused by the change, but it's my ship now and I couldn't stand listening to it."

"I'm shocked. The Bishop I remember was a notorious cheapskate. So what's the cybernetics budget like here?"

Ethan chuckled and took the good-natured ribbing. "You'll be pleased with it, trust me. I've got more personnel coming over in the next couple of days, several with implants of some kind. It should keep you busy."

They passed through a maze of winding corridors, twists and turns down polished steel paths, taking a stairwell down to another passage instead of the lift. Xander tried unsuccessfully to memorize the way. "Each ship is so different. Space vessel architects are masochists in disguise."

"Well, you can rest assured that all these new Lexar cruisers will be the same. They're built to stay out longer and travel farther before refueling is required. We'll be hitting up all the border colonies and new terraform projects to check in on their progress. Make sure they're safe."

Concerned, Xander glanced at Ethan. "Is this because of those abandoned settlements they found?"

"Good, you're keeping up with the news. I have a feeling your medical experience will be needed on the ground assault team. The queen wants to know why her people are vanishing."

Xander had been a combat medic before he became a doctor, one of the corpsmen sent down on ground missions to keep their marines alive. He nodded, eager for any action that didn't involve a desk. "What about the Lexar? Are they helping?"

"They're allowing us to make the investigations, since only human colonies have been affected."

"In other words, it's our problem."

"Yep."

Fifty years had passed since the human race came into conflict with the sovereign alien presence in the Nova galaxy. The war between humanity and the Lexar had been brief, a crushing and humiliating defeat in which almost all United Nations of Earth had surrendered. There'd been no winning against the technologically advanced race of giants.

They'd had little choice but to fall under Lexar rule if they wanted to keep the new planets they'd colonized since leaving Earth. Once the peace treaty had been ratified, not much had changed, except their military had been absorbed into the Nova Force.

Ethan and Xander approached a group of medical personnel collected near the hydraulic doors to the infirmary. Three of the five automatically stood at attention. The other two drank Xander in like thirsty women crawling through a vast desert until their associates nudged them.

"Some things never change," Ethan muttered under his breath.

They moved into the medical wing's lobby, an open space painted canary yellow and lit by artificial solar panes spanning the walls. Those were designed to resemble windows, replicating sunlit scenes like serene forests or a lake bordering a flowering meadow.

"Smells a bit like a garden, but—"

"Oh, don't listen to him, sir. The Commodore didn't complain much when he was down here with the twilight flu two months back." A redheaded woman in a white lab coat joined them. She offered her hand. "Kathleen Hart. You must be the new cyberneticist Oshiro is so excited about."

"That's me. Pleasure to meet you, Doctor Hart." Xander glanced toward Ethan, grinning broadly from ear to ear.

"He won't admit it, but he likes the downtime away from command."

Ethan muttered beneath his breath, then cleared his throat. "Hart is our genetic technician and responsible for the care of our splicers. According to the bunk assignments, which I had *no* part in creating, you're also sharing a bathroom with her. So good luck with that."

Experience with his fellow officers of the female persuasion had taught Xander to never look forward to sharing bathroom assignments with them. They were brutal when it came to using the last of the hot water and showed no mercy to men who forgot to put the seat down.

"Ah, so he has finally arrived," the friendly voice of Xander's greatest mentor spoke from behind them, the man who was the father he'd never had.

The trio turned to face the chief medical officer. Little about the small man had changed since their last reunion a year ago, Oshiro standing a few inches shy of reaching Xander's chest—though considering his great height, the same could be said of most humans. Ethan was one of the few exceptions.

Oshiro smiled up at him. "Always a pleasure to see you, Xander." He glanced at Ethan and allowed a broader grin to surface. "I will take things from here, Commodore. You are relieved from our effeminate infirmary."

"Fine, but I get his company for breakfast."

Xander laughed and rubbed the back of his neck. "I'll be there."

Breakfast was the least Xander owed him. God, had it really been twenty years since Ethan recommended him to United Command as a prospect for medical school? Time had flown.

"Coming off shore duty, Xander? Ready for ship life or

wishing you were boots to ground again?" Hart asked after Ethan left.

"I like ship duty. Glad to be with the crew."

"Well, you can relax. The *Jemison*'s crew is bloody brilliant, so you have nothing to be anxious about."

"I think I'll take Xander around now, Kathleen." Oshiro touched Xander's arm.

Disappointment flitted briefly over the woman's features, but she nodded and stepped away. "It's almost end of shift, so I'll lead him to his quarters once you're done, if you'd like."

Oshiro nodded. "That will be fine." He gestured for Xander to follow and then led him down the wide corridor.

A uniformed young man strode toward them, the kind of guy who looked like he spent too long in front of a mirror styling his hair into a perfect pompadour before reporting to shift. He offered Oshiro a thin tablet.

"Doctor, I have the inventory review you requested. I just need your signature."

"Thank you, Jean-Claude. Please welcome Doctor Vargas. Corporal O'Reilly will be one of your technicians, Xander."

"Excellent. It's a pleasure to meet you, O'Reilly. I look forward to working together." Xander shook the corporal's hand firmly.

"An honor, Doctor Vargas. Your work in cybernetics has been inspiring. I heard you pioneered the recent advancements in synthetic veins and live nerve connections in artificial limbs."

"Jean-Claude has an interest in your field, as you can see." Oshiro passed the tablet back and smiled.

"I even read your article in the Galactic Cyberneticists Journal about neurocybernetic modification. Do you think they'll ever repeal the laws prohibiting cybernetic brain enhancement?"

As far as the UNE was concerned, brain modification was a strict no-no. It was one of the few medical morals the Lexar agreed with—to them, the brain was the sacred home of the soul. They didn't approve of humans using splicing to enhance themselves, but any alteration of the mind was blasphemy in their eyes.

"We made small steps in completely curing Alzheimer's Disease and epilepsy using cybernetics long ago, and I think, given some time, we can convince them to allow supervised research into other studies."

The kid brightened, hero worship in his eyes, words bubbling from him like a font of enthusiasm. "Amazing. I hope to be there when it happens. We have lots of cyborgs coming onboard, so I'm really looking forward to working with you, sir."

Oshiro cleared his throat. "Thank you, Jean-Claude. Please make sure everything is secured for our departure then report to Doctor Matthews before you check out. That will be all."

"Of course, Doctor."

When Jean-Claude ducked away to return to his duties, Xander glanced down to Oshiro and grinned. "That was a nice change from the ordinary."

"If it relates to the synthesis of man and machine, you won't find anyone more passionate." Oshiro brought him to a wide door which opened smoothly at their approach. Lights brightened inside.

"Welcome, Doctor Vargas, to your new laboratory," Jem announced.

One glimpse of the spacious cybernetics lab assuaged the remainder of Xander's worries. An array of lights hung suspended from the ceiling, connected to a retractable beam that repositioned on voice command, fully-automated by the ship's intelligence program.

It was physician's porn, the stuff of dreams that doctors like Xander wasted hours ogling on social media and hoped to work with at some point in their careers.

He stared, mouth slack.

"I suppose it's safe to assume you did not see anything of this sort on base," Oshiro commented.

Xander slowly turned his head to regard the older doctor, his eyes large. "No. I expected the usual from Ethan. Back where they stationed me in Valencia, the lead medical officer decided voice-assisted surgery was an unnecessary expense."

Though that had been a lie, hadn't it? He suspected the truth of the matter was that they hadn't wanted any Lexar tech on their base, shunning the alien race's advancements as much as they loathed the people.

"He's truly happy to have you aboard and so am I." Oshiro placed his hand on Xander's shoulder. "You have been missed."

Xander released the breath held in his chest and, for the first time in almost a year, felt the stirrings of hope. Of acceptance.

HART ATTACHED to him the moment he appeared in the hall following Oshiro's tour of the medical wing. "You don't know how much of a relief it is to have another adult among us, Xander. So, what are you like?"

"Excuse me?" he asked her in confusion.

"Tell me something about yourself. Doc's kept his

mouth shut tight and wouldn't utter a single word about you for good or ill."

"Well, that's a relief. What do you mean about having another adult in medical, though? Aren't we all adults?"

"I suppose so. Lilibeth arrived about two months ago from Sargossa. She's some sort of bloody prodigy, I guess you'd call her. Only twenty."

"That's young," he commented, maintaining his careful neutrality.

"Aye, it is. We'll soon have a full complement of Royal Marines onboard. Plenty of splicers for me and cyborgs for you. All right, the Wardroom is that way and staterooms form a horseshoe around it. The food's not bad and fried chicken night is always the busiest. Starboard side is where you'll find the CO, XO, and distinguished visitor suites. Port side is the rest of us. We're about halfway down."

"Thanks for the walk up, Doc—"

"Kathleen's fine, or Hart. We're all going to be good chums, so I'm all for canning rank and title formality if you're that sort. You seem that sort, at least." Something about her friendly smile encouraged him to do the same.

Xander grinned. "Astute observation."

"Anyway, I s'pose we'll all talk in the morning. Enjoy your new digs." And without so much as a flirtatious glance, Kathleen Hart turned and jogged away.

He liked her. No bullshit, and she hadn't flirted once.

Inside his assigned bunk, a blank canvas with sterile walls greeted him, waiting to be personalized. Crisp white sheets wrapped a double-sized mattress tucked into a headboard with a shelf. An oval viewport overlooked the upper reaches of the ship's bio-farm, displaying leafy treetops that swayed in the park's generated breeze. Compared to the enlisted berths, it was practically a mansion.

Xander found his belongings lined up neatly beside the small desk. With minimal possessions to unload from his luggage, he powered on the computer rig and flopped down on the bed. It finally set in. He had a new home and new patients.

Before he could unpack any further, Ethan rang him on the comm system and ordered him to mingle with the crew. Resigned to his fate, Xander ventured reluctantly from his room. It didn't take long to reach the Wardroom. The distance was conveniently close without being so near that the smell of cooking food would flood his room. He'd already had a bunk like that before on his old ship, and he'd quickly tired of smelling boiled vegetables and overcooked meats during all hours of the day.

All eyes turned in Xander's direction when he stepped through the door and he progressed to a lone table, where he observed the crowd until a blinking holographic menu urged him to make a choice. He blindly pressed one of the entree options without reading the choices. It promptly vanished.

A dark-skinned officer with gorilla arms, a barrel chest, and closely trimmed black hair crossed over. Too deep of a breath would burst his uniform at the seams, turning buttons into lethal projectiles. "Commander, welcome. You the new Operations officer?"

Xander's gaze fell on the man's rank insignia, also a commander. "Actually, no. I'm Doctor Vargas. I'm the new cyberneticist in Medical."

"Ohhhh, right. I saw the CO giving you the tour earlier. Didn't get a good look at you then. Good. When old Doctor Price retired, I wondered how long it would take to get a replacement."

"Your CO stole me from the Valencia base on Paradiso.

I'm as glad to be here as you are to receive me," Xander joked.

The guy looked him up and down, scrutinizing. He probably wasn't used to meeting anyone taller than him, but Xander tended to tower above everyone he met like an English oak in a field of bushes. "You're kinda big for a doctor."

Xander laughed. "What can I say? I take fitness seriously."

"Daniel Viljoen, by the way. I run the Combat Department. Mind if I sit here?"

"Please." Xander gestured him to an empty seat. "What do you think of the *Jemison*? This is my first time on one so large."

"The ship is good. Top-notch facilities. Some of the crew needs whipping up, but that's my job." Viljoen grinned, flashing white teeth.

"Guess that means I should expect a high visitation rate in medical? I'm not used to having a lot of work."

"Heard they're sending us a bunch of mutants and mechies. That'll keep your hands full right there."

Xander stiffened at the slur. "Cyborgs dislike the term mechie."

Viljoen only smiled. "I guess you'd be the expert on that."

A blonde sergeant arrived with their trays before Xander could snap out an irritated reply. And then she drank them both in with unabashed, unmistakable interest. He'd seen her type before. There were always at least a handful on every ship. Nothing ever changed, but he'd learned to be polite without encouraging them.

"Thanks," Xander muttered, dismissing her.

Viljoen leaned close and lowered his voice. "That one's the leading rank-tagger around here."

Another filthy term twisted his stomach, sent daggers lancing through his gut. Guys like his dinner companion deserved a hard right hook in the mouth. Xander forced down bites of mashed potatoes to stall his response, and it worked until he stole a glance at Viljoen, to see him hanging on anxiously. "Yeah? Every command's got to have one, I guess." He didn't particularly want to become a notch on anyone's figurative bedpost.

"The Jemison has her fair share."

"Know it from experience?"

The man smirked. "I don't kiss and tell, but there's plenty who do. Besides, nothing in the rules against mingling. Heard there was back in the olden days."

The tension wavered and diminished, disintegrating with each bite of food and forced sip of water. "As long as they don't bring it to medical. You don't want to know how many requests I've received to perform gyno services since my licensure. It isn't even my field." He gulped down the water that accompanied the meal and took a quick glance at his watch.

"Ha! I'll just bet."

"Anyway, thanks for the lowdown of the ship. Guess I'll be seeing you around." Combat guys always ended up in medical eventually, prone to taking their training beyond safe limits.

"Nice chatting with you, Doctor."

Xander stood and strode from the Wardroom, in no rush to chat with Daniel Viljoen again.

CHAPTER TWO

Thandie Kruger had only served on a single vessel since her enlistment seven years ago, but the chance to transfer to a ship with its own cybernetic specialist was an opportunity she couldn't miss.

What had startled her the most was that the request had come in from Commodore Bishop himself, a damned hero from the Terran-Lexar Rebellion. Having a cybertech onboard his ship had only sweetened an already awesome deal.

As an added bonus, the Jemison was a damned beautiful ship, far more advanced than her last command vessel.

After checking in with the ship's administration and receiving her bunk assignment, she spent her first couple days learning the layout between her duties in the armory and meeting her peers. Her direct supervisor was a chief with a reputation for his laid-back demeanor, the sort of guy who didn't put a lot of pressure on his division as long as they were on time and worked hard.

And then there was Commander Viljoen.

Like the ship's commanding officer, Viljoen had made a

name for himself in battle a few years back when a few societies broke free of the United Nations of Earth and decided they'd go and join the Lexar's sworn enemy—the Zaecady, a race of insectile beings with a hunger for all humanoid flesh.

Looking back at history, she wondered why humans enjoyed working against their own self-interests.

According to some of the tales out there, Commander Viljoen had saved an entire human colony from becoming overrun with drones. She'd actually looked forward to serving with him, but the ideal in her head hadn't matched up with the reality. He'd taken one look at her service record before summarily dismissing her like she was trash.

"We'll see if your upgrades are worth a damn in the ring. Gear up. Training begins in five minutes."

An hour later, after a grueling physical, she stood in sweat-dampened shorts and a tank alongside a line of her fellow marines, both her living and cybernetic fists wrapped in sparring mitts while Viljoen kicked off the day's combat instructional by hurling a poor new guy across the mat.

Thandie winced. "Is he always like that?" she whispered to the young man beside her.

"Oh yeah. Guy's intense. He really takes our training seriously. Says he'd rather be the one to fuck us up in a closed environment than to see us die out in the field, you know."

"I suppose that makes a morbid sort of sense."

"Yeah it does, plus I kinda get a sick sense of pleasure when the guy he has facedown is an asshole."

Thandie laughed quietly.

"Anyway, you're new, right? Name's Lopez. I'm on the ground assault squad."

"Thandie, and I hope to join you."

The next sparring match began. While she appreciated

that the commander didn't pull punches for the females, she dreaded going up against him. He took down his next opponent in under two minutes, pinning her to the mat with his knee pressed into her spine. Thandie winced.

And so it went for the other half dozen members of the training session. Lopez held his own, but he was nursing a swollen jaw with an ice pack held to his face.

"Kruger, you're next," Viljoen barked.

"Good luck," Lopez muttered.

She stepped into the training ring and studied the muscular man across from her. Wherever Thandie was stationed, she was always among one of the tallest women on the ship, measuring in at a little over six feet. Despite that, this guy had about three inches on her and a good hundred pounds of pure muscle. And despite going up against the other marines, he still hadn't broken a sweat.

"Let's see what you've got, Kruger. Come at me."

Without further prompting, she moved in, choosing to focus on her speed and agility versus his strength. She ducked his first swing and went in with a precise jab to his left kidney, maneuvering around and behind him instead of making the obvious blow to the solar plexus. Cheers went up from her fellow crewmen as she danced out of reach again.

For a man built like a living tank, Viljoen whirled with unexpected speed, nothing about his expression betraying the fact that he'd just taken a hit that would incapacitate a lesser man. She threw up her cybernetic arm to block his strike and grunted. He hit like a hammer. Put on the defensive, she moved back and regained the space between them.

They both advanced at the same time, Viljoen leading with a kick she knocked aside with her strengthened arm, twisting at the same time to kick his knee. Back and forth they went, exchanging blows. The first trickle of perspiration rolled down the officer's brow.

About damn time.

Spotting an opening, Thandie went for his side again, sacrificing her defense to get a hard strike in. Viljoen's fist hit her square in the sternum and knocked the breath from her, but she came back with a lip-splitting uppercut. The commander wiped the blood from his mouth and narrowed his eyes.

He chopped her in the shoulder, the side of his hand pounding the seam of her living bone and cybernetic implant, sending pain resonating through her nerves. She blocked it out and thrust him back from her with a palm-heel strike from her throbbing right arm.

She recovered in time to weave to the side and avoid another left-right combo. She swept aside his right cross like she was batting away a kitten, finding a pattern to his attacks. And since her kicks were her greatest strength—next to her implants, anyway—she used them to her advantage by going for his thighs and shins, each blow brutal in execution and too fast for him to get an attack in. She had to keep him on his toes.

"Holy shit," someone muttered from the sidelines.

The longest anyone had lasted in the ring with Viljoen so far was two minutes. Someone clocked their spar at three.

Just as she prepared to triumph over the commander, Viljoen surprised her with a shin scrape, grabbed her by the arm, and dragged her in close enough to headbutt her. She stumbled back, temporarily blinded by the pain as blood trickled down her face.

He capitalized on her moment of weakness with a brutal punch to her cybernetic shoulder. The strikes came hard and fast, and it would have been punishing to her forearms if not for the benefit of the reinforced metal limb shielding her. Thandie grunted and yielded ground a step. The man must have lifted weights ferociously for hours a day to compete with cybernetic muscle.

He didn't aim anywhere else.

The shoulder took another hit, and before her blurring vision clarified, he planted the sole of his boot in her shoulder with a hard kick that sent pain rocketing down her spine. All of his weight must have been behind it, every ounce of his power dedicated to one strike. She hit the mat, trying to scramble to her feet the moment it was under her.

But Viljoen was on her again, strapping her arm between his powerful legs.

Trying to pry apart his thighs was like moving two boulders. She squirmed and fought, hitting him with her left fist, pulling with the right, but he'd damaged something earlier and the arm malfunctioned instead of effortlessly sliding free.

He wrenched again, and something in her shoulder popped. The zinger traveled up and down her back, sparking little explosions of pain everywhere from her fingertips to her hip. She hadn't even known all of those things were connected.

Her world was misery and fire, worse than the injury that had taken the limb from her in the first place. Agony paralyzed her, froze the rest of her body until she couldn't comprehend breathing, let alone moving.

Viljoen twisted again. "Yield!"

The spectating crowd was on the proverbial edge of their seats. No one spoke. They were waiting for her to masterfully escape a crippling hold that was five seconds from reducing her to tears. Weakly, she tapped the mat with her left hand. She didn't trust her voice enough to speak.

He released her and stood. Didn't even have the decency to pull her off the floor.

"Dismissed."

The commander strode from the training room. The second the doors closed behind him, the overbearing silence shattered and everyone started talking at once.

"I totally thought you had him, Kruger."

"Are you all right? You looked green there for a second."

"That was amazing."

She wished they'd all shut up. The words blurred with the pounding in her head. Lopez chased off her nearest admirers and knelt down beside her. "Want me to walk you to medical?"

"No, I'll be fine."

"You sure?"

"Yeah. A few aspirin and some sleep and I'll be fine."

Four hours later, after she'd taken the max dosage of aspirin, Thandie's black and blue shoulder disagreed.

Bright lights activated across the training room, and intermittent blips glowed from holograph apertures scattered around the expansive room.

"Is this honestly necessary?" Xander asked. "It's only my second day aboard the ship and I've been in medical all day."

"I know, but I can't send you out into the field without verifying that you're not soggy around the middle, mate," Ethan replied.

Xander patted his flat abdomen. "Soggy?" All that those months spent on Paradiso had given him nothing but time to hit the weight room and vent his frustration. "You wish you looked as good as me."

"Put your money where your mouth is, Xander. I do this with all my officers. Lieutenant Shahid holds the speed record for the course, by the way."

"Haven't met him."

"Her," Ethan corrected. "Intel. Nice Astreyan girl. Pretty, too. You'd like her."

"Ethan."

"All right, all right. I was only saying. Besides, she's seeing some bloke in Navigation, I think. So that ship has sail—"

"*Ethan.*"

"Sorry. Are you ready?"

Despite his friend's good intentions, Xander held no illusions about involving a woman in his future on the Jemison. He wanted to work. Romantic entanglements, no matter how casual, weren't in the cards.

"I'm ready."

Ethan tapped in the final sequence and the empty chamber immediately morphed into a full military training course. Cubes, ramps, stairways, and ladders rose from the floor and slid from the walls and then a holographic overlay gave them the appearance of a mountainous stronghold. A synthetic sun blazed overhead, with lights so intense that sweat beaded on Xander's brow.

"You don't do anything half-arsed do you, Ethan?"

"Nope."

A buzzer activated and they took off at a sprint down the room's length. Xander's longer stride gave him an advantage and he reached the first station ahead of Ethan. A series of human silhouettes popped up behind various obstructions and opened fire on the pair. Bright red paint splattered against his side, accompanied by a sharp, breath-stealing punch in the ribs. The painful rubber bullets within the paint capsules reminded their marines that errors came with a price.

"Five second penalty," Ethan whooped, ducking past him. He aimed his training pistol and fired at the programmed assailant.

How did a man in his fifties move so quickly? Xander swore under his breath, loathing Ethan a little more with every step.

They raced through the obstacle course, ducking into cover, bobbing and weaving as necessary, sliding beneath shelter and surviving make-believe hazards. Droids sprang from nooks and crevices to perform hand-to-hand combat maneuvers while automated turret guns attempted to mow them down with a hail of agonizing, non-lethal rounds.

Holographic projections paired with physical components created a realistic scenario without live opponents. Xander blocked the merciless, rapid-fire assault from a four-armed mech, staving off punishing strikes aimed at his face and upper torso.

"You dancing or fighting?" Ethan taunted from fifteen feet above him.

Xander blocked a hit with his left arm and struck with his right. A green flash cleared him to continue forward after the penalty ended. Ethan had moved ahead of him, and he clung precariously to a wall designed with as few handholds as possible. He didn't use a harness. Those wasted precious seconds.

Not to be outdone, Xander ignored the climbing rig and hurried up the rocky surface.

Xander gained better time on the thirty-foot wall, and they were practically neck and neck when they each heaved over the edge. His booted feet pounded the ground for the finish line. He lunged for it, powerful legs launching him across the end zone seconds before Ethan's arrival.

Fuck yes.

While Ethan slumped over with both hands on his knees, Xander feigned nonchalance, like a few moments of their match hadn't been a close call. "I haven't run one of those since battle school. You make everyone do this?"

Ethan laughed. "Only the best on my ship. This is a better way to assess them than that jargon in their personnel records. It's personal."

"Fair enough. C'mon, let's see the results."

Xander took a long drink then activated the computer panel on the wall, prompting a holographic display of their course and stats.

Ethan grimaced at the readout. "Damn. You always have been a better aim than me. Still, you ended up with more holes in you. I know you've got Lexar blood in you, mate, but I hope you don't take these risks on actual missions."

"Never. Anyway, have I proven to you yet that I remain up to performance standards?"

"I'll allow you to pass."

"Appreciated," Xander replied dryly.

"By the way, I have plans to run through a secret quest I found in Spellbound. Our usual tank said he'd be on tonight and we could use a healer who won't stand about with his thumb up his arse when we need him. Interested?"

Xander considered the offer. He and Ethan both participated in the same guild of a popular online video game. It was a hoot when their schedules matched together. "That isn't a terrible idea. I could use the R&R."

"You also have nothing better to do than to join your

good friend in a heroic virtual reality game. We can never find a better healer than you."

Xander grinned at Ethan. "Well, when you put it like that."

"Hit the showers and have a brief kip on your cot before meeting up with us. You've earned it."

"I would, but Oshiro organized a medical staff meeting I'm going to be late for, thanks to you."

Ethan chuckled. "Give Oshiro my apologies for delaying you. See you tonight in game."

Long after Hart, Oshiro, and their techs left the meeting, Xander remained behind with Dr. Matthews to discuss the latest discoveries in microbiology. She seemed like such a nice girl—young woman, he corrected himself—but her interest in nanite technology impressed him the most. Cybertechnology and Nanotechnology were like bastard brothers to one another sometimes.

Needing to be in his room within the hour for game night with Ethan, he hurried from medical to the Wardroom to grab a bite to eat. Maybe even take a sandwich back to the room with him. With that plan in mind, he veered for the quick-grab line rather than sit and order a meal.

The broad-shouldered blond ahead of Xander offered his hand. "You must be Commander Vargas, right? Heard a fair bit about you. I'm Lieutenant Etherington. Engineering."

"Pleasure to meet you."

"Care to join us?" Etherington gestured toward a nearby table.

"Well..." Xander glanced down at his watch, aware of

scrutiny from the table's occupants. Every eye was on him, but he had enough time to sit with his fellow officers for a few minutes. "Thank you. I'd love to." He moved up in the line and stacked his tray with a pre-measured bowl of soup and a sandwich, ignoring the crowded dessert line at the end.

The moment Xander sat down at the table, a young lieutenant leaned forward, eyes shining with enthusiasm. "Is it true you're qualified to work on the latest series of implants? I heard we're getting people with tech that hasn't been released yet for normal distribution among the civilian population or the rest of the military."

"I am," Xander confirmed, a broad grin on his face. "I recently completed a twelve-week course on performing spot maintenance while on Paradiso, too, so I'm also a certified cyberware mechanic. Quicker repairs, no need to send it out."

"Holy shit," Etherington breathed. "No more weeklong turnarounds to receive our shit back from the repair depot?"

"That's right. I can manage most repairs myself here and in the field. Including the newest stuff."

"And the staff?" another officer asked, wrinkling her nose. "How do you like your fellow doctors?"

Xander chuckled. "I feel welcome. Oshiro and I have known one another for a very long time. He was my mentor."

The same officer raised both brows. "But what about the Sargossan? I still can't believe they let her onboard."

"Should they not?" Xander asked, puzzled.

Etherington grimaced. "Her kind don't have any place on our vessels. Don't you think so, Doc? Hart doesn't say much about it, but it has to be a nightmare in medical. I mean, aren't you one needle stick away from infection?"

Xander sighed. "It doesn't work that way. It requires prolonged exposure to the organism, over a period of years. One contaminated needlestick won't be enough. The average human body would fight it off, even an infirm one."

"We're exposed to her every day, aren't we?" the second officer asked. Her name tag identified her as Lieutenant Porter. "She has no business among us. Especially in medical where things need to remain sterile."

"They'll regret overturning the law as soon as there's an outbreak on one of our ships. I hope to God it isn't the Jemison, and that her plague doesn't spread to the rest of *us*," Etherington said, shaking his head.

When settlers had first colonized Sargossa, no one detected the microscopic organism that lived deep in the soil and rock. After twenty years, colonists fell prey to the first symptoms—sensitivity to sunlight, anemia, and unquenchable thirst. The development of secondary canines wasn't seen until the first generation of Sargossans were born.

"Well?" Etherington persisted. "She has no bloody place among the rest of us. It's a joke that she even received a commission. Sargossans are practically alien."

Porter snickered suddenly. Xander followed her gaze, twisting in the seat until he saw Lilibeth at the table behind them. She pushed up from the table to leave.

Xander lost what remained of his composure, his words spat out with vehemence. "Your fellow marine and peer deserves respect. She's a fine officer."

"Sir—"

"Finer than any of you," Xander interrupted. "Doctor Matthews doesn't gossip about her peers and cares for each of you equally, and in my opinion, that makes her an exceptionally fine *human,* as well."

Lacking the patience to tolerate more of their ignorance, he left his sandwich on the table and hurried after the retreating woman. "Lilibeth, a moment," he called out. She paused a few feet from the door, her back ramrod straight. Xander offered his arm. "Walk with me?"

A couple officers gaped at him, as if horrified to see the commander offering unprotected physical contact with the "alien" Sargossan.

Lilibeth blinked but slipped her arm through his and allowed him to escort her from the room.

"I want to apologize for the shit you overheard," Xander began.

"You have nothing to apologize for. Etherington and his friends will always be jerks, and there's nothing I can do to change that. They're no better than high school children, and clinging to anger doesn't hurt them, it just hurts *me*," she explained.

"You're a wise young lady."

"And you are a kind man, Xander." They paused outside a stateroom, where she gently extracted herself and leaned up to kiss his cheek. "Remember my words for yourself."

Before he could ask what she meant, she smiled and crossed the threshold. The door shut behind her.

When Xander turned, a dark-haired young man was standing not too far away, features those of a native from one of the many planets colonized by China. Or perhaps Japan. "That was a pretty nice thing you did for her."

"I didn't really do anything at all."

"I was working on the communication system in the Wardroom and saw the entire thing. Anyway, I'm Chief Lockhart. Gareth Lockhart. It's a pleasure to meet you, sir."

"Pleasure's all mine."

"You're also much nicer than the rumors indicated."

Xander raised a brow. "Mean isn't *usually* on the list of false attributes assigned to me. They must be coming up with new stories to tell." Crazy perhaps. Psychotic. He'd even accept violent, but mean?

"You should have heard the tales going around about my brother and me. People were convinced before we ever stepped foot aboard our first command that we'd read every mind on the ship and sell secrets for quid."

"You're a psychic then?"

"Apt assumption, sir. But, uh, don't worry. I'd never violate someone's privacy like that, and I can't read minds without physical contact. Not anymore." Gareth's smile faded. "Anyway, Commodore Bishop wanted me to check on your netlink and guarantee you'd have a stable connection. He says you were always lagging out when he needed to be revived in game, and to make sure your shit was on point here."

Xander groaned. "Did he really?"

"Okay, he didn't admit it openly, but I've seen it with my own eyes."

The two men laughed and made their way to Xander's stateroom. Gareth immediately moved to the interface panels and crouched beside them to begin his work. He whistled. "Nice gear, Doctor. Now you'll have a connection to match."

Less than five minutes later, Gareth had made the necessary alterations in the information currents. The chief closed up the panel and slipped his tools away. "There. All finished. You shouldn't die the next time we're raiding the Hell level."

Xander's eyebrows rose toward his hairline. "You were there?"

"Didn't you gather that much from my comment about reviving Bishop?" Gareth exaggerated a sigh. "You're on the commodore's private network now like the rest of us in the guild, so you won't be dragged down into the laggy abyss again."

"Thanks, Chief, I appreciate it."

Gareth hesitated at the door with his fingers against the cool metal. "Commander?"

"Yeah?" he answered absently while unpacking his virtual gear.

"It wasn't your fault."

Tension straightened Xander's spine and locked his shoulders. His fingers clenched around the edge of the case. Better that than the delicate equipment within. "Excuse me?"

"It wasn't your fault," Gareth repeated without making eye contact. "I just thought I should say as much. Couldn't leave without saying it. I don't see what's bothering you—it doesn't work that way... but there's an aura of guilt surrounding you so deeply that your soul is drowning in it, and I *can* see that."

Words died in his throat, choked back by the upwelling storm of emotions. Xander didn't think his dry mouth could form them anyway.

"Things will get better. I know you've heard that before. Trust me, I've heard it a hundred times myself. But one day, there'll be a moment when you wake up and realize you can breathe again."

"I don't think..." Xander swallowed and dragged in a breath.

Although Gareth was already across the room, the impression of a warm palm settled against Xander's shoulder. Encouraging, and somehow pleasantly supportive.

"Give it all the time you need. I think I know why Bishop insisted for me to install your netlink personally. And I'm glad that he did. You and I have something in common, sir... and I'm around any time you need an ear."

The psychic excused himself from the stateroom and took the familiar, friendly presence with him. Xander remained seated at the edge of his bed for a while longer, too captivated by his own deep thoughts to do anything else.

CHAPTER THREE

The *Jemison*'s medical suite had to be one of the nicest Thandie had ever seen, but she chalked that up to Lexar ingenuity. Her last ship had been a human made clunker ready to fall to pieces.

"Got a patient for you, sir," the on-duty medical technician called, announcing Thandie's arrival at the examination lab. "Lovely piece of arm work on her."

"Thanks, O'Reilly. I'll be right in with her."

Thandie peered through the doorway left open by the corpsman. Her unpleasant experiences with military doctors consisted of assholes rushing her in and out of the exam room. Occasionally, one asked about her eyes, questioned her headaches, and prescribed useless pain meds that didn't even scratch the surface of her migraines.

When she had been selected for the splicing program, Thandie had leapt at the chance to undergo genetic therapy and become one of the best snipers in the Royal Marines. Youth had clouded her judgment and downplayed the potential negative side effects.

Her gaze dropped away from the hall and down to her

boots. When footsteps announced the arrival of her doctor, she didn't look up. They all tended to look the same—bland and judgmental. Arrogant.

"Sergeant Kruger, right? I'm Doctor Vargas. Nice to meet you."

The unusually cordial voice drew her gaze upward where it froze on the medical officer's face. It took her mind a moment to realize the handsome sight in front of her was a doctor and not one of her fellow enlistees. She blinked at the Commander insignia shining against his lab coat collar.

In all her life, she'd never met a doctor who filled out a lab coat the way he did, with broad shoulders and a chest defined with chiseled muscles under his scrub shirt. The body beneath it had to be rock hard and sculpted as finely as the infantrymen she'd trained alongside. Never mind that the man towered above *her* and had to be somewhere in the neighborhood of six and a half feet tall, maybe a little more.

His reassuring smile melted her insides until she recalled their surroundings and that he was her damned doctor. "Uh, hello, sir."

His grin didn't fade. "This says you're in for shoulder pain. Let's have a look at you, shall we? What happened?"

Her mind didn't want to cooperate with her mouth and it took a moment to shake off the fuzz. "I was throwing punches with Commander Viljoen yesterday in training, and now my arm is all out of whack."

"Can you describe it to me? Where is the pain localized? Does it spread? Is it difficult to pinpoint?"

Thandie raised a hand to her shoulder and kneaded the spot. "It begins right here, like stabs from a knife in the cartilage. Then it radiates into my back."

The doctor moved closer and flashed a sympathetic smile. A *gorgeous* smile below the prettiest set of gray eyes she had ever seen. For a moment, she thought they glowed like the sun behind fading storm clouds. And they were so damned familiar. Had she met him before?

"All right if I check it out?"

Thandie jerked her gaze away before she stared too long. "Er, sure thing, Doc."

One hand touched her shoulder and the other took her elbow, fingers warm, unlike the usual icy physician's touch. "Why did you wait so long to come in if this happened yesterday?"

"Figured that was normal enough at first, all things considered, but it lingered through to today. First it only hurt when I raised my arm. Now it's constant. I feel it zinging toward my spine."

He flexed the joint a few times then lowered the arm to her side again before drawing a nearby screen closer. "I see."

When the two most frightening words to ever be spoken by a medical professional left his lips, she winced and waited for his diagnosis.

"According to your medical history, the entire right arm is a prosthetic?"

"Yeah, they fit me about two years ago. I took an incendiary round to the bicep. My arm was burned, and they couldn't save it." She mumbled the last bit and glanced away. Everything was in her files, but doctors had a nasty habit of making her repeat it aloud. When the request for details didn't come, she peeked back up. Doctor Vargas smiled warmly.

God, he looked like a model from Paradiso someone had thrown into a lab coat.

"Shoulder reconstruction. How's that working for you?"

"Great. The doctor who did it was magical, they said. A

real wizard with a scalpel and nanogel. It didn't feel like it at first, but three months later it was tougher than ever."

"And some bone plasteel lacing augmentation of your left hip after taking a bullet. You seem to be a magnet for those."

Heat raced up her neck. "Comes with the job. But, yeah, that's it for the implants," Thandie confirmed.

His brows raised. "Have you ever had a problem with *any* of them before? Any sharp stabs, aches, irritation beneath the skin? Grinding?"

"Not until Commander Viljoen kicked my shoulder and wrenched it in a hold," she grumbled under her breath.

"You're in luck. Received my cyberware mechanic cert while on Paradiso this past year, so I'm familiar with these. The Royal Guard seems to be fond of this brand, too…" he mused out loud while reading the specifications. "Newest model. Very nice. It's not a bad device, until some prick decides to play dirty in a sparring match."

Thandie's lips turned up at one corner. "Some people take losing very seriously."

"Guess that means you were winning."

"Yeah, 'were' being the operative word," she responded dryly.

"I need to have a look, Sarge. Mind unfastening your coveralls and lowering them to your waist?"

She nodded and unzipped her suit to reveal the fitted tank top beneath. The faint surgical scar had diminished over the years, barely a discolored line where lab-grown skin grafted to her natural body.

"I swore when I signed up for this, I wouldn't let any of you ship-boys talk me out of my clothes."

Her doctor resembled a deer staring into hovercraft headlamps.

Thandie shifted restlessly and bit her lower lip. "Sorry, I tend to blurt out stuff when I'm nervous."

"Understandable. Medical makes everyone nervous." He recovered and flashed her a grin. "I don't like undressing for strangers either. Maybe that's why I'm the doctor." He guided her back gently against the table. A machine hung overhead, dangling from rails installed in the ceiling. He grasped hold of it, guided it above her body at torso height until the lens was aligned with her shoulder, and he peered into the screen.

Her booted feet fidgeted, then she crossed one ankle over the other to still their swaying. She tried to stare up at the ceiling, but her gaze drifted toward the dark-haired man peering at her skeleton.

"You're probably familiar with this, but I like to talk everyone through what I'm doing anyway. I'll start by shifting your limb as needed to see if any of your connectors came loose from the nerve plates."

He didn't fill the empty seconds with meaningless conversation, speaking only when necessary. It was during a silent lull that subtle notes of classical music teased past her hearing.

"Is that your music?"

"The ship's A.I. likes to chase me with music ever since it found out I play the cello." He chuckled. "You're going to feel a jolt in a second." He wiggled the pads of his index and middle fingers against the joint of her shoulder. Then he rotated her arm, stabbing unforgiving lances of pain into the socket, a hot poker sizzling into the core of her bone and sending molten metal down every nerve fiber.

Thandie bit back a scream, but it was a close thing.

"Sorry, Sarge. He got you pretty good, but you're in luck. We won't need any invasive procedures to go in and surgically adjust it, at least, and the worst of the pain will be over by the time you leave my office."

"Good," she wheezed, quickly clearing her throat afterward. "So, it'll just settle back in then or...?"

"No. I'll nudge it and send you back to your bunk with a sick note. You can have a couple days off for it to heal. Sound good to you?"

"Not how I'd hoped to make my debut at a new command, but I guess I have little choice in the matter."

"Absolutely no choice, really. Unless you'd prefer to go under the knife. I have some new surgical lasers I'm very excited to try."

"No!" She flashed a quick, bright grin up at him. "Absolutely no need for you to play surgery with me, Doc."

"Are you certain about that? This is only my second week, and I'm dying to do some real work."

At least he had a sense of humor. "Rain check."

The heel of his right palm pressed flush against her body, effectively pinning her to the table. He stared at the screen, completely unaware of her awkward mood.

Thandie braced herself for the pain. It hurt. It hurt every bit as much as she'd expected when his fingers pressed bone deep. He kneaded and palpated, until the loosened connectors met with their sockets. Each time, a wild zing of electricity raced down her nerves to her spine.

"Be still," he warned her. His voice had changed, husky and thick. Or was it her imagination?

Thandie gritted her teeth and refused to cry out. As he completed the final pop, sensation exploded beneath the bone and raced down her spine to the tips of her toes.

"Finished." When she glanced up, anger flashed in his eyes. "Next time Viljoen comes after you with an invitation to spar, I suggest you accept and begin the match by kicking him in the groin."

"So unsportsmanlike, Doc." Moisture clung to the corners of her eyes, trapped by her lashes.

"Hey." The hands that had hurt her so much became tender. A comforting weight that stroked down her bare arm. "If you thought half the things about me that I think you did just now, then you know I'm right. Go ahead and sit up, roll your shoulder."

Thandie's head swiveled around to face him again. She stared, wide-eyed and alarmed. "You're not a psychic, right?" Between her lusty thoughts and her wishes for him to walk out of an open airlock, she'd never find a hole deep enough to hide in.

"Not at all, Kruger. I just know how to read faces. I've been a doctor for a while now. I've also been called a lot of things in plenty of languages over the past couple years, and facial expressions are more honest than words."

It took a moment to roll up into a seated position. Thandie quickly swiped at her eyes when she thought he wasn't paying attention.

"I might have thought some unflattering things for a minute there. Sadist came to mind." She smiled to soften the admission. "But it does feel better, so thanks for that."

"You probably won't think that in a couple hours." He plucked up his tablet and scribbled with the stylus. "Let your supervising officer know that you'll be off duty while that settles. No sparring, all right? There's a prescription waiting for you, as well."

"I'm guessing target practice is also out?" Thandie shrugged back into her coveralls and zipped them up.

"You guessed right. Maybe you should apply to med school."

She rubbed at her arm and slipped down to her feet. "Funny, Doc."

"Glad to be of help. I fixed the misalignment, but the damage Viljoen dealt to the tissues needs time to heal. If it doesn't feel right after two or three days, come back and I'll make time to see you."

"Yes, sir."

Thandie's medication waited for her at the counter. She signed for the pills and headed out. The lift took her three decks down and she headed directly for her supervisor's open office door. After checking in with her medical orders, she headed for her room.

At the first water station along the way, she paused to take her allotted pain meds, looking forward to a painless, drugged slumber.

Like all other enlisted personnel, she bunked with five other people. Three shared the day schedule and the others worked nights. Thanks to the personalized sleep bays in each dorm, the ladies could chat and use the communal space freely without waking their slumbering companions.

That especially counted for rendezvous with crewmembers of the opposite sex. Or sometimes the same sex. Opaque glass partitions surrounded each bed. Adjustable settings could make them completely soundproof and absolutely private. At least, they were private until some half-dressed serviceman stumbled out with his uniform over his shoulder and his boots in one hand.

"You're back early."

"Doctor Vargas took me off duty," Thandie replied.

"Hottie Vargas? Do tell. What's he like up close? I've only seen him while serving his meals in the officers' mess. I swear, it's about time we got a male doctor who wasn't a thousand years old."

"Er...."

Daksha didn't wait for Thandie to answer. "My cousin Padma is on the *Glenn*, and she recognized his name immediately. All the girls were crazy about him there too, right? Guess what she told me. You'll never guess, Thandie."

"Guess what? He seemed nice enough. Fixed my arm right up."

"A few years ago, he was supposed to marry some hotshot captain on the ship. Supposedly, he dumped her a month before the date for—get this—an Eloran!" Daksha announced.

Angela wrinkled her nose. "He's into aliens? That's *disgusting*."

The intensity of their reaction took Thandie by surprise. She blinked at them. "What's wrong with aliens? Some of them are very nice."

Angela cleared her throat and focused on her painted nails. "There's nothing wrong with them, I suppose. Personally, I don't see the appeal. Do we even have compatible parts? Elorans are fish peope, and I mean, the Lexar may look like us, but I heard they have *two* dicks."

Daksha mimed gagging. "Ew. I heard that, too. I guess that explains a lot if he's a xenophile. He'd rather have gills and scales over a real woman."

"Come on, Thandie. You've met him up close and in person. What did you think?" Angela persisted.

"I think he knows his job." *And he has a nice smile.* "I was there in pain. Staring at the good-looking doctor wasn't high on my list of priorities. Sorry."

"Oh you're no fun. C'mon, tell us. Are his hands as nice as they say? I saw him once after he arrived, but it was for a cold. But if he was looking at your arm, he must have touched you." Angela leaned forward eagerly.

"Like I said, pain. Pain I'm still feeling, so if you'll excuse me, I just wanna get changed and hit the hay. These drugs are making me loopy." The drugs had yet to affect her coherence, but she had no intention of continuing the current conversation.

Angela sighed. "Oh. Okay, I guess we can talk about it tomorrow then. Get some rest."

Thandie nodded, forced a smile, then moved over to her assigned bunk.

"Oh, Thandie?" Angela piped up before Thandie managed to crawl into bed. "Do you think I could borrow that gold top I spotted in your locker at our next port?"

Thandie eye-rolled and pretended not to hear her, shutting the door to the privacy pod surrounding her bed. As she settled down, she did have to agree with one thing: Doctor Vargas was extremely easy on the eyes.

Ten minutes after Thandie Kruger left his exam room, Xander was still hard as a fucking probe. There was something about her smile—no, not just the smile, it had been the entire package, including those dimpled cheeks and her honey-brown eyes.

He retreated to his office and sank into the desk chair, breathing hard and waiting for the Mating Frenzy to subside. He'd made it through a thirty-minute exam with her. He could make it a few minutes longer. Just wait it out. Let it fade.

Xander dragged in deep breaths through his nostrils, let his lungs expand, and tilted his head back with his eyes closed. Think of surgery. Sterile, boring, run-of-the-mill surgery. Something mundane.

Ingrown toenail removal. Dull as it came. He'd done two of those since coming to the *Jemison*.

Thandie's feet were probably perfect and flawless. Kissable.

Ugh. What the fuck? He wasn't even attracted to feet. That was the problem with the Frenzy—it was wild and unpredictable, wholly irrational.

Intentionally putting her through pain had been a sort of hell. Her every wince had shot through him like a knife and he could only be grateful she hadn't cried out. He might have stopped altogether and been unable to perform his job.

Then again, her pain had been the only thing that kept his demeanor professional and prevented him from whipping his dick out. He didn't need to be court-martialed for exposing himself to a patient.

Breathe, man, breathe. This time, it did fade, though it left him exhausted and drained in every way, emotionally, physically, and mentally.

This had never happened before. Hell, he hadn't even realized he had enough Lexar DNA to succumb to their strange mating rituals. In the alien culture, men entered a sort of male heat when around a special female, and they'd do anything, including battles with rival males, proving their sexual prowess, hunting for her, or displaying an aptitude for her favorite arts if it meant she might love him.

But from what he'd understood, that only counted for Lexar females.

He pulled up Thandie's file again on his personal station. Not a drop of Lexar blood in her ancestry. She was completely human, aside from the splicing.

In fact, he'd seen her before, though that was two years ago when he'd stepped into the OR to assist the surgeon tasked with rebuilding her shoulder. The man had been an arrogant asshole, claiming the shoulder couldn't be saved—that she wasn't a suitable candidate.

One of the nurses had rushed to get Xander from his office at the facility before old Commander Wilhelm canceled the procedure and had her wheeled to recovery.

He still remembered the asshole's words to him.

"Waste of time."

"It'll never withstand shock."

"You can't rebuild that shoulder. It'll be kinder to discharge her now."

Xander had taken one look at her face and known somehow that she was a woman who wanted her naval career, and then he'd spent almost eighteen hours piecing together and reconstructing her shoulder from fucking scratch because even the bones attached to it had been damaged to all hell.

Not once throughout the entire surgery had he felt attracted to her. Had it been because he'd already been in love at the time?

Or was it because Thandie had been passed the fuck out?

Times like this made Xander wish he'd known his father better. Made him wish all the more that the man hadn't been murdered in cold blood, or that his mother hadn't died in a shuttle wreck years afterward. Made him wish he knew something more about the people who shared 50% of his DNA than the standard shit they learned about them in textbooks.

She was a patient. It couldn't go anywhere.

He didn't need another wife.

Losing one had been enough.

CHAPTER FOUR

Cool light gleamed from the debriefing room's ceiling, illuminating the faces of stoic officers gathered to discuss plans for their next mission. Ethan and Amelia, his second-in-command, had called the emergency meeting only minutes ago.

An oversized map dominated the room's center, displaying a three-dimensional representation of the galaxy and its countless systems.

Ethan tapped a button on his console and zoomed in, then tiny pinpricks of light blinked to life, interspersed with radiant suns and an assortment of planets. One glowing blip depicted the *Jemison* and another bright yellow icon displayed their next destination three days away. "Yesterday, United Command received a request from the capital city on Loki 4 to check their sister colony on the orbiting moon. They're unresponsive."

"Do they lack ships of their own?" Xander inquired.

Oshiro turned in his seat to look at him. "Loki 4 is a green civilization site. The moon colony was founded with help from the Lexar to reduce overcrowding on the planetary surface."

Commander Viljoen folded his arms against his chest. "Figures the Lexar would stick their noses in where they weren't wanted then beat it without offering further help."

Amelia's disapproving look silenced him. Xander decided he liked his new executive officer. A lot. "This isn't the time, Commander."

"Right. Sorry."

"Now that we're back on track, let's discuss the mission. We will investigate the issue and lend aid if required. Commodore Bishop and I have discussed possibilities at length for your squads." Amelia swiped a hand across her tablet and brought up a holographic display that projected over the center of the table. An identification photo of a young blonde appeared above a list of military achievements.

"Saskia DuPrie is one of the splicers we picked up from our rendezvous with the *Noriega* five days ago. She's been trained for reconnaissance and her camouflage ability is one of the best I've ever come across. Took me weeks to get her transferred to my ship," Ethan said.

Viljoen grunted. "Acceptable."

Ethan clicked again. Another photo appeared. "Sergeant Thandie Kruger. Sniper. She underwent voluntary gene splicing after her enlistment and came out with eagle vision. Doesn't need a scope to hit her target."

"I'd rather take Henley," Viljoen disagreed, arms crossed over his chest. Another photograph hovered above the table.

"I examined Kruger's cybernetic arm. It's top of the line," Xander spoke up. "She can handle a lot of weapons without stress."

"Maybe so, but she hasn't seen combat since she lost her arm," Viljoen replied.

"Then the young woman must feel anxious to return to combat duty," Oshiro said mildly.

"How about Upstead?" Amelia suggested. "Steadiest arm I know. His upgrades aren't the latest model, but they're still good and reliable."

Viljoen shook his head. "Steady arm, true, but too slow. I need someone who isn't weighed down by implants."

So that's his game, is it? Xander squeezed his coffee cup a little too hard. The crushed cardboard sloshed hot liquid over the side that dribbled over his fingers.

Ethan snorted. "Sergeant Kruger will be your sniper. That is why I had her transferred here. Deal with it."

Viljoen assumed a professionally neutral expression and nodded. "Aye, aye, sir." The next names met with his taciturn approval while Xander howled with laughter on the inside.

Afterward, Oshiro and Ethan fell into discussion about combat medic protocols and support.

"Will four medics be sufficient?" Ethan asked.

"I don't require many. I'll happily accept quality over quantity," Xander spoke aloud while reviewing the suggested marines. A few of the names on his personal list coincided with Ethan's recommendations. "I'm happy with the four, but I'd be pleased if you add Elizabeth Fairchild, too. I spoke with her in medical this morning and she's a brilliant nurse with a second degree in microbiology. Perfect asset to the team."

"Done."

"Appreciated," Xander said courteously. He stole a glance at Viljoen. The quiet man still sat back in his chair with his arms folded against his chest.

Eventually, they concluded their meeting and began to file from the room. Viljoen stepped into line behind Oshiro, but Xander found it increasingly difficult to bite his tongue.

"Viljoen. A word with you?"

The other commander hung back and shut the door, as if he'd expected the request. They didn't return to their seats. Xander opted to lean by the table while his fellow officer waited a few steps from the door.

"Something wrong, Vargas?"

"You tell me. Do you have something against cybernetics that I should know about?" Xander asked.

"They're a crutch. An easy way to cheat their way past doing the work themselves."

"Whether it was elective augmentation or not, they are here to serve the Empire the same as you and me."

Viljoen smirked. "Of course, you have a soft spot for them. That's the only reason you're here."

"No. That is where you and I differ, because I see them no differently than our men who have the blessing to remain completely flesh and blood. You, on the other hand, appear to have something against Thandie Kruger in particular. If it's about wanting to avoid any claims of favoritism toward another native of your home planet, you've taken it a few steps too far."

"Not really. This doesn't have anything to do with her originating from Tallulah." Viljoen paused and glanced at the watch fastened to his wrist, as if he'd spared too many seconds of his precious time already for Xander. "Like most mechies, she needs to pull her weight without relying on her shiny new upgrades. She'll get herself killed if she goes into a fight thinking that arm will save her."

"She's a sniper. Her job is to kill before the enemy knows she's there. I doubt she relies on the arm to save her."

"My job is to make sure they can handle any combat situation."

"That's odd, because I've taken the liberty to speak to half a dozen other cyborgs after the second complaint entered the medical bay yesterday. Three complaints, since my arrival, of joint and nerve damage. The commonality between them is that you are the trainer. Are they handling combat situations or discrimination?"

"I'm not having this discussion with you, Vargas."

Heat spread over Xander's face. "I saved your ass when I salvaged Johnson's hand in the repair lab. You won't have me to speak to if you wreck a twenty-thousand-quid prosthetic—you'll be taking it up with Bishop when the budget has to replace it."

Without another glance at the other officer, Xander slammed the door behind him and stormed to the elevator. The moment the doors closed, he leaned against the wall and shut his eyes.

Deep breaths. He counted backwards. He tried to center himself, tried to imagine the shores of Elora with turquoise water gliding over pink sand beaches. If anything upset him, it was bullies, and Commander Viljoen was no exception.

But he couldn't afford to lose it again. Couldn't jeopardize this second chance.

Xander had to keep it under control.

THREE DAYS LATER, a shuttle bearing the *Jemison*'s ground assault squad descended toward the surface of Loki 4's single moon. Xander led his team of medical support while Viljoen commanded the Royal Marines. And because

Thandie was among the latter, he counted himself fortunate that his combat suit concealed the persistent hardon she inspired until he got himself under control.

Lieutenant Rogers landed the rockskipper at the settlement's outskirts on a landing pad designated for supply ships.

"You okay to wait here?" Viljoen asked the pilot.

"Aye, sir. I have a rifle." Rogers patted the stock and smiled. He didn't look old enough to pilot an aircraft, ginger-haired and freckle-faced. "I'll be right here if you need me and prepared to offer aerial support with the rockskipper's canons, too."

"Excellent," Viljoen said. "We'll need a reliable eye."

Thandie stared at Viljoen until Xander touched her shoulder in passing.

Once they all moved outside of the rockskipper, the silence of a dead village greeted them. Windmills moved in the distance and water crashed through the hydraulic power plant by the thin river cutting through the rock bordering the town. No one came to greet their ship.

"DuPrie, you're up," Viljoen called out. "I need a quick in and out to know what we're up against."

Saskia nodded. A combination of spliced squid DNA and technological advancements in combat suits rendered her practically invisible seconds later. She became impossible to track once she moved away, blending with the ruddy red and brown rocky terrain all around them.

After Viljoen split the whole team into two groups, mixing medical personnel between them, he assigned each a search pattern while they waited for word from their scout.

"The place is a ghost town." Saskia reported over the comm. "I'm seeing no signs of life. We're safe to go in."

A haunting atmosphere hung thick in the air. They passed empty gardens and silent buildings, the orderly sweep through the peaceful settlement eventually discovering homes with smashed furniture, ransacked closets, and empty pantries. Abandoned toys littered the streets and vegetable carts rotted beneath the sun in the village square. The group split to cover more ground, each commander taking his share of marines and combat medics.

"What happened in the western pasture?" Abernathy, one of the marines with Viljoen, questioned over the commlink.

"Maybe the livestock began to cannibalize? Villagers appear to be gone and there's no one here to feed them," Fairchild replied.

A waist high fence portioned a great space beside the village. Beyond the wooden structure, remnants of several mauled livestock carcasses cooked beneath the midday sun. They might have been a variant of cow native to the nearby planet.

Abernathy shook his head. "Those are herbivores, Fairchild. They won't cannibalize. Something else did that."

"Doctor," Thandie said in a low voice, tone urgent. "Don't move. *Nobody* move."

Xander took her advice at face value and froze. Scanning his field of vision, he scrutinized every detail of their surroundings. The dwindling sun reflected light off a glossy softball-sized eye two yards to his left.

The rest of the mottled red and gray creature came into view. Like Saskia, its skin mimicked the rough stone surface of the rocky ground.

Don't move? What else am I supposed to do? I can't very well wait for it to eat me, he thought. One adjustment of his shotgun muzzle would place the creature on the receiving end of military retribution, at least. He swung his firearm toward the monster and discharged the shell, point blank, into its chest. It shook off the shot and lunged. The carrion scent of its breath blasted his face.

At the same time, Thandie slammed into Xander and took him down to the ground, despite him outweighing her by more than a hundred pounds. Something sharp scraped past his cheek and left searing heat in its wake. One second later, and it would have been worse than a graze, beyond what even his Lexar genes could help put back together.

The feral creature appeared to be as large as a horse when his eyes focused on it again. Hard to track, it lunged left and right, snarling and feinting as the marines opened fire.

Thandie leapt to her feet and put her rifle to her shoulder. "God, that thing is ugly."

Xander lurched to his feet and leveled his shotgun at the beast. The weapon bucked against his shoulder, then the shot deflected off the creature's tough skin.

So much for our reliable eye. Instinct placed him in front of Thandie—he didn't know when he moved, only that suddenly, he was there, shielding her and taking on the creature. He pumped the firearm and blasted it again, hobbling its foreleg at point-blank range. It recovered swiftly and lunged with the intact front leg, its claws open and ready to strike.

Xander danced back, faster than it. Lexar genes were good for something, after all. The second shot crippled its remaining forelimb, though it appeared unhindered, doggedly pursuing them by bounding on its powerful hind legs.

"Down, Commander!" Thandie cried.

As Xander dropped to one knee, the sniper aimed her

rifle over his shoulder and fired. The creature's eye socket exploded in a spray of blood and gore. Dead, it crashed to the ground, though one of its claws twitched a death rhythm against the dusty ground and saliva drooled from its open mouth in a slimy puddle.

"Holy shit, we've got more of them, guys! Two more on your six," Saskia reported.

"Man down!" Fairchild cried through the comm. "Lopez needs immediate surgical assistance."

"Rogers, this would be the time to provide that aerial support you mentioned," Xander barked into the frequency.

Gunfire echoed across the square and the comm chatter revealed the other team faced similar assault. Mirroring his earlier gesture, Thandie squeezed Xander's shoulder before she moved away.

"Lopez is hurt. Go, I'll cover you," she informed him.

But how could he leave her?

He had to. It was his job. He strangled the crushing drive to become her protector and sprinted across the wide lane. A lithe form twisted around, lunging in his direction. Before it became necessary to raise his own weapon, rifle fire peppered it. Thandie covered his flank while he dashed toward the downed man.

Four barbed spines protruded from Lopez's leg, but their presence kept the bleeding to a minimum. Xander dropped to one knee beside him and tore open his equipment pack. A thin trickle of blood dribbled down his numbed cheek, and he closed his eyes to steady his head.

He shook off the feeling and dove into his bag.

Saskia and Chang took cover nearby and concentrated their fire on a third beast.

As the shuttle swept overhead in a low pass, strategically placed detonations from the rockskipper scared off the remaining creature, forcing it to rear back and expose its softer underbelly. Xander filled it with scatter rounds. The pulse of battle pounded in his veins as he ejected the charge and slammed another into the weapon.

"More incoming from the mountain range," Rogers announced. "I'll keep them off you."

"What *are* they?" Viljoen demanded. "Four have us penned by the corral."

"They're only wargs. I thought you had it covered," Rogers said.

Viljoen didn't sound amused. "What the hell is a warg?"

"They're predatory mountain dogs. Like wolves. Native to Loki 4, but probably domesticated and brought here by the settlers for hunting. By the way, try not to let one gore you. There's a neurotoxin on the tusks, and it'll put you down on your ass," Rogers said.

Viljoen's brusque voice filled the comm channel. "Get these things off our asses, Rogers, then scare off the rest."

By the time things settled, Xander had cleansed Lopez's leg, staunched the blood flow, and took the marine's blood sample. His vision swam in and out, but he blinked it away and glanced down at the results.

"Fairchild!"

"I'm on it." She knelt down beside Lopez and administered an anti-toxin from her kit. Within seconds, the man's color returned and his wheezing breaths eased.

"You're a lifesaver, Fairchild. I knew I wanted you on this team for a reason."

"Thank you." Her quick smile dimmed and her gaze settled on his bleeding cheek. "Your turn, Commander."

"I'm good," Xander insisted. "Save your injections for the people who need it."

"But your face—"

"It's just a scratch. I feel fine."

After an uncertain look, she closed up her kit. By that time, the others were moving in on their position. No one else required an antidote

Viljoen eyed him. "You good to continue, Vargas?"

"I'm good." Xander shook it off and rose to his feet as Thandie arrived, too stubborn to let her see him in a moment of weakness.

"No offense, sir, but I saw you take a tusk to the cheek."

Viljoen glanced at him. "That true?"

"I'm good," Xander repeated. "Do I *look* like I've been affected by a neurotoxin?"

"True. All right then. Fairchild, you stay behind and help Lopez to the rockskipper. I'll take my team through the west buildings as planned. We'll meet up on the northern strip."

They swept through the village, occasionally picking off a straggling warg that came bounding from cover. Rogers covered them from above with his rifle. Occasionally, he hit one.

"Next time, we leave Kruger in the shuttle, too. I see why that kid is the pilot." Xander muttered over the comm.

Viljoen grunted something that sounded like agreement.

"Hey! I'm doing the best I can while piloting a bloody hovercraft."

A nervous chuckle passed over the divided squad. They reported to each other over the wireless commlink, pointing out the signs of ambushes and assaults. Bullet holes marked a few wooden market stalls, and blood stained the stone walls.

Their continued search in the stifling heat turned up few answers, and even more empty buildings.

"Not a single child. Usually in a raid, someone gets away to hide in a closet or a basement storeroom," Xander muttered as the group met at the city hall's stone-carved steps. "At least one."

"Have you witnessed that often?" Chang asked.

The commanders glanced at each other, but Viljoen spoke first. "Not recently, but a few years ago during the war with the ASR, my team found a little girl hiding with her mother in the closet. We almost left her behind, too. She was playing dead under the corpse."

Abernathy groaned. "Shit. That's awful."

"We're performing vital scans in every room we enter. There's nothing here so far," Xander spoke up. "We'll spread out and continue to sweep toward the outlying farms."

Ten minutes later, Davis called the commanders to a large house bordering the central square. She met them inside, her face solemn and pale.

"We found six corpses, sir. All were killed execution style with a single bullet to the back of the head," the medic informed them. "One of them is the governor."

Viljoen swore and stopped on the threshold, grimacing. "What a stench."

The bloated bodies formed a haphazard line across the middle of the floor in a large office. "These corpses are several days… ripe," Davis muttered. She removed masks from her kit for the members of the assault squad who'd come unprepared.

Xander hastily placed his filtered mask over his nose and mouth. His enhanced sense of smell took offense to the odor of rotting corpse. "Could it be pirates? The homes were also looted."

"Pirates aren't usually murderers, too. They rob and dash."

"Could be slavers. The city hall indicated this settlement's documented population is 594 people," Abernathy said. "That makes 588 unaccounted for individuals."

"Slavers wouldn't trouble themselves with looting," Xander said. "An adult human male goes for five thousand quid on the market. Ten if we're doing our bloody jobs and they're unable to meet the current demand."

"Would take a pretty big ship, too, abducting that many people." Thandie chimed in. "Most slave rings I've come across in the past were small operations. Fifty people taken at most, but usually more like ten."

"Two ships." Saskia stepped into the room without acknowledging the dead bodies splayed out on the floor. "I followed rover tracks out to the canyons. Based on the ground marks, I'd say they had two ships land out of sight."

"That's more info than we had before," Viljoen said. "All right, we'll take the bodies onboard with us. Maybe you can learn more from them in your medical labs."

Xander cleared his throat. "In every old horror movie I've ever watched set in our era, taking corpses aboard a ship is a recipe for disaster. We'll examine them here, Commander."

"He doesn't want chest-busters." Thandie bit back her grin. "Can't say I blame him."

Xander winked at her. "Damn straight. We brought mobile scanners with us. We'll make this quick."

He and the rest of the medical crew ran basic scans over the corpses without finding any clues, underlying diseases, parasites, or trauma. Even forensic examinations failed to yield anything pertinent and lacked any useful physical evidence about the perpetrators.

And then he found one different from the others. "Here. He's the only one who lacks an exit wound. And the point of entry is also cauterized."

"Yeah, so?" Viljoen asked. "What's that mean?"

"This is typical of bullets prior to the Lexar Annexation forty-nine years ago. A combustible round," Thandie explained.

Xander raised both brows at her.

God. She was gorgeous *and* she knew her gun rounds. Somehow, that made her double attractive.

Viljoen thoughtfully stroked his closely groomed goatee. "Means we're probably working with space pirates then."

"We found the rest of the colonists," Lopez reported over the comm. "The school gym is packed full of bodies. Fairchild's preliminary scans indicate there are no survivors."

"I thought we ordered you back to the shuttle," Viljoen said.

"Sorry about that, sir. We spotted the building on the way to meet up with Rogers and had a look."

"We're on our way."

The numbers in the school gymnasium totaled one hundred and sixty-two in all. Xander went from body to body, checking for signs of life before taking a DNA sample to compare against the registry on file for the colony.

"Loki 4 is home to an unusually large number of psychics among their population. Since these people are overflow from the planet, some of them should have the same traits," Fairchild pointed out.

"What are you getting at?" Thandie asked. She worked to move the bodies into neatly laid out rows with the assistance of her fellow marines.

"Well, I've scanned almost everyone in the room and not a single one is registered as a psychic."

Xander glanced up from his readout. "I haven't noted any cybernetics among the victims either. Statistically speaking, we should have had at least a handful by now, even if they are from a green planet."

"So we have slavers taking their choice of cyborgs and psychics now?" The frustration in Viljoen's voice carried over the comm.

"Seems like it. Kids, too. Not a single body under the age of thirteen among the rest," Fairchild added.

"Then this was more than a common raid," Xander said. "It was a culling."

CHAPTER FIVE

From his medical station near the airlock, Xander observed the endless sea of crewmen awaiting their chance to exit the *Jemison*. Liberty days were a rare but pleasant breath of fresh air, enjoyed by everyone granted a couple days' respite from their duties.

Except for medical. Being a member of the medical department only meant there was a dramatic *increase* in work before they had their break, due to frequent changes in immunization requirements. He'd spent hours inoculating crewmen.

Not that Xander planned to leave the ship for more than a quick visit to the market so he could restock his preferred sweets.

"You plan to come along on your first liberty with the *Jemison*? After that business on the lunar colony, you certainly deserve it." Ethan grinned at him.

"Try it some other time, Bishop. I don't want to go."

"Oh, come on. How will I draw the ladies without my best wingman?"

"You can drink yourself into a pit of despair without me

present. You've always been a magnet for all the pretty girls eager to find a sugar daddy. Unbeknownst to them, you're as cheap as it gets."

"When's the last time you slept with a woman, huh?" Ethan's expression softened. "It's been a while, mate. You'll feel better once you get back in the game and—"

"Listen, I don't need to get laid." Even if every time he spotted Thandie in the passageways, he couldn't think of anything else. Time hadn't eased his desire for her, if anything, it wound the tension even more until he wondered how much longer he could endure before losing his mind.

Ethan's touched Xander's shoulder. "I'm sorry, but I am telling—not asking you—to enjoy freedom from your responsibilities for a while. I don't care if you spend it drinking, not-shagging, or reading in a cafe. Just get the fuck out of here."

Xander exhaled. Ethan had always been a good friend. The best friend he could ask for despite the decade gap in their ages and differing authority aboard the ship. He still remembered Ethan's words from the day Xander finally summoned the nerve to ask him why he cared about a scrawny, underfed kid like him.

"You remind me of my brother," Ethan had said. "He ran away to find a job on another planet when I left for the Royal Navy. Fell out of touch with the rest of us. So I guess I always hoped that someone out there was looking after him like this."

Xander hoped so, too. Sometimes it was difficult to believe they were serving aboard the same vessel again for the second time.

"All right, you win this time. I need a few to get out of my scrubs."

"Don't be late!" Ethan called behind him.

"Wouldn't dream of making you wait, sexy." Xander rolled his eyes and pushed his way through the thinning medical bay crowd.

The flashing lights and pulsing beat provided the perfect atmosphere for the crowd down on the dance floor. Xander sat at a table on the balcony overlooking the writhing mass of half-naked youngsters shimmying to the hypnotic noise. He shook his head and quietly nursed his drink.

Techno clubs and loud bars weren't his usual scene, but Ethan appeared to be enjoying himself. The commodore had a woman on each side.

"Evening, Commander," Gareth spoke up, dropping into the seat to Xander's right.

"Chief Lockhart, are your migraines any better?"

"Aye, sir. Whatever you did fixed me right as rain again."

"I'm glad. I know I'm a cyberware doc, but I've learned some tricks for people with your predisposition toward them. Feel free to come in anytime your usual pain relief isn't cutting the mustard."

"Appreciate it. Was that the CO I saw you come in with? Looks like he's living it up." Gareth peered down at the dancers.

Xander laughed and nodded. "He's as much of a ladies' man as ever."

"I think he's having enough fun for both of us."

"You're young. Why aren't you dancing along with them?"

Gareth shook his head. "You're not much older than I am, si—"

"We can leave the sir and title on the ship, Gareth. Please. I'm just Xander right now. A sad man drinking all by my lonesome because my friend intends to abandon me and fuck two hot ladies. Probably at the same time. He likes to live dangerously."

Gareth laughed. "I'm not much of a dancer, and it's nice to get away from the ship's two-drink limit sometimes."

Xander raised his glass in a silent toast. "I don't mind dancing. Just not this sort of stuff."

They spent most of the night tossing back drinks while Gareth pretended he had enough sobriety to shoot pool. What he lacked in dexterity, he made up for with humor, and Xander realized he'd come to really like him in the handful of weeks since his arrival on the *Jemison*.

Suddenly, three hours had passed and Gareth was well on his way to needing someone to carry him back to the ship.

And still eager to play bar games.

"Aw, don't tell me you're too much of a coward to play Guess That Drink. C'mon, Xander."

Xander snorted. "No, I'm too smart to play it."

"Fair enough. I'll wait 'til you're drunk then ask again."

Before Xander could warn Gareth that he'd be waiting a while, raucous laughter reached them from the adjacent game table, where the drunken group of marines in civilian clothing made more noise than the pounding music.

Viljoen and Etherington were among the revelers, which told Xander everything he needed to know about that crowd.

"So I have to ask, and if you don't want to say anything,

I'll understand, but what's the deal with Commander Viljoen?"

"Don't get me started on that bastard," Gareth muttered. "If you're not in a skirt or some prick who hefts around heavy things, Viljoen won't give you the time of day."

"Ah." *Should have known as much.*

"The man knows his job. That much I can say positively about him, but he's... brutal in his methods."

Xander made a noncommittal grunt and finished his drink. "You enjoy the rest of your time off, Gareth. Gonna head back to the ship."

"Really?"

"Yeah."

"But I didn't get a chance to outdrink you."

"It wasn't happening. Trust me." He clapped his friend on the back. "C'mon, I'll walk you back and we can plan a rematch."

LIKE MOST SHIPS, the *Jemison* followed Universal Standard Time, which was a 24-hour day set to their original world's 365-day year. The UNE hadn't yet discovered the perfect duplicate of Old Earth's cycle and orbit patterns, but its calendar was a popular tool used aboard ships to help regulate the work day and keep track of time.

At 0300, after helping Gareth to his rack, Xander had nothing better to do than dominate the crew lounge. He loved ancient movies and especially enjoyed comparing the science fiction films prior to 1980 to modern reality.

The wee hours of the morning became a delicious reverie of bad acting, terrible special effects, and deep-fried bread products. He'd have to hit the gym the next night to make up for the perfect storm of calories.

"Tea and cake at this hour? Really?"

Xander nearly spilled tea all over his sweatshirt. His gaze darted toward Thandie's voice and adjusted to the dim interior lighting. Desire struck him straight in the gut and it took every ounce of self-control he had to remain in his seat. Thandie studied him with an uncertain smile.

"Sorry, didn't mean to startle you, Doc. Sir."

"It's fine. You caught me deep in thought." Those deep thoughts took a dangerous detour into wondering how it would feel to be balls deep inside her.

I've had too much to drink for this. Shit. Deep breaths, man. You can do this.

Except each breath filled him with her scent until his erection was a pounding, excruciatingly rigid presence beneath his popcorn bowl, and he didn't dare to set it aside with her nearby.

"Well, don't mind me. Figured being bored here was better than being bored in my bunk. Least I can watch the sunrise." She gestured to the large viewport and settled in the seat beside him. "Guess I'm not the only one with the idea, except you came prepared."

If there was a god, he must have hated Xander. He cleared his throat and offered her a snack cake. "Would you like one?"

"Thanks. Er..." She took it while eyeing his pile of wrappers. "You know, for a doctor, this doesn't look like a very healthy meal. Sweet tooth, huh?"

"Are you implying I'm not in shape?" The incredulous tone of his voice accompanied a raised brow.

"Sweats really aren't the most flattering," she quipped back while unwrapping her treat.

The Lexar side of him took it as a challenge, commanding his hands, while his brain and the very human part of his body fought to regain control. Vainly, he adjusted his shirt above his abs and exposed lines of hard muscle. "Nope. Looks fine to me. I can refer you to the eye specialist if you want."

"They're just fine, thanks." Her carefully measured tone deflated his mood a little, too bland for him to easily determine whether she referred to her vision or his physique. "I'm surprised to see anyone awake, really. So, are you an early bird sort then?"

"I don't sleep for long usually, but the truth this evening is that I haven't been to bed at all yet."

"Fun night out, huh?" Her expression brightened, and the twinkle returned to her beautiful eyes. He was lost in them, staring. "Doc?"

He jumped. "Sorry. Lost my train of thought again. I was kidnapped and dragged away on liberty against my will by Bishop." He hoped Ethan was in a ditch puking his guts out.

"Ah, I see." Thandie chuckled softly. "So... kidnapped. You don't look too worse for wear."

"I have an unusually strong drinking constitution."

"Lucky you. All those colorful drinks knock me on my ass."

Xander's mind took another improper turn, wondering how it would feel to have that gorgeous, perfectly rounded ass cupped in both of his palms.

It was hell on him to think of her in any way that wasn't sexual, and he hated himself for that.

"So why aren't you passed out in bed like a good escapee?" Thandie propped her chin on her upraised knees and regarded him with open and friendly amusement.

"You make it sound like so much fun."

"Going out with friends is supposed to be, and you're avoiding the question."

Xander chuckled. "I couldn't sleep, so I decided to entertain myself with a good movie on the Holovision screen here. Normally, I volunteer to stay aboard and wait in medical for you people to come spilling in."

"You shouldn't have more than a few drunks and busted lips, right?"

"Oh yeah. Someone is bound to return with a broken nose or a couple of loose screws," he agreed easily. He sipped his tea and stole a glance at her, aware of the urgency dulling from an intense throb to a tolerable ache. For a while, the comfortable silence had no interruptions save the rustling noise of pastry wrappers and the movie.

"How's the arm, by the way? I should have asked before our mission."

"It's been good, thanks. The tenderness went away a couple days after you mauled me, and everything appears to be in working order. See?" Thandie held out her right hand and wriggled her fingers for his inspection. Xander set his tea aside and ran his fingers along her limb for a quick assessment. Nothing at the shoulder felt out of place and the joint smoothly rotated with guidance. Comfortable, natural warmth radiated from her flesh. Even the fine hairs reacted beneath his fingertips. If not for his experience, Xander would never guess it wasn't her natural-born arm.

"Yeah, seems good again. I probably shouldn't be telling you this, but I had words with Commander Viljoen about his training methods. If you can avoid him in the ring, it's for your best interest." During his time as a doctor, Xander had met a lot of officers high on their own power trips.

Daniel Viljoen didn't impress him in the least. "I don't think I'm on his Christmas list anymore."

Thandie eyed him dubiously. "Sorta hard to avoid the person who's teaching you. That'd be like telling me to avoid *you* if my arm malfunctions."

"Heh. Well, you could, technically." Xander realized that he still hadn't released her arm or taken his hand from her shoulder, so he quickly dropped both hands and turned to face the movie.

"Avoid you?" Thandie drew her arm back and clasped her hands loosely in her lap. "You're the reason I chose this assignment."

Xander blinked. "Me?"

"Well, not *you* exactly." Hints of color flushed into her cheeks. "I just mean that they said one of the fleet's leading cyberneticists would be aboard, so that swayed my decision when I was offered the assignment."

"Yeah. I graduated top of the training class when they sent a bunch of us off to get our certification. I guess cybernetics kind of resonates with me. I intend to finish out my career here until I'm as ancient as Oshiro. I've known him and the CO since my enlistment."

"So, you didn't start out an officer. That's actually sort of nice. Respectable. You must have enlisted young though, if you went on to school and became a doctor."

"You could say that. I enlisted at sixteen."

And he didn't regret a day of it. Enlisting had gotten him off the streets and given him a home. He gazed through the window to pick up the first rose-pink shades of color spreading like coral fingers against the midnight skies.

"Pretty, isn't it?" Xander asked, smoothly directing the topic away from himself. The longer he remained in her presence, the easier it became to control his urges. Or maybe it was enough just to be in Thandie's company and bask in her radiance, like a flower beneath the nourishing sun.

"I've heard about the sunrise here, but it's my first time to this planet. It really is beautiful. All the shifting colors are stunning."

Xander dared a glance over to see her enraptured gaze focused beyond the viewport. The gilded light bathed her face, bringing out the warmer highlights amidst her dark hair. His eyes lingered on her thoughtfully pursed lips and hazy fantasies of tasting them surfaced in his mind. That came to an abrupt, screeching halt when she turned her bright eyes toward him.

"What? Do I have crumbs on my face?" She hastily wiped her lips and chin.

"No," he blurted. "Guess I'm daydreaming to make up for the sleepless night. I better get going." Xander wadded up the wrappers and tossed them into the bin without looking at her again.

"Oh. Well, at least you can sleep all day without worries." She smiled up at him again. "Thanks for the snacks. Guess next time I bump into you it'll be my time to share."

"For your references, I like anything with pecans," he told her. "Unless they're in chocolate."

"Pecans, no chocolate. Noted."

He stretched and ambled toward the door. He paused there and glanced back at her one final time. "Don't you plan to do something on your liberty days?"

"I'll probably go out for a little bit with Saskia, but I have plans in Realm of Spellbound this evening, so..." She shrugged.

"You play?"

"Doesn't everybody these days?" Thandie laughed softly and waved. "Get some sleep, Doc."

"You, too. See you around." Because it was inevitable that he would see her again, which meant he had to figure out how to handle his reactions toward her.

There wouldn't always be a popcorn bowl to hide behind.

Xander abandoned the idea of continuing liberty after he dragged himself from bed. Four hours of fitful sleep weren't enough to recharge him for work, and he couldn't legally scan into Medical for a shift when recently intoxicated, even if he did have a Lexar's drinking constitution.

After a few sleepless hours in his bed, he capitalized on the empty gym and private time with the heavy-weight machines. By lunch, he couldn't stand it any longer and poked his head into the Medical department. Three crewmen waited in the lounge for treatment and looked as though they might hurl at any moment.

"Hey, hot stuff, come back here and sit with me."

"Keeping busy, Kathleen?"

She wrinkled her nose and frowned at him. "I've already tended several black eyes, one case of alcohol poisoning, and two people came in with Indari Blue Rash." She paused a moment for dramatic suspense then added, "On their dicks."

Xander snorted back a laugh. There was no logical reason for anyone to have had a poisonous native fern anywhere near their privates. "Sounds like the usual. I'd be let down if we had anything less to look forward to. I promise I'll be back on duty tomorrow."

"Of course you will. I want to get honking drunk, too, goddammit. I only stayed on today to help Oshiro." She grinned brightly from ear to ear. "Even Lil takes a walk off the ship during liberty. Promised her we'd shop together tomorrow."

"I wish I'd spent the evening souvenir shopping instead of drinking. I feel like shit."

"You look like shit, too, Xander. You're also not scheduled to return from liberty for another day. What happened?" Oshiro spoke up to announce his arrival, the small man lurking in the open passage between reception and the offices.

Xander winced. "Nothing happened. Why do you always assume something's happened? I only came to chat with Kath during her break."

"Because I know you. You throw yourself into work when you need a distraction from whatever foolish things you've done."

"I didn't do anything yet..."

"Oh? Now it is *my* lunch break, and Kathleen's has ended. Come into my office and tell me about it."

"Damn, I miss the good stuff," Hart teased as she waved him off.

A padded armchair awaited Xander in the spacious office, and his old mentor poured him a cup of tea while he slouched in the comfortable seat.

"Perhaps this will lighten your hangover troubles, as well," Oshiro murmured.

Concealing the truth from Oshiro was about as plausible as holding water in a leaky pot, so he accepted the tea and uttered his woes without further prompting. "Something is happening to me. Something unusual."

"Oh?" Oshiro's brows drew together.

"I met a nice young woman."

"Not so unusual."

"True, but what happens when she's around is what's unusual. I think I've been feeling the Lexar Mating Frenzy. Whenever she's in my presence, I can barely see anything but her. I can't smell anything but her. Every ounce of my attention hyper-focuses on only her and it takes all my concentration to notice anything else. It fades after a while, but only enough that I'm not pounding any male who looks at her into paste."

"That *is* unusual." He set his cup aside and pulled up a screen on his terminal. "This has never happened before?"

"No. Never. I didn't think it was even possible, considering I'm half human." He paused, then added, "And she's human."

Oshiro blinked, a brief—*incredibly fleeting*—moment of surprise surfacing before his compassionate- therapist expression returned. "Is there trouble in that?"

"She's one of my patients."

"All on board the *Jemison*, even myself, could claim you as our doctor, son. There's no protocol against relationships."

"You don't understand. I put that arm on her a couple years back."

Oshiro raised both brows. "That means nothing. If she seems nice—"

"I can think of other women who seemed nice, too, until they realized what was wrong with me. That I'm a freak of nature."

"Has *she* done anything to make you question her sincerity?"

Xander shook his head. "No. She hasn't."

"If the young woman has not shaken your trust, what else is there to bother you?"

"It's... Ylona. Barely a year has passed and looking at other women feels like betrayal." His throat tightened even as he said the words. His genes were playing a cruel trick on him, forcing an attraction to a young woman who deserved more than a broken half of a man. "She brought me out of a dark place, and now she's gone because of me."

"Experience is the mother of wisdom, Xander. Your troubling past has made it difficult for you to trust again. Perhaps you are correct to give it time, but you must also consider taking opportunities when they are given to you."

"You sound like an ancient Chinese master in a bad historical martial arts flick."

"Japanese. My ancestors came from Japan. Not China. Now, what would your Eloran say, were she present to guide you?"

Xander glanced away without giving a verbal answer. Unyielding discomfort settled in the pit of his stomach. Twisting. He already knew the answer to that. Ylona would be distraught to know her memory had become a hindrance. "She'd tell me to be happy again."

The older doctor spread his hands and smiled gently. "I would listen to her."

"I can't. She'd be alive and well on her home planet if not for me."

"And you would have never known her love. What happened to Ylona was nothing more than a terrible accident, but an unpredictable accident, nonetheless."

"She boarded that ship to surprise me. If I hadn't voluntarily deployed again, I'd have been home with her. She died a terrible, excruciating death because of my choice."

"No one could have known what would happen,

Xander. You were away serving your duty to the galaxy, and she loved you for that. It is natural to feel pain, to grieve, to mourn, and no one—not even me—can limit your time to heal. Just remember that Ylona made her choice, and she chose you."

Xander closed his eyes. He imagined her face before him, the large, dark eyes framed in an oval face of such breathtaking, alien beauty he'd been humbled by the sight of her during their first meeting.

But it hadn't been a relationship born from lust. He'd never felt such unrelenting and painful male urgency until the day he met Thandie Kruger. He'd had to beat off in his office restroom before attending the remaining afternoon patients.

"Have you spoken with her family?"

"A few messages over the year. After what happened, I didn't exactly feel worthy of talking to them. Ylona would have been ashamed of me."

Oshiro placed a hand on his arm. "No. You were put in a horrible situation, and many others would have lacked your restraint."

"Restraint? Yuki, I put that man in the hospital."

"You stopped. While I do appreciate you've taken complete responsibility for your actions, punishing yourself long after the deed for a crime of passion serves no great purpose."

"Maybe, but it's how I feel."

"If you had it to do over, would you do it again?"

Xander swallowed. "A good person would say no."

"You *are* a good person. Emotions such as anger are human emotions, and in people like you, with Lexar blood, you're fighting against genes. Had he repeated such a vile, irredeemable thing to a Lexar, he'd be dead. That is how things are in their culture."

"But I'm not a Lexar."

"Only half, but..." Oshiro studied him from across the table. "How do you feel about that these days?"

"Like a monster, more often than not. This new development doesn't help." Especially when he had to fight against instinct during their mission to Loki 4, constantly resisting the urge to drag her beneath him and out of danger. Thandie was a marine. She didn't need his protection.

"I will pull up whatever information I can, but you should speak with one of the Lexar. I could get in touch with—"

"No, that's all right. I'll figure it out."

Oshiro nodded. "Very well. If you change your mind, you know where I am. Now, go and enjoy your day off the ship, Xander. You'll appreciate that you did. I am told the new romantic comedy is worth your twenty quid."

Oshiro was right. Xander even paid to watch it a second time. Afterward, he wandered the city streets and breathed in the fresh, unrecycled air. No matter how much he loved ship life, nothing compared to the feel of the sun on his skin. Nothing beat the fresh breeze on a spring afternoon.

"Evening, sir."

Xander jerked around and came face to face with a member of the assault team. Lopez had his arm around a gorgeous woman in a gold-trimmed cream tunic. A crimson shayla covered her hair, hanging loosely around her face before wrapping neatly over her shoulders. Her skin carried the rich and warm tone associated with the desert people inhabiting Astreya, and she resembled her Persian ancestors as much as Xander resembled the people of 21st century Mexico.

"Evening, Lopez. How's liberty been for you? You recover okay?"

"Never better, man. Thanks for getting me back on my feet. Have you two met?" Lopez glanced from Xander to his companion. "Most of us assume all you officers know each other and share laughs behind our backs."

Smiling, his date offered a slender hand to Xander. "Not officially, no, though we exchange many reports."

"I suppose I'd be correct to assume you must be Lieutenant Shahid. Pleasure to finally make your acquaintance."

"Nisrine," she corrected him gently. "We're all off-duty now, are we not?"

"Nisrine it is. Just make sure you call me Xander in return to make us even. Both of you. I hear enough Commander this and Doctor that while on the *Jemison*."

"Wicked. We were just about to catch a movie," Lopez told him. "She picked some rom-com that I'll sleep through, but you're welcome to join us, mate. I'd appreciate the company."

Nisrine swatted him. "You are not allowed to sleep through the movie, but Xander is allowed to join us if it will keep you awake."

Xander grinned. "Actually, I saw that one twice already this afternoon. You'll have to suffer with your girlfriend alone." It didn't sound like a horrible offer, but his rumbling belly demanded sustenance. Overpriced popcorn wasn't enough. "You two have fun. It's really not bad."

Lopez shot him a betrayed, pleading expression as the couple headed off.

He enjoyed supper for one at a family diner by the seaside. There was fresh salt on the wind and the crashing tide washing over the shore reminded him of Elora and distant, fond memories of when he'd had another home.

He nursed a glass of wine and watched the sunset, its canvas of deep colors inferior to the pastel sunrise he'd enjoyed that morning. Or maybe it had something to do with the shared company, of having Thandie at his side. Briefly, he envied Lopez and Nisrine until he swallowed the bitter taste of jealousy.

The right company improved everything. With that bleak thought in mind, Xander returned to the ship alone.

CHAPTER SIX

At the end of his relaxing day, Xander elected to visit his favorite online videogame over an hour or two in the gym. He showered, changed into fresh shorts, flopped into his desk chair, and donned his virtual reality equipment.

Realms of Spellbound had been the most popular virtual reality online game in the UNE for ten years running. Users played out fantastical roles as magicians, legendary creatures, or dark entities in a setting replicating 21st century Earth.

The game was the perfect escape from reality, his subscription a gift from Ethan to get him through his year-long desk sentence at Valencia Naval Base.

Within seconds of activating the neural components, weight gradually settled over Xander's limbs, comparable to falling asleep after a long and exhausting day. He surrendered to the sensation of falling backward through the air. Weightlessly, he floated until the digital world suddenly snapped into existence.

He awoke on the other side in a crowded city zone

teeming with fellow gamers. He'd picked a popular place to log in, sitting beneath a cafe awning on the side of a crowded street bustling with pedestrian traffic. His current location was styled to resemble downtown Los Angeles.

An urgent message accompanied Xander's party invite from Vincent Knight, Ethan's role-playing avatar. Accepting the in-game teleport delivered Xander to Olde London, where he managed to team up with Ethan and Gareth, arriving on the tail end of an argument about the game's class options.

"Look. Everybody knows that Templars are just overpowered paladins," Ethan grumbled.

"Whatever, man. You guys would have gotten your arses kicked if I wasn't there with the holy water on the last raid."

Ethan opened his mouth to fire off a witty retort but noticed Xander approaching. "Look who finally decided to show up. Get lost along the way, mate?"

Xander snorted derisively and brought up the HUD menu. The holographic user display allowed him to see a 3D representation of the map.

"I'm surprised to see you here after your hard partying last night. Feeling all right, or should we worry about you keeling over at the first mob we meet?"

"Shut it," Ethan grumbled. "I'm online in cyberspace, which technically means I'm resting and asleep."

"Not the same kind of rest. The digital world creates constant stimuli that—"

Ethan stared at him. "Can you not?"

"Fine. You ready to hit this storyline quest?"

"Completely ready. My assignment says we need to take out a warlock landlord of an apartment building in Newham. Boss is in the penthouse level."

Xander nodded. "Gotcha. I've been there before to hunt for magical components, but I've never explored beyond the streets. The quests in that area are rated for groups of three or more."

Taking the lead, Gareth guided them to a dark and dirty side of London where the smog stank of chemicals and filth. The darkening night sky pulsed and undulated with magical flickers as they fought their way through the undead guarding their destination.

Skeletons and zombies were child's play, an easy task to vanquish despite a hoard of them ambling through the streets. Xander dispatched one after the next until Ethan's fireball spell cleared the stoop, wiping out a zombie doorman. Once defeated, the monster disappeared and left behind its gear.

Gareth plucked a black coat up from the ground. "Either of you want this? Looks nice."

Ethan glanced at it wistfully. "I've got too many costumes already. I don't wear half the shit I paid out-of-game money to buy."

Xander shook his head. "You keep it. I'm cool wearing my character's uni... Hey, what's that?" A gilded gleam from the empty coat's pocket caught his eye. He dragged a key out. "Guess we've got our way inside now."

Except the large door didn't have a visible keyhole and they spent another ten minutes feeling it from top to bottom and shining flashlights over it. Xander scratched his head and leaned down for a closer inspection, while the other two searched the wall for a secondary hidden entrance.

"You'll never get in that way," a feminine voice chimed from behind the group.

Xander turned to face the speaker behind them and

came face to face with three nymphs, nature spirits in female form with shamefully sexy bodies.

The redhead of the group stepped forward, voluptuous and curvy in a maple-leaf gown. A second dryad stood behind her, a brunette covered in green moss resembling a lace bodysuit. The third woman appeared to be a sylph, the type of magical creature associated with wind and storms. Her pale blonde hair danced around her face on an ethereal breeze, as did the scant silk covering her body. Name bars identified them as Varine, Annalise, and Zephyr.

In the digital world and the real one, Xander went rock hard.

Dammit. Had it really been that long that his body was reacting to digital pixels?

Gareth scoffed. "Like you know how to get in."

"You need a rogue with a high enough search skill, or a powerful disillusionment spell," the redhead continued. "The keyhole is there, but they have it trapped."

"Ah, sexy triplets. Wanna join us?" Ethan offered without consulting his mates. Gareth kicked him indiscreetly. Xander wanted to tell him to do it again, because he recognized Annalise from a large raid two months earlier, and she'd almost gotten their party wiped.

"I hope you learned how to play better since last time we met," Xander said. Ethan elbowed him where his kidneys belonged. It didn't hurt, failing to register as more than pressure. A group message flashed across his lower field of vision, telling him not to be rude. Xander rolled his eyes.

Annalise's porcelain face contorted into a scowl. She swept a hand toward Gareth. "Your tank rushed the room and drew the whole horde on us. Don't blame me for being squishy and attractive to mobs. Besides, we've gained levels since then."

He glanced at her viewable stats. "Yeah, I see. You ranked up. Congrats."

"Anyway, Zephyr can see the lock, so why don't you give her the key?" Varine cut in. She wriggled between Gareth and Ethan, choosing to link arms with the latter.

"Hell, why not?" Ethan said.

Xander frowned but even he could see the logic in having more people alongside them for the dungeon ahead. Sighing, he passed over the key.

They didn't have to wait long once Zephyr used one of her abilities to release the trapped entrance. The heavy metal doors slid open to reveal the gore-stained lobby occupied by warlock sentries. The moment Xander stepped inside, the computer-controlled enemies took notice.

The game had been designed with faction play in mind, undead enemies the intended prey of Templars like Gareth. He unloaded a hail of bullets at the approaching targets, putting his real-life military prowess to good use.

Plantlife burst through the floor to their right, a barrier spell cast by one of the nymphs. From that moment, the fast pace of battle didn't allow them much time to communicate beyond occasionally shouting commands or begging for Xander's healing spells.

Together, the six of them swept through one floor after the next, making quick progress through a dungeon rated with a two-hour completion.

"Do you have to lag behind so much to explore?" Gareth hissed at Varine.

"It normally takes her longer," Zephyr muttered while Annalise nodded in agreement. "She's still getting used to the controls."

"Do you know how many resources and good gear you're passing up?" Varine held up an enchanted amulet to prove her point. "Anyway, our Beast Charmer can use this more than me. I'm not even the right level."

When she dropped the golden disc in Ethan's hands and batted her lashes at him, Xander bit back a snicker. Even in a game his friend attracted the ladies.

"Thanks. I appreciate it." Ethan swatted the dryad's ass and palmed one cheek. She wiggled against him in a sensual shimmy, dragging her fingers down his chest and taking her role as a seductress of men seriously.

"No problem. Better it go to someone who can use it."

"A gun would be more useful," Gareth grumbled.

Ethan rolled his eyes. "I don't know how Flidais tolerates you in her group," he said, referring to Gareth's usual gaming partner, "if you complain nearly as much around her as you do with us about the item drops."

They ascended and cleared five more levels before reaching the top where the dungeon boss resided. Zephyr scouted ahead and returned, manifesting in a cool breeze. "He's huge," she whispered. "He had two health bars, guys. *Two*."

Ethan threw his arm around Xander's shoulders. "We can take him. We have the best healer in the game. What sort of cover are we looking at in there?"

"Furniture, most of it broken. A long kitchen counter to the left when you first go in. A doorway behind him, if you can get past. I have a friend who completed this run twice, and she said as long as the healer is on point, it's golden."

"So, a basic penthouse layout. Got it. Xan—Juan, you try and get behind that counter so you can cover us for healing," Ethan directed, nearly slipping in what name to use.

"Hayden and I will keep him locked on us while the ladies add the Damage-Over-Time spells."

"Sounds like a plan."

Ethan summoned a bear as his animal companion. The large creature stepped through a dimensional rift that looked like a molten circle of glass, then stood protectively beside him. "Let's do this."

Zephyr conjured mist to conceal their charge through the penthouse door then propelled Xander toward his assigned cover with a gust of wind magic.

Before Ethan and Gareth made it halfway to the boss—a demon-summoner named Landlord Kuminor—three imps appeared in puffs of flame. The warlock chanted, then Gareth turned his gun on Ethan and shot him in the chest with a critical hit that depleted a third of his health bar. The telltale sign of a mind control spell surrounded him in shades of red.

One of the nymphs swore.

Xander cast a healing spell on Ethan. Meanwhile, Varine cast a cleansing over Gareth while Zephyr darted in toward the imps with her blade drawn. Once they had Gareth back on their side, they took the fight to the boss and defeated it with teamwork. As much as he hadn't wanted the ladies to join them, it had become painfully apparent that they'd have never survived without their magical spells.

The warlock collapsed to the floor as a motionless silhouette that smoked and glittered with bullet holes before vanishing. It left behind a pile of loot, gold coins, and gear to be split amongst the party members.

Satisfied with the experience points and his share of gold, Xander passed on the other items.

Zephyr shook out her designated prize and grinned. "I've needed a new set of robes."

"Like it matters," Gareth said. "Once you put them on, they'll just become a set of leaf-shaped nipple pasties and a flower-petal thong."

Xander struggled to hold in his laughter. "Good game, everyone. We need to meet up again soon sometime." The alarm timer flashing above his HUD warned him that it was nearly time to log off for bed. He wanted to rise bright and early for his duties the next day.

"Certainly. I gotta work tomorrow, so how about seven p.m. standard, Saturday?" Annalise asked.

Xander thought ahead briefly. Logging on to clear his head and get Thandie off his mind had worked. "Brilliant idea."

"You guys have fun. I'm booked on Saturday," Zephyr said with an easy smile.

Varine remained by Ethan's side, held close with his arm around her waist. The two exchanged quiet whispers and flirty glances. Gareth sent Xander a private message, predicting the inevitable outcome.

"Varine is still new to the game. I promised to offer her a tour of the local common areas," Ethan said, oblivious to their secret conversation.

Then Gareth sent him a message. *What did I tell you?*

Xander rolled his eyes. *You didn't have to tell me anything. I guessed it myself.*

Ethan was lucky that STDs didn't exist on the galactic net.

"Thanks for allowing us to join you," Annalise said. "This was an absolute blast. See you soon."

Xander logged off and lay back in his seat for a moment until he awakened completely from the virtual world. The feeling returned to his limbs and fingers, banishing the paralysis of lucid dreaming. Eventually, he pulled off the headset.

A message reached his console from Gareth less than a minute later.

Are you going to be all right, Xander? it asked. *Something about you seemed off a few times tonight.*

Had Gareth sensed that through the game, with the shield of the internet between them? The man was a stronger psychic than Xander had anticipated. Inhaling deeply, he waited a moment before he typed out his response.

For once, he didn't lie.

No, I wasn't. But I will be soon.

"That was fun last night, don't you think?" Thandie closed her locker and crouched down to lace her boots.

"Not as much fun as what this little tart had," Saskia teased. "C'mon, Lizzie. Don't hold back. Tell us how your virtual romp went."

Elizabeth Fairchild stuck her tongue out at them. "There's no need for jealousy just because I got some and you didn't."

"Please," Saskia said. "I'd rather have a real cock. The virtual sensations just don't do it."

"Meaning you've tried it," Thandie pointed out. Saskia's reply was to shrug and grin.

"Who hasn't? We're on ships for months at a time between ports. I don't know about you, but dating our fellow military men—*especially* the ones on the *Jemison*—doesn't do it for me, either," Saskia replied. "They're a rather childish sort, with the exception to a limited few."

Elizabeth laughed. "You've barely been on the *Jemison* a month."

"More than enough time to weigh and judge these guys."

"Fine. I'll give you that. Speaking of dating fellow crewmen, I can't believe O'Reilly asked Thandie to join him on a date in the bloody lounge." The combat medic stood in front of the locker room mirror, gathering her white-blonde hair into a neat bun.

Thandie grunted and finished wrapping her wrists. "I managed to avoid giving any sort of answer. Medical didn't seem the place to laugh in his face."

"I've been here long enough to know he's a womanizing creep. Do yourself a favor, love, and stay away. These twenty-four-month deployments turn them into randy losers."

"No worries about me, Saskia, I've been through ship tours before. Now I'm just trying to plan how to whoop the commander in the ring."

Saskia smirked. "You almost had him, until he took that cheap shot. Anyway, the way he treats you reminds me of a boy on the playground picking on the girl he has a secret crush on."

"Kick his bloody arse today, Thandie. We'll all be cheering for you. I dated Viljoen for about a month when I was new to the ship, so I know what an asshole he can be," Elizabeth muttered.

Now that they were on the assault squad, Viljoen put them all through fifteen hours a week performing high-intensity physical training routines. And during those fifteen hours, they each received his undivided attention in the ring while their squad mates ran endurance, lifted weights, or sparred against each other.

Saskia squinted around. "I don't see Commander Vargas."

"Oh, he has duty in the medical wing today," Elizabeth said.

Viljoen already stood in the center of the sparring ring. "Davis, you're up first!"

Thandie began her training session with a timed run, while the trainer started calling them into the ring one at a time. After three laps, she moved on to the climbing wall, followed by a round on the mats practicing blocks and strikes until Viljoen barked out, "Kruger, get in here."

Thandie bumped fists with Saskia, then they exchanged places. Allowing her no time to get situated in the ring, Viljoen launched a spin-kick into Thandie's rotator cuff the moment she moved within his reach. She rolled with it this time and let his foot glide off her arm to minimize the force.

Bastard. The strike knocked her off balance, but she blocked the next with her natural arm to avoid granting Viljoen access to her prosthetic again. She had to keep it away from him before he capitalized on the same weakness.

"Afraid I'll shatter your toy again, Kruger?"

"No, sir."

Viljoen moved swiftly for a man of his considerable bulk, and his blows were devastating, whether she blocked them or not. He bruised her forearm and her shin as they traded strikes and kicks across the mat while eager comrades watched and held their breaths.

Literally. Saskia was blue in the face.

"Come on, Kruger. What are you waiting for? What if I wasn't a trainer and I pulled a gun on you or a knife? You can't drag the fight out and keep that arm away from me forever."

His taunt goaded Thandie into dropping her guard.

Viljoen pressed his advantage and caught her across the face with a right hook. The coppery taste of blood filled her mouth and she retreated out of his reach.

"Accept that you're going to lose and don't deserve the spot on my team. Give it up, and let me teach the rest of my squad—"

The commander's words filled her with white-hot fury. She lunged at him with her cybernetic fist, but he stepped aside of the blow, grabbed her by the wrist, and cracked her prosthetic over his knee. Thandie screamed. Desperate to remain in the fight, she drove her flesh and bone fist beneath his chin, cracking his teeth together.

Blood and spittle flew from the man's mouth as he staggered back off balance, pulling Thandie with him. He recovered quickly and wrenched her arm, then he used it like a tether, taking her wherever he wanted to lead her on the floor.

Regaining her footing, she maneuvered close enough to slam the back of her head into his nose. Suddenly, Viljoen didn't want to hold on to her anymore.

They traded blows back and forth across the sparring mat, one blocking and the other receiving. She searched for an opening in his defense, determined to end the intense exchange between them.

Viljoen's weakness became apparent with crystalline clarity. It had dangled before her all along, but she had never considered it with any seriousness. Thandie feigned a strike with her left and stepped in close, turning her cheek so that his punch skimmed past her face. It hurt but failed to lay her out on her back. With only a second to spare, she aimed her right hand downward for his balls.

Thandie's strike was colossal, the sort of blow that made a spectating crowd sympathetically wince along with the recipient. The heel of her palm collided with the commander's crotch, and she held very little back, allowing him to experience *almost* the complete might of her cybernetic limb. Anything more would have squished his grapes into jelly. Viljoen convulsed and relinquished his grip on her shoulder.

Without wasting a precious second, Thandie took him down to the ground into a locked grapple that placed the commander face down on the mats. He puked, but she lacked the sympathy to ease up on her restraint. She kept him locked by both of her strong legs.

"Tap out, Commander."

Viljoen struggled, but in the end, he slapped his hand down on the mats. Thandie released him to the sound of cheers.

CHAPTER SEVEN

"The marines must have had a great sparring match, sir. You have Kruger *and* Viljoen this time," O'Reilly reported.

"Really?" Xander tapped the screen and pulled up the patient-waiting list. He blinked.

"They look feckin' awful. Especially the commander. I, uh, sent him to the showers first, sir. Kruger is waiting in your lab."

"What's wrong with him?"

The medical technician struggled to maintain a straight face. "Read his chief complaint, sir."

Xander tapped the screen with his finger and expanded the digital record. "Testicular contusion..." *Christ. She actually did it.* A broad grin spread across his face, and then he leaned back in the seat, chortling with laughter.

"They brought him in covered in his own vomit."

"Ha!"

Thandie waited for him in one of the exam rooms, sitting on the edge of the table in form-fitting workout attire.

Bruises littered both forearms and dried blood crusted her lower lip.

For the first time, his cock didn't rise up to greet her, too. He had it under control. Instead of unearthly beauty, he saw a marine who had apparently been through hell in the ring. He grinned.

"You're looking a little rough around the edges, Kruger." He held both of his hands beneath the sanitizer and a perfect pair of gloves molded to his hands.

"You should have seen the other guy."

Xander chuckled and gestured for her to lie down. She knew the routine and remained still as he guided the biometric scanner above her and activated it. "I will soon. Did you take my advice?"

"It wasn't bad advice, and he didn't leave me much opening for anything else."

His keen eye picked out most of Thandie's injuries without use of the device. A swollen lower lip appeared to be the least of her troubles.

"Does that hurt?" he asked.

"Which bit?" Thandie looked up at him from her reclined position. Her smile tugged at the tear and quickly dropped the expression from her face.

"That bit," Xander said. He smiled back at her. "Hold on, I'll clean that up first."

Xander used a damp cloth to wipe the dried blood away, careful not to further agitate the split skin. "Any pain in your prosthetic?"

"Not as bad as last time, no, but…"

"What?" he asked while using an applicator to smear a dollop of anesthetic gel over the split skin of her lip.

"I heard a crack, I think. And my fingers sort of tingle. Things don't feel right."

"I thought so, but I wanted you to verify it." Xander turned aside and opened a drawer to remove his surgical scalpels.

Thandie squirmed. "Um... Doc? I see lots of sharp things."

"He separated a nerve and I can't reconnect it by touch this time, Kruger. If you want complete sensation back, I'll have to go in."

"Oh. Right. Okay." She focused her gaze straight up at the room's ceiling, tension in her lean frame.

"Relax. You're familiar with this, right? I'm going to make a small incision here, and here," he explained patiently, marking the spots with a green marker. "For the duration, your pain receptors will remain deactivated in this arm. I won't let you feel a thing."

A pent-up breath spilled from her, accompanied by a terse nod.

Xander numbed the arm all at once by deactivating the sensors beneath the skin. He knew them by memory on her arm's model and could do it without the use of an x-ray. Once it fell limp against the surgical table, he positioned it as needed and began making small and precise cuts to yield access to the mechanicals bits beneath the human skin. It parted easily, welling small amounts of blood to the surface that he wiped away with a cloth.

The repair took less time than the conversation preceding it. At the end, Xander sealed the small cuts and reactivated her arm's nerve sensors. "You're done. How does that feel?"

Thandie rolled up and flexed her hand, touching each finger in turn. She pressed her palm against the table and then ran her fingers down her pants before she seemed satisfied with her tactile sense.

"Thanks, Doc. Viljoen hits like a drake."

"He should. He was a former MMA champ before he enlisted. You should feel proud."

Xander patted her on the back in passing on his way to the next patient room.

Commander Viljoen lay on his side in the fetal position, ashen gray and shaking.

"So... My chart tells me that you walked groin first into someone's hand. Bad luck, mate." Xander grinned broadly and stepped into the room. *Karma is a bitch,* he thought cheerfully as he shut the door.

Something told him Daniel Viljoen wouldn't be challenging Thandie to the ring again anytime soon.

A DOCTOR like Commander Vargas deserved to be spoiled. After an impromptu visit to the commissary to purchase a sack of sweets, Jem directed Thandie to the crew lounge to find her benevolent prey.

For a moment, she lingered in the doorway and watched him. Like the other night, some old and unfamiliar film played on the holographic display. Teenagers ran screaming from a knife-wielding monster and creepy music played from the surround sound audio apertures.

Thandie dropped the bag of glazed pecans over the back of the couch next to Xander. He jumped, startling badly enough to slosh tea over his hand.

"Sorry, didn't mean to scare you."

Xander stared at her. Even in the dim lights, his eyes still shone like silver. A moment passed before he shifted on the couch. "It's all right," he said slowly.

"Are you sure?"

He scrubbed his face with the heel of his palm and exhaled. Then he eyed the bag and plucked it from the cushion, expression warming. "Why are you awake at two in the morning?"

"I told you. Night owl. Sometimes I wonder if it's a side effect from the splicing." She rounded the couch and dropped down beside him, drawing her legs up. "I used to be a terrible sleep-in, Doc."

"Xander. We're both off-duty, so the name's Xander."

"All right... Xander." She tasted the name on her tongue and decided she liked it. But probably not as much as she'd like tasting *him*. Shit. She pushed the naughty thought away and shyly swung her gaze to the video. "You're always watching these old shows. And eating sweets."

"Is there something else to do at two in the morning?"

Before she could rein in her dirty mind, it spilled out of her. "I can think of a few activities that are ideal at two in the morning." Thandie waited a beat, long enough for the understanding to dawn in his eyes, before she added, "Like the gym or the bio-farm."

Xander eyed her. "Right."

"Seriously. The gym isn't crowded at this time."

"Depends what you consider crowded. Viljoen and Etherington like to visit the gym around three and leave by four. That's when I head inside. As far as the bio-farm goes, the trees are a little too popular at night for my liking."

"Not one for intimate strolls, Xander?" Thandie snagged a couple sugar-glazed nuts from the bag. Their fingers brushed together, the touch lingering longer than what was considered polite or appropriate. She glanced up to find the doctor's gaze fixed on her mouth, with the kind of sensual intensity that sent heat curling through her core—

the kind of intensity that made her wonder what fantasy was running through his mind.

Seeming to realize he'd been busted, Xavier cleared his throat and glanced away. "I'm not one for tripping over two marines fucking in the bushes. There's kind of an unspoken vow between us officers and the rest of the crew to remain away from a few locations during certain hours of the day."

"Is that so you don't have to bust people, or so they don't try to lure you into mischief?"

"Both."

Her heart did a little double beat as she settled back against the cushions. "So, what's your story? Anyone waiting back home? A wife? Kids?" On the inside, part of her was praying he was just another handsome, *single* officer, and flirting with him wasn't shitting on another woman's marriage. What other reason could there be for him avoiding the risk of an entanglement?

Something in Xander's expression changed, the desire wilting like she'd poured ice water over his lap. "No. I'm not married."

"Sorry. Your private life is your business."

He waved it off. "It's fine. I don't mind questions. The military life doesn't suit marriage, and since I prefer living on ships, it wouldn't be fair."

"Oh, I don't know. Some people seem to make it work. Look at the residential deck. Abernathy has a wife onboard. She works in one of the science labs, I think."

"No, I wasn't aware."

Silence fell between them. When the easygoing, flirtatious mood didn't return, she searched for something to say —anything, really—to resume conversation between them. "So, if it's *really* okay to ask, why do you prefer a stateroom and mess food to a house and cooking your own meals?"

He chuckled. "I was born on Paradiso but grew up in a large city on Albion where no one gave a shit about anyone else. This is nice and personal, the people are reliable, and I know that for every Viljoen, there's someone supportive like Doctor Oshiro. He mentored me into the Royal Navy."

"Oh. I suppose I can understand that then. I grew up in the capital city on Tallulah. Not as big as the cities on Albion, but not small. Just enough that most everyone knew everyone else's business."

"No husband waiting back home for you?"

"Me? Hell no." Thandie shook her head vehemently. "Actually, if you want to know the truth, I joined the marines to *escape* marriage."

"I'm told that the word 'no' also works." A big grin spread over his face. "Poor bastard. I suppose he didn't take that well."

She shrugged. "His family didn't, but arranged marriages are an archaic tradition my planet decided to bring back into practice. I was seventeen and I didn't want to be thrown at a stranger to become a... proper housewife."

Xander raised his brows. "That's respectful. I couldn't imagine marrying without feeling an emotional attachment."

"Exactly. So my folks practically disowned me, and we didn't see each other again 'til after..." Thandie nodded at her right arm. "Funny how tragedy reunites people sometimes. They didn't approve of my choice to remain in the service, but they didn't fight me on it."

"Lucky me."

Her brows shot up. "Oh? How's that?"

"I mean, lucky for me and the squad."

"Uh huh... So, tell me what we're watching, anyway."

He took a moment to explain the premise of the old

horror flick, a dream demon who liked to prey on kids in a particular neighborhood, and then they fell into a companionable silence. There was something comforting about sitting beside him in the dim room sharing snacks, and he smelled good, something unidentifiable and spicy, like warm rum, leather, and cinnamon. She relaxed enough to lean in against his side and breathe him in. Xander curled his arm around her waist.

At some point, Thandie must have dozed off, because the soothing caress of fingers through her hair stirred her awake. She rubbed her cheek against his shoulder.

Wishing she could remain against him for hours longer, simply wrapped up in his arms, snuggled against a contrasting blend of hard muscle and the softness of his sweats, she burrowed in deeper and swept her arm over his chest.

The drowse carried Thandie away again until the moment her hand fell in his lap.

Her palm landed on an unmistakable bulge. Xander hissed in his breath, definitely not asleep and definitely aware of her accidental fondling. She jerked her hand back then darted her gaze up to his face and discovered their cuddling session had placed their lips mere inches apart.

"Sorry, I—"

Xander covered her mouth with a kiss that scorched her to her soul, burning through her with profound and merciless desire. She moaned beneath his lips and curled her hand against his sweatshirt before stroking downward and returning to the prize. He hardened beneath her touch, a few layers of cotton a poor shield for the arousal throbbing there.

Daring to take the risk, Thandie flicked the roof of his

mouth with her tongue, encouraging what he'd already began.

He made a low, deep sound she could only describe as a growl and seized her, fingers tangling in her hair. Her wildest fantasies of kissing Xander Vargas hadn't lived up to the delicious reality. Each expert stroke of his tongue sent her imagination into overdrive, wondering if it would be as skilled between her thighs.

If they'd been anywhere else, she might have tried to find out.

Maybe Xander came to the same realization. He pulled back the moment her fingers crept toward the waistband of his sweats and relocated her hand, while uneven breaths fell heavy and warm against her cheek. "Shit. Uh, guess we both got a little carried away."

Her gaze dropped to his lap. The man had to be hung like an Astreyan stallion. The longer she stared, the more difficult it became to tear her attention away from it.

Chest still heaving, Thandie scooted to the edge of the couch. "I should probably get going. Armory watch in an hour."

"Yeah, the time crept up." Xander not-so-discreetly adjusted his sweats. It didn't help.

Seconds ticked by and threatened to become minutes. The holovision started its next feature presentation, but they remained in their seats, each waiting for the other to move first. Thandie reluctantly stood.

"Will you be joining us for training this afternoon?"

"I'll be there. Though I don't imagine Viljoen will be doing his usual matches. I plan to fill in for him."

Chuckling nervously and avoiding direct eye contact, Thandie glanced away and rubbed the back of her neck. "Yeah, I guess we'll see. Catch you then, Xander."

"Hey, Thandie," he called out, catching her before she reached the door. "Thanks for the company."

She twisted around to see the unmistakable lust in his eyes hadn't faded. It lingered like an unspoken promise. "Same to you."

That promise lingered with her for the remainder of the day.

CHAPTER EIGHT

DESPITE BEING ONE OF THE MOST CROWDED PLACES ON the ship, the *Jemison*'s bridge was also the quietest. Ethan's command seat dominated a raised section at the back of the room, overlooking the various stations and personnel below, including the pilot.

Xander needed the distraction there. The past three days had been hell on him, because if he wasn't slammed with frivolous medical requests, his mind was on Thandie and how much they *didn't* belong together.

Didn't she deserve better?

Hadn't he vowed he would never throw himself into another romantic entanglement on board a ship after the massive shitstorm he'd endured while deployed on the *Glenn*?

He'd managed to keep from bumping into her since their kiss in the lounge, but it was only a matter of time.

"I owe a favor to Lieutenant Shahid for her help identifying our killer," Gareth said, bringing Xander's attention back to the present matter. An intergalactic identification file expanded on the holographic display, featuring the bearded features of a man in his sixties. "Jarvis Crane, leader of the Black Jackal Brotherhood."

Ethan leaned forward in his seat and studied the report. "So you tracked him by the gun?"

"Yes, sir. As you can imagine, there aren't many .40 caliber pistols on the open market equipped to fire combustion rounds. They're old tech."

"So what makes you think he's our guy?" Viljoen asked.

"Lieutenant Shahid tapped some connections, so we know that he purchased a Smith and Wesson model 2040 Ignite off a black-market weapons dealer out of Astreya a year ago. It's a pricey piece. About a half million quid, as there's less than a dozen in working condition these days."

Xander whistled. "So it's only a possibility that he's our man?"

"No, I'd say it's about 98 percent." The communications chief minimized the window and pulled up Crane's list of crimes. "He's wanted for countless violations, and the least of them are murder and burglary."

"Unlawful trade of children..." Ethan read out loud.

"Forced prostitution," Xander continued, swallowing heavily afterward.

Gareth nodded. "And he fits the forensic team's profile. We're looking for a big sonuvabitch about as tall as Commander Vargas. Crane is six-foot-six."

"Contact United Command and tell them we've identified our man, Lockhart. If he's still in this area of the galaxy, I want Crane and his ship found."

"Yes, sir."

In an effort to calm his troubled thoughts, Xander sucked in a deep breath and leaned against the side of Ethan's chair without concern for what was proper or professional. He expected Ethan to complain or order him off, but he didn't.

"Commodore?" A young woman at the communications terminal spoke up from her station. "We have an emergency transmission from Athena. You might want to hear this, sir."

"Patch it through to my terminal." A second later, he tapped his console. "This is Commodore Bishop of the HMS *Jemison*. What—"

"Oh, thank God!" A frazzled voice sounded over the comm. "Please, you must help us. We need immediate evacuation!"

Xander raised both brows and exchanged glances with Viljoen.

"What's the nature of your problem?"

"I've spent bloody hours searching for someone, anyone. I'm an engineer, and I work for Hephaestus Tek, the manufacturing plant on Athena. Pirates landed about three days ago. Killed most of the technicians and took others off-world about an hour ago. God only knows where. There are wounded people everywhere. Pregnant women in labor. One popped during the attack, and I don't think she can make it much longer. She's real tired and weak."

Ethan maintained an even voice but gestured for his navigator to input new coordinates. "I need you to remain as calm as possible. Tell me everything you know about your captors."

"Pirates. Well-armed pirates, equipped with cybernetics unlike anything I've ever seen. They overwhelmed our security force—" A single gunshot rang out before the communication link went down.

"Shit," Xander muttered.

"I'd put fifty quid on this bein' him," Gareth spoke up.

"I'll contact United Command and find out whether we've got more ships in the area."

"You do that. Agosti, give me a time frame for arrival."

"I can have us there in two hours, sir."

"Get us there in one. Time to see what these Lexar engines can really do." Ethan turned to Xander and Viljoen. "Get your team geared up. We'll send you down in the shuttle and pursue Crane's ship by radar if we can locate her in time."

"Right away, Commodore." Viljoen turned about face and strode off the bridge.

Ethan input a set of commands into his terminal and the ship went into alert. Red lights flashed overhead. "All hands to their stations. Alpha team, gear up and report to the shuttle bay."

Xander waited until Ethan closed the ship's comm line. "Did he say pregnant *women*? Plural?"

"You're going to have your hands full, Xander. Good luck."

ATHENA ORBITED a gas giant in a yellow star system. The barren moon held little of interest aside from a subterranean colony developed beneath its rocky surface for two purposes: mining and technical production.

Rich fields of liquid valerium beneath the moon's surface provided a clean-burning fuel for manufacturing plants across the galaxy. In its solid state, valerium formed the basis for plasteel, the galaxy's most profitable metal. Since it was as light as plastic and stronger than steel, it was favored for cybernetics and space vehicles.

Unfortunately, Athena's inhospitable atmosphere

required masks for surface work and travel between civilization hubs.

"Masks on! Be prepared for gunfire when we exit the shuttle," Viljoen called out to the squad. "If they expect our approach, they'll flood the surface landing pad. Kruger, I want your gun on that door."

"Will do, Commander." Thandie rose from her seat and activated a button on her combat suit. The individual pieces of her helmet slid from the neck of her form-fitting combat suit and created a functional re-breather mask.

When the rockskipper's side door opened, a shimmering energy barrier manifested in its place to maintain the interior atmosphere and pressure. Thandie clipped a line to her belt, placed her rifle to her shoulder, and then leaned out of the protective shielding.

Below them, rocky terrain rushed past the descending shuttle. Xander eyed her vulnerable position and moved closer. Then he remembered their surroundings.

Thandie didn't need him to baby her. Instead, he tried to see her as his war Valkyrie, powerful and capable of defeating any foe who dared to oppose her, a true Royal Marine who needed no man's coddling or protection.

The longer he mulled it through his thoughts, the more he liked it, until he was grinning with anticipation and his Lexar blood was hungry for the sight of seeing her in battle again. Had he ever seen a marine with an aim like hers? Some of it had to be her eyes, but the rest was pure skill and muscle memory, things which no amount of genetic therapy could help.

Xander didn't know what disturbed him more, that he thought of Thandie as *his* Valkyrie or that, for the first time in his life, he was actually anxious for violence.

Head back in the game. Mentally chastising himself, he

put his thoughts where they belonged, suppressing the Lexar hormones racing through his blood. Xander cleared his throat and raised a hand for the squad's attention.

"There's a fair chance that they have pain dampeners. Pirates and merc bands like them. That means that no matter where you shoot, they won't feel it." The devices were hot on the black market, desired for their ability to numb all sense of pain and discomfort.

"You heard the man. Let's go for headshots," Viljoen said.

An ear-splitting gunshot rang out before they touched down. Two more followed and a round sparked off the kinetic barrier a few inches from Thandie's body. She returned fire, never once flinching from the shots aimed at her. Five feet above the surface, she unclipped and leapt down.

"Move out!" Viljoen ordered.

Xander led the support team. During firefights, he and the three field medics in his squad had a single task—to save as many lives as possible while supporting the primary assault squad. They had a difficult job, keeping their eyes on the hostiles while also maintaining constant vigilance for their teammates.

Six men emerged from the blast door leading into the facility. They had the advantage, despite being outnumbered, and utilized low walls for cover, as well as personal shields.

Viljoen deployed his team to positions with mobile bulwarks to defend against the onslaught from the facility, but for every three rounds fired from the marines, only two penetrated an assailant. Half of the incoming pirates didn't even blink, despite the military rounds chipping into their armor and sinking into them.

Xander hated to be right.

"I said headshots, marines!" Viljoen yelled over the gunfire.

"Davis and Fairchild, switch to armor-shredding rounds!" Xander ordered.

"Shit," Thandie swore over their communications channel. "Rogers, get out of the shuttle!"

Xander whirled to face the shuttle, but Thandie's warning came too late. A rocket tore through the air and struck their transport, ripping through the kinetic barrier and disabling it. A column of fire and black smoke rose, then flames rushed over the portside wing.

Blown back by the resulting shockwave, Xander rolled across the ground. He pushed to his feet and maneuvered around to the shuttle door where automatic extinguishers sprayed the flames with foam particles.

Trusting his combat suit to protect him, Xander rushed in and knelt beside the motionless pilot before the metal even cooled. "Rogers is down but alive. But I don't think we're getting off this rock anytime soon."

"Stay with him, Vargas, while we mop up this mess," Viljoen relayed over the sound of gunfire.

"Acknowledged." Like he needed to be told.

The kid was in pain, and his left leg resembled charred steak below the knee. He'd lose it for sure, and without a full medical laboratory on hand and a lot of grafts, there was nothing Xander could do. "Hang in there, Rogers. You're going to be just fine. Can you hear me?"

Rogers groaned but continued to lie frightfully still as Xander worked over him. He dosed him with a premeasured shot of nanomorphone and applied antimicrobial ointment to the burns.

The rest of the battle faded to obscurity, adrenaline flooding Xander's veins.

"They're wearing stolen armor," Thandie relayed from her position. "If their helmets deflect your rounds at this range, aim for their joints. The plating is weak there since it's not made for them. Pain or no pain, they can't stand on a shattered knee."

A gunshot punctuated her point.

In the time it took for Xander to stabilize his patient, Viljoen and the others had secured the landing pad. No one else on the squad appeared to require his services. The pirates were another matter.

One crawled on bloodied arms toward the fallen missile launcher that had blown the rockskipper to shit. Before he reached it, Viljoen walked toward him and squeezed the trigger, executing the man with one round to the head.

"Bishop to ground squad, do you copy?"

Viljoen canted his head. "We hear ya, Commodore."

"We've located the Jackals and are in pursuit. Do you require immediate assistance?"

The squad of marines all exchanged glances. Getting dumped in the middle of a warzone was nothing new for them, an expectation they'd taken on years ago when they all enlisted to serve their galaxy as part of the Nova Force.

Xander spoke up. "We have one injured man."

"Stable?"

"He'll live."

There was a pause on the other end of the comm. Xander didn't envy Ethan for having to make the difficult decisions that came with having command of the ship. "Keep him comfortable. Stay safe down there."

Moments later, the *Jemison* left communication range.

They may have been on their own, but nothing about their mission had changed.

"Jackson," Xander spoke over the comm link. "Fall back and stay with Rogers in the shuttle. I can't do anything else for him at this time."

"Williams, you stay with them, too," Viljoen added. "Hold this position and see if you can get this bird flying again."

The brutal firefight continued inside the facility, where they encountered heavy resistance, a dozen well-armed men who eventually fell beneath military firepower. Once the last pirate fell, Viljoen took charge of his marines with the calm authority of a man accustomed to bloodshed.

"Kruger, get up on that catwalk. Abernathy, you maintain watch on our entrance. Chang, I want you on the door across the room. Lopez, accompany Commander Vargas and his medics on a sweep through the side rooms."

Xander stole a side glance at Thandie's retreating form. She swiftly scaled a utility ladder and took her position above them. Then he got his head back in the game and overcame the call of his Lexar blood urging him to claim his warrior bride.

Not now.

Defying the Lexar Mating Frenzy again, Xander quickly barked out orders to his men. The medics fanned out as commanded, sweeping from the entrance and tagging the deceased with prominent orange markers in passing on their way to the injured.

"I found a survivor over here! This man's alive!" Davis called.

"You tend to him. Jefferson, come with me. We'll sweep the next room."

It didn't take long to discover the whereabouts of the

remaining colonists. They'd been herded like cattle into a dormitory bunker while pirates raided their homes and businesses. Because the pirates had destroyed all surface communication towers with their ship, the colonists couldn't call for help until the engineer had rigged a signal to the *Jemison*.

As for the colony's savior, they found his body in a communications lab next to a smashed console.

"Damn shame that this had to happen this way," Xander said.

"We finished our headcount. Most recent census indicates this is a colony of 631. We have 182 survivors." O'Malley pulled up the report on his holographic display.

"Christ. What of the others?" Xander's stomach twisted in knots. So many lives extinguished for nothing.

"It's like the transmission said, Doc, most colonists were taken off-world. Maybe the *Jemison* will find 'em on the ship if they catch them," O'Malley replied.

Davis stepped into the room and cleared her throat. "Commander Viljoen and his people went to scout the rest of this facility. We're getting the colonists fed and cleaned now with supplies we found. Jackson and Williams have brought Rogers inside. He's still stable."

"Good. Keep an eye on him and let me know if anything changes."

Fairchild dashed up to him, her ivory face flushed pink and sweaty. "Sir, confirmation on the pregnant women. All three in labor."

Xander tossed one of his kits to her. "Here's the sterile gloves."

"But—"

"You can do this, comm me with any pertinent information. Comfort them in the meantime. Unless they're a minute apart or hemorrhaging on the floor, I don't want to hear anything else about it."

"Aye aye, Commander." Fairchild bowed her head and stepped away to return to the laboring women. They were her patients now, and Xander became all the more thankful that he possessed the foresight to invite her to the medical squad.

CHAPTER NINE

Bleeding from a minor gunshot wound, Thandie opened her medkit and set it on the kitchen counter of an empty apartment. All members of the Royal Navy, regardless of whether they were ground assault teams, boarding parties, or medics, carried the necessary supplies for basic medical care.

She removed her damaged body armor and peeled up the bloody tank top beneath to take a look. The bullet had gone straight through, carving a deep groove through her side. It wasn't the worst wound she'd ever received, but it still hurt like hell and was bound to leave a scar.

And if Xander wasn't overwhelmed with work, she'd take the injury to him.

Viljoen had assigned her and Chang an easy job, tasking them to clear a residential building of the expansive complex. Deciding to split up and cover more ground, they'd each taken one wing and stormed it floor by floor until Thandie got the drop on a pair of pirates.

One had gotten off a lucky shot, shattering a chink in her armor with his high-powered, illegal round.

It must have been damaged during the earlier firefight.

She cleaned away the dark, clotting blood first, then pulled out the nanogel antimicrobial dispenser, angling the tip of the tube toward her side.

"Okay, I can do this. Nothing to it." She swiped it over her injury and bit back a scream, grunting instead. The disinfectant solution was like an inferno in her wound, burning mercilessly through her injured tissue. Within seconds, it formed a protective seal over the tear.

Sagging in relief, she drew in a few deep breaths through her nose until the pain faded and blissful numbness spread in its place.

"Yo, Thandie, you okay?"

She glanced up to see Chang in the doorway, his concerned eyes trained on her face—not her exposed skin. "I'm good now. Startled a pair of looters."

"Ah. I found another a few units down. Need any help?"

"Seriously, I'm good. These things are *marvelous*."

"The Lexar surgical gel? Hell yeah. I mean, it burns like Satan's asshole when it's a deep wound, but when the anesthetic hits you, it's great."

Thandie laughed. "Not the kind of imagery I needed."

Despite her claims, Chang helped her fit the molded armor plate to her torso again before they headed back to rejoin the rest of the squad. Until the *Jemison* returned from hunting down Crane's ship, they had no choice but to hunker down with the survivors and hope for the best, keeping the civilians safe in the meantime.

With all of her security tasks complete, Thandie reported to Viljoen. They had a long day ahead of them, and it was only beginning.

Sometime the next day, Thandie ended her security patrol alongside Jefferson and Chang after being on her feet for eighteen hours straight. Rather than accompany them to get food—several grateful colonists had opened the facility's food court to serve them—she went to check on their downed pilot in the makeshift medical center.

The smell of stale sweat and coppery blood invaded her nostrils before she stepped into the room. Every bed had an occupant, the survivors with minor injuries laid up on cots elsewhere.

After Thandie slipped in, she made her way over to Rogers's bedside. "Hey. You bein' a lazy bum already?"

"Heeeey," he slurred. "You got pretty, Doc."

She laughed. "Yeah, well, we'll have to disagree there. It's me, Thandie."

"Thandie?" He squinted.

"Yup. He must have you drugged up pretty good, huh? I remember that feeling."

"Feels like I'm drunk, but better." Rogers attempted to nod but his head lolled instead. His eyes rolled in his head without ever focusing on her face. "Don't hurt, at least."

"You'll be on the painkillers for a while. They'll take good care of you, and our doctor is one of the best." She stole a glance over one shoulder toward Xander to see him performing an exam on one of the newborns. When he straightened to speak with the mother, a big smile broke across his face.

Good. The baby must have been okay.

"Get a brand-new leg, huh? More impressive than your wussy arm." Rogers laughed weakly. Thandie looked back and nudged him in the shoulder.

"Nah, I'm way better. But we can compare rigs once you're all situated. Deal?"

Rogers passed out before she received an answer.

"Gave him a solid dose of the good stuff. He shouldn't be in any pain for a while," Xander said, stepping close to the bedside. He leaned over and scanned Rogers's vitals. "Thanks for that. Speaking to him, I mean."

"I remember what it was like..." Trauma had flash-burned it into her memory, everything from the fire to waking up minus a limb. The excruciating pain, the numbness, and the way people tiptoed around her afterward.

Thandie shook off the old memories. "Least I can do is talk to him some. Let him know what to expect."

Xander's warm smile set off butterflies in her stomach. "I appreciate it and so will he." He moved from Rogers to the next patient, lingering long enough to scan vitals. "How long would you say we've got to wait before we hear word back from the *Jemison*?"

"A day, maybe two. Best thing to do, Doc, is find a spot to catch some rest."

"I suppose so." He smiled wistfully. "I haven't been in the field like this in a while. I prefer it, actually. Feels like I'm really doing my job and making a difference when I'm planetside. Don't get me wrong, I meant what I said about fancying the ship over living on the ground, but after a while... Most of what I see from day to day are the petty things. Someone with the flu wants out of their duties. A case of the clap. Or some unlucky woman goes toe to toe with Viljoen and learns he's an asshole. This is more like home to me."

"Yeah, well, not too many battles anymore, thanks to the Lexar."

"You sound like you admire them."

She paused and considered his observation. "I guess I do, in a way. I mean, look at how far the human race has come since we joined their coalition."

"A lot of your fellow marines would lose their shit if they heard you with a pleasant word to say about them."

"But not you?"

He shook his head. "Not me."

"Guess we're the rare ones then. Anyway, I feel pretty comfortable in speaking for the crew when I say we're lucky and thankful to have you on board. Which is why I also feel justified in telling you to get your ass to a bed and let the other medics handle things for a while."

His brows shot up and he looked from his rank tag to hers. "Really."

"You're beat, and if those pirates come back before the *Jemison*, we need everyone at their best. That includes you."

"I'll hit the sack when Viljoen gets up. But for now, I have two more babies to check on. Unless you want to help?"

She backed off, hands up. "I think I'm gonna follow my own advice. I'll catch you later."

Xander's laughter followed her from the room.

Another day passed without either incident or word from their ship. Thandie spent most of her hours on the surface, maintaining the watch while her fellow marines worked on the damaged shuttle. Several workers from the colony volunteered their services for the repairs, and their mechanical expertise expedited its completion.

The rest of them worked on repairing the recent damage inflicted to the quantum relays, hoping to extend their communication range to the *Jemison* or any other passing ship.

By the third day, tempers among the colonists flared. Some were convinced the *Jemison* had been destroyed by the pirates. They wanted someone to take the patched shuttle and make a run for help, but Commander Viljoen quickly squashed the idea, with Xander's agreement.

The angry mutterings stopped completely after a garbled message came in from the *Jemison*.

While they had caught up to their quarry and damaged the pirate ship's engines, the military vessel had also sustained a surprising hit to her own barriers. Jem had been overloaded, leaving them dead in the water.

The good news was that they'd sent a boarding party over on a shuttle and gained control of the mercenary ship to liberate the pirates' human cargo. Unfortunately, it wasn't Crane's flagship and the *Jemison*'s engineers needed time to repair their systems before they could return to Athena. They estimated thirty hours.

Just one more day until the assault team received their rescue.

WEARINESS WEIGHED Thandie's limbs when her shift finally ended, and she'd never thought it possible to miss a ship bed so badly until she'd gone with nothing more than a pile of blankets for three days.

Her body ached, and her swollen feet protested taking another step, but she had one last job to complete before retiring to her makeshift bunk. Rubbing her tender side, she picked her way through the debris-strewn dormitory halls toward the manager's flat.

Thandie knocked and lingered hesitantly in the hallway. "Knock, knock, it's Kruger."

Nudged by her metal knuckles, the creaking door swung inward to reveal a motionless shape sprawled on the low, sleigh-style bed with enough blankets draped over it to cushion a crashing shuttle.

"Doc?"

Poor Xander. According to Viljoen, he'd been dead on his feet, at last exhausted enough that he didn't argue about taking a break from command.

"C'mon in."

It felt like stepping into another world. Opulent decor drew her gaze from one item to the next. A large oval window offered a view of the moon's violet-tinged surface. On the horizon, the planet Apollo hung like a multicolored marble. Despite the beauty of the planet, Xander made the better sight, his body long and lean, unarmored from the waist up. He wore a dull gray military-issue t-shirt, the cotton stretched taut over chiseled muscles.

Xander cleared his throat, dragging her attention back where it belonged. His alert gray eyes made him appear less tired than she'd originally thought at first glance. "There a problem out there?"

"No, no problems. Viljoen sent me to make sure you were okay. Sorry about waking you."

"Nah. I was drifting in and out of sleep. Had a movie going for some background noise."

"Sorta figured. You always have music or a show on."

"Yeah," he chuckled softly and ran a hand through his hair. "So, what is it this time? Is Viljoen lost without me?"

"The commander asked me to pass on that all is clear and secure for the night in the infirmary. He didn't want you to come up earlier than needed."

"Sounds good. Let him know that—" He glanced briefly toward her and abruptly ended his polite dismissal, his gaze focused on the bulky pad of gauze outlined beneath her black tank. "What's that?"

Thandie made a poor attempt to conceal it, her hand rising reflexively to rest over the padded area. "This? Just a graze. Nothing to worry about. Scrubbed it clean and bandaged it the way we're taught. It's a little tender, so I slid a gauze pad over it so it wouldn't rub." A graze that hurt like all sorts of hell, but she hadn't wanted to bother him while there were so many other serious injuries requiring his *immediate* attention.

Xander paused his movie and set the tablet aside. "C'mere and let me have a look."

She stepped through and shut the door behind her. "Really, it barely bled or anything. Considering you had a lost limb and stuff to deal with, I was pretty low on the totem pole."

"Yeah, yeah, yeah. There's no rule of battlefield triage at the moment, so lie down. Shirt up. You know the drill, Thandie."

"I should be insulted you're disparaging my field skills." She rolled her eyes, but she didn't disregard the order. The familiarity of their relationship didn't extend to insubordination. Thandie sat gingerly on the edge of the low bed then laid back, enveloped in the warmth his body had left behind against the covers. She didn't have to tug the fabric up far to reveal the bandage to the right of her navel. "Bored or do you just delight in torturing me in particular?"

"My movie was a little more entertaining than you."

Xander crouched beside the bed and rifled through his supplies. The contents of his medical case had been dramatically reduced since their arrival only three days before. Earlier, she'd overheard both commanders discussing whether they had enough ammo charges and medical equipment to hold out if another shuttle of pirates arrived with a desire to retake their new home.

"And here I thought this was our thing." Thandie sighed and focused her eyes upwards. "Seriously, though, it's not so bad."

"Why are you so stubborn? What do I tell you whenever you make a visit to the medical department?"

"Come see you if my shoulder hurts again," she replied cheekily.

He didn't reply immediately, but his jaw tightened when he lifted away the bandage and exposed a shallow groove with red, tender edges. "It's infected."

"Stupid black-market bullets. It didn't look like a big deal."

"You don't make that determination."

"Doc—"

"I am the doctor, and you are the gunsmith. When my rifle is jammed, I will give it to you. When you're fucking hurt, you come and tell me whatever's wrong."

"Your accent comes out when you're angry." His sexy accent ran chills up her spine.

"Sometimes." Xander fell silent for a moment, his touch professional as he applied a cold compress over the affected area.

"How bad is it?"

"Nothing some meds won't fix, but I *am* low on the good stuff. One of the moms had a wicked infection." He flicked out a prepared syringe from the bag and took the cap off with his teeth. "Hip, please."

Thandie's smile wobbled and fell. Damn, she hated shots. Despite all the scientific advancements over the centuries, needles remained one of the most effective ways to introduce medicine to the bloodstream.

Reluctant to further irritate an already frustrated man, she obediently rolled to one side and nudged the waistline of her pants down. She didn't think he'd appreciate her cutting the tension with an immature joke about preferring a meat injection from him instead.

The cleansing agent was cool against her skin, but Xander's fingers left heat in their wake. She barely noticed the puncture of the needle.

"None of you marines seem to understand how deadly an infection can become on an unknown planet when we've only had time to issue a basic broad-spectrum inhalant."

"You're right. I'm sorry." Disappointing Xander left a sick feeling in her stomach. "I found a couple of mercs hiding out and one of them got a lucky shot. You were so swamped, and I didn't think it would get this bad since I used the field kit."

He kneaded the spot he'd injected, the warmth of his palm easing the knot beneath her skin. "Sorry for losing my temper with you."

"It's sorta sweet." The words slipped out and she didn't mind them. A lovely flood of comfort spread from her head to her toes. "I feel like I'm floating."

"Yes. I may have mixed in something for the pain, so that means the medicine is working. Now relax and watch the fucking movie. Doctor's orders."

Xander settled beside her, sitting up with a pillow propped behind his back, and resumed the movie.

"But I don't want to rest."

"Too bad."

She made a valiant effort to watch the movie, but her gaze frequently shifted to study Xander's handsome profile. No one knew much about him, and his career on the *Glenn*

—aside from sparse tidbits of gossip related to his previous engagement—was shrouded in mystery

"What?" he asked, looking down at her

"I'm trying to figure you out."

"Trust me, there's not much interesting about me."

"Oh, I don't know. I can think of a few things. I mean, I know almost nothing about you except that you like chocolate and nuts, unless they're mixed together, and that you're an amazing doctor." She pushed up on her elbows and wriggled backward into a reclined position. Xander frowned but he didn't stop her.

"What more did you want to know?"

"Tell me about your assignment before this. Why were you stuck on a small planet command when you have such needed skills?"

He grunted, the sound low and displeased.

"I'm not asking anything too much, am I?"

Xander sighed. "I... fucked up about a year ago before coming here to the *Jemison*. Got into a fight with an admiral's son and almost lost my commission altogether."

"For *fighting*?"

"I put him in the hospital. Nobody could pull me off the little fucker, and it damn near killed him. They stationed me at a shit base on Paradiso instead of doing their worst, until Bishop rescued me and arranged my transfer to the *Jemison*. That's it in a nutshell, Thandie."

"Oh, a fresh start. I can respect that, but..." Thandie drifted off, her brow furrowed. Nothing about Xander's situation sounded as cut and dried as he tried to make it seem. "I'm sure you had a valid reason. You don't seem like the sort to fly off the handle."

"Doesn't matter. I was bigger, and I should have ignored him."

She reached over and smoothed her hand down his shoulder. "Can I ask one more question?"

"I can't promise I'll answer."

"Why'd you pull away from me that night in the lounge?"

"Didn't seem appropriate to dive balls deep into you in the crew lounge."

That blunt answer took her by surprise. She blinked at him, and unquenchable lust curled low in her belly. "Well, in that case, I should admit the same thought crossed my mind. More than once."

The same desire she'd seen that night burned in his bright eyes. Thandie drank in the sight of them and yielded the fight against her impulses, closing the distance in a hungry kiss.

The logical part of her brain told her to end it at only a kiss, that anything more was irresponsible while they were deployed to ground. Her impulsive side insisted there was no time better than the present to take advantage of the privacy ship life had denied.

Encouraged by his matching ardor, Thandie shifted her position until she straddled him.

With the damned combat suit in her way, she couldn't feel him swelling and hardening beneath her, but she could *hear* the low, primal groan of pleasure he made against her mouth. His hand closed over her ass and squeezed. For the first time, she became aware of the size of his hands and how it covered her entire cheek.

As far as Thandie was concerned, Xander had a mouth made for kissing and abs worthy of worship. Her fingers crept over each plane and dip, learning his shape as her mouth committed his taste to memory.

She swept her tongue past his lips again, and the return

flick made her imagine how good it would feel lapping her clit. His head dipped down, then his lips traced an invisible pattern on her neck.

"Thandie," he moaned against her throat. "We shouldn't."

"We should. Definitely should."

Archaic fraternization laws had been dissolved when United Command instituted two-year deployments in space, although it had been done at the behest of the Lexar government.

They were sensible people. Logical. Rational. Except for their quickness to anger.

The narcotics warred with the endorphins rushing through her body. Would she be brought up on assault charges if she ripped the suit off him plate by fucking plate until he was as bare as she needed him to be?

It seemed worth the possible court-martial, though something told her that if Xander wasn't amiable to her suggestion, nothing could make him.

"Thandie, you need to rest."

"I'd rather be doing this." To emphasize her point, she kissed him again.

Quicker than she'd realized he could move, Xander flipped her beneath him on the mattress. As he kissed his way down her throat, his stubbled jaw abraded her sensitive skin. One flick of his fingers unfastened the snap to her fatigue bottoms, then the zipper descended and he worked them down her thighs with ease. Her boots wouldn't allow them to go any lower than her mid-calf, not that it was necessary.

Talented hands slid beneath her black panties and tugged, baring her. Naked skin against naked skin, his fingers stroked over her mons then lower.

Only a week ago, on impulse, she'd made a spa appointment with one of their civilian ladies, the wife of one of the lieutenants on board the ship who happened to have an aesthetician license. Thandie hadn't been waxed completely smooth, but it was close, sleek and softer than suede, with a narrow runway strip.

Gazing down at her, he sat back on his heels and drank her in until she'd never felt sexier. A feral growl rumbled in his throat that didn't sound human, so low and husky a tremble clenched through her core. Heat curled in her stomach, a low and dull throb that ached for any part of him inside her.

A strong digit curled against her pussy and fulfilled her desire, gliding into her with ease. She shuddered and reached for one of his wrists, hoping to pull him down for a kiss.

"Xander—"

His thumb flicked her clit, and all that she'd wanted to tell him evaporated, her ability to form cohesive thoughts breaking apart like motes of dust on the wind. Her hips raised, following his fingers, straining to resume contact, then he sprawled between her spread thighs and pressed his mouth against her slit, tongue parting her with an eager stroke.

Thandie jolted on the bed, startled by his enthusiasm. Then her back arched, and she spread her thighs wider, and moaned each time he traced a wet pattern with his tongue. Throughout it all, one of his fingers remained inside her, never ceasing its effortless in and out plunge. Another digit joined the first, ratcheting up the tension drawing tight inside her.

"Xander, oh God, oh God, please—"

His breath whispered against her dewy skin. "Please what?"

"Please." She repeated herself, groaning in frustration and raking both hands through her own hair, needing something she couldn't voice. "I need... fuck, I need you inside me."

His tongue circled around her clit, touching everywhere but the delicate bundle itself until she cursed his name, and he laughed, the delicious sound of his amusement a caress around her heart.

How could she love one man's laugh so much?

The sound of it, rich and warm and alive with sensuality caressed her with the same talent as his tongue. And when it finally curled around her clit, he sucked—a tiny fraction of suction all it took to thrust her into orgasm—and she came apart while crying his name, praying no one heard. She clenched on his fingers over and over, moaning into the pillow.

Limp and floating in the stars, Thandie sprawled on the bed, unmoving at first, gathering her wits.

He dressed her again with surprising tenderness for a man who had to be giving himself a set of blue balls. "Get some rest."

Her eyes opened. She reached for him, fingers harmlessly skimming past the fastening on the left hip of his combat suit. He removed her hand and set it aside.

"But, we didn't—"

"You'll pass out any moment, I'm sure. Would you respect me any if I had my wicked way with your unconscious body?" Damn him for his logic and that shot. "C'mon. Get some rest, Thandie. Our watch will come sooner than you think."

He had a point. They were technically relieved of their

duty posts after working grueling hours with little rest and only a handful of comforts. But there was a time and a place. She'd hate to be caught with her pants down, literally, if returning pirates engaged their squad in battle.

"You play dirty, Xander. Don't think this is over."

His warm breath feathered across her brow, quickly followed by a gentle kiss. "Wouldn't dream of it."

CHAPTER TEN

Once the squad returned to the *Jemison*, Xander became inundated with work. He spent days performing tune-ups, repairs, and helping the other medical officers with the men and women injured on the ship during the space battle and emergency landing.

Refugees from Athena filled their aft cargo hold, and the three new mothers and the severely injured survivors occupied rooms in medical. As for the pirates, they had been detained until United Command's prison ship, the HMS *Bridewell*, arrived to take them away.

For lack of a better place to house the survivors, the *Jemison* flew for a week to reach the nearest major post equipped to handle a few hundred refugees.

Fuck, Xander was glad to lose the additional medical responsibility. He may have enjoyed making a difference in those peoples' lives, but babies were *not* his forte. Their fragile little bodies distressed him, as did the reminder that he had never had kids of his own. But it had also been nice to care for them during the short time, a double-edged sword that was both pleasure and pain.

Being the ship's only certified cyberware technician also meant he'd returned to an abundance of appointments, enough to spend almost four days making up for cancellations.

A small part of him missed running into Thandie during the ship's night hours. He even peeked into the lounge once or twice against his better judgment, but his sniper hadn't been present.

So he hit the gym for a couple hours, pumping iron so hard he impressed a pair of marines from the boarding team when he outlifted them, then retired to his bunk for a shower, where he stood under the steaming spray and ruminated over the recent events.

The memory of her body writhing on the bed haunted him. And then there was the taste of Thandie in his mouth, her sensual scent everything he needed and wanted. He stroked himself, with both dicks pressed together in one hand, hot water pounding against his tired back, and replayed every perfect moment from the brief liaison. Each breathy moan and soft cry. He closed his eyes and imagined her mouth wrapped around one of his cocks, the fantasy taking on a life of its own.

During his early life as an enlisted man sharing the communal shower, guys had joked about how lucky he was to have two penises. What they didn't see were long and frustrating masturbation sessions, because he had to jerk both to climax at the same time if he wanted real relief.

Hart impatiently hammered her fist on the door. "Wank on your own bloody time, you big twat!"

"For Christ's sake, I'm getting out now!" he bellowed. If he joked about her shower "massager"—that he could sometimes hear buzzing through the walls—she wouldn't speak to him for a week.

Xander turned the water off and stepped out of the stall, giving up the fruitless effort to blow his load with memories instead of female skin wrapped around him.

The restroom lock clicked behind him once he was toweled off, dressed, and gone, followed by the noisy drum of the resuming shower head. He'd have been smarter to give Hart the first shower and wait his turn later.

Before he could pick up where he'd left off, two knocks tapped against his door.

"This better be an emergency," he muttered under his breath. He slid the door open and peered into the hallway, expecting news from the medical bay. Instead, as if his thoughts had conjured her, Thandie stood in the hall.

"Aren't you a little far from your berthing?"

"I suppose so. I..." Thandie's gaze froze on his bare chest and she shifted her weight from one leg to the other. Uncertainty briefly flickered across her features, then her posture straightened, and she clasped her hands loosely behind her back. "I wanted to come clear the air on something. Please."

"What is it?"

"Oh, um..." Her glance darted down the passageway, then back to his face. "Not exactly a conversation for the public."

"Well, come on in. I have plenty of privacy."

"Thanks." She stepped past him into the room.

Xander stole a glance into the hallway in time to see his fellow commander attentively watching their exchange. Viljoen glowered at him before disappearing into his own room. Xander sighed.

What the hell had that been about?

"What's on your mind, Thandie?"

Thandie turned from her casual inspection of the space

XANDER

and tilted her head to look up at him. "I wanted to talk about what happened on Athena."

He hesitated to answer and erred on the side of caution. "What about it?"

"Is there any chance of it going somewhere or was that a one-time deal?"

A tense silence fell between them, and when she didn't yield first, he bit his lip and played cautious. "What exactly did you want it to be?"

Her eyes narrowed. "Okay, before we get into answering questions with questions, let me just cut to the chase. I like you and I would be happy to take this further, but if you don't wanna, I'll step back now. I just don't want to be played with, that's all."

"I'm asking for a specific reason. Give me the benefit of the doubt, at least. Have I ever done or said anything to make you think I'm playing with you?"

"No, you haven't."

He drew in a deep breath, filling his lungs before he continued, "Then answer my question. What did you hope would happen when you came here?"

"I hoped to find out that you felt the same way I do." She took a step closer. "That you'd want to finish what we started."

Xander met her step with one of his own, moving in close enough for their bodies to touch, to breathe the same air. "I do, trust me. I can barely focus on anything else lately, but there's a lot you don't know about me."

"Not for lack of trying. You're awfully tight-lipped about yourself."

"For a good reason." He spread his fingers over her hip and caressed through the layer of coveralls, wondering what, if anything, she'd worn beneath them for the impromptu visit. "You've been on my mind since the day you first came to my exam room. I can't get you out of my head. When we're on missions, I have to give myself a fucking pep talk just to keep focused on what's going on around me."

She blinked but didn't pull away. "That's pretty damn flattering, but I'm not sure I understand."

Sharing anything about himself had become difficult over the years, the number of times it had gone wrong more numerous than he could count. Still, he nudged his hips forward, pressing pelvis to pelvis, then dipped his head down and claimed her mouth, kissing her with all the pent-up desire that had been building since Athena.

Thandie melted in his embrace, curving her arms around him, and it felt only natural to heft her up in his arms. Strong legs wrapped around his waist and her fingers curled into the corded muscles of his shoulders.

"That's not an answer," she said, punctuating the words with a playful nibble.

"It is for now." He bumped into the end table beside the couch, and settled on the cushions, with her nestled on his lap.

The moment her lips parted to speak, he smothered her words, his mouth as demanding as she was curious. Both hands curved over her ass and yanked her in until his pajamas and her suit became their only barrier, a few scant layers of cotton between her heat and his rousing cocks.

"Fuck it feels amazing to kiss you again."

"I sense an unspoken *but*."

"But I need to come clean. About a lot. And it's the kind of stuff I don't tell just anyone, even *gorgeous* anyones, because it's also the kind of thing that can fuck with my reputation here." His pulse thundered in his veins.

"Gorgeous, huh? Are you fishin' for a return compliment?"

"I wouldn't say no to a few kind words."

Her smile widened and she dipped forward, laying a path of soft kisses and nibbles up his jaw. "You are, without a doubt, the sexiest man I've ever laid eyes on. But there's more to you than that."

Her lips reached his ear and a pleasurable tremble made its way down his spine. Thandie traced the curve with her tongue and skated her teeth against sensitive spots he hadn't even realized he possessed.

"Yeah, like what? Thought you just said I was tight-lipped about myself."

"Stuff anyone can see. You're smart. Kind. Hell, you're even sorta bossy and I actually like it. But I'm willing to take things slower, if that's what you want."

Slower was the last thing he wanted, rather, the last thing his Lexar DNA wanted. His bottom cock twitched, hardening slower than the one on top. He made a noncommittal grunt instead of answering.

"How about a massage?"

Xander rolled his left shoulder. He'd still be in the shower under the hot water if not for Hart. "Sure you aren't a mind-reader?"

Thandie slid from his lap. Once she settled behind him, her hands smoothed across the breadth of his muscular shoulders, somehow finding the aches and discomfort from his overenthusiastic exercise routine. "Positive. I just have good eyes, and you looked awfully tense. Have you been working nonstop since Athena?"

"Aside from a brief visit to the gym today, I haven't had much leisure time since we returned to the ship. Hell, I logged on Spellbound last night for about an hour and got chewed out by half my friend list. I don't make it known that I'm military, and when I miss our scheduled raids, they think I'm skiving off."

"Been there. Done that. I don't really game enough to have a regular group, though I've found a couple good ones to team up with sometimes. They were probably just worried about you is all. Friends do that."

"Yeah, they do. I'd log on tonight if the day hadn't caught up to me. Guess I'm getting old."

She scoffed. "You're far from old. You're just overworked and stiff."

"Almost forty, hon. I only look good. Too bad I don't feel it, too."

"Like I said, overworked." She applied even pressure despite her cybernetic hand, working out a knot with competence.

"Where'd you learn to do this? You're better than some of the people I've paid for a backrub."

"Long story short, I enrolled in a masseuse class during my implant adjustment leave. After I got the new arm I had trouble with managing the strength. The occupational therapist had me try everything from pottery to model ships, but I sucked."

"So, you thought people were a better medium?" He glanced over his shoulder and cocked a brow. "Maybe I need to rethink this."

"I'm not going to pulverize you. Geez. Anyway, my little sister suggested it and offered to be my practice dummy. Not hurting her was a strong motivator."

Silence fell between them as she worked on his knotted muscles and soothed the low burn lingering from the gym. The placid notes of classical music began, woodwinds and cello spilling from the room's audio aperture.

Thandie's amusement was equally musical to his ears. "Jem must like you. Is this helping any?"

"It feels great, but..." He reached up and took hold of her right hand, then traced his fingertips over her skin. Warm, alive, and sensitive to his touch. "Do you trust me?"

"I do."

Xander pressed gently with his thumb above her wrist where veins belonged on a flesh and blood limb. "You loosened a nerve connection again. Probably during a fight. How's that?"

Thandie flexed her fingers. "I barely even noticed. How did you...?"

"I'll spare you the medical jargon and say that my job is to notice when things are not as they should be." He laid a kiss inside her palm before releasing her.

"I'm impressed. Thank you."

Her praise sent warmth coursing through him. Then his eager upper cock jumped again, the bottom almost as firm. Unable to help himself, he rubbed one palm over the prominent bulge tenting out his pajama bottoms.

Done with his shoulders, Thandie moved in close behind him and slid her hands down his arms then up again. The next pass moved down his chest, then below his midsection, a stroke of her fingers tightening his abs with anticipation. He closed his eyes and reveled in her touch.

She was bound to find out eventually.

And there was no time like the present.

THANDIE FOLLOWED the dark trail of hair below his navel, even as Xander's abdomen tensed. His breath quickened, desire thick in the air, a palpable feeling her fledgling empathy picked up the moment her fingertips breached the elastic band of his pajamas.

Her exploration encountered hard, smooth skin. She delved further, breath catching as she measured his length. "Um..."

Xander stilled, frozen like a statue, and suddenly she understood his trepidation and reluctance to let her in his pants.

Because there was more than one dick there above his heavy balls, both of them hard and throbbing under her questing fingers. She smoothed her index and middle finger over the one on top, then its lower twin, the breath caught in her throat. "Holy shit. You're a Lexar."

"Half."

The revelation shocked as much as it fascinated. She stroked him again, earning another low groan, but it wasn't enough to satisfy her mounting curiosity. Now that she knew the truth, she wanted—no, *needed*—to see everything.

After moving around the couch, Thandie knelt between his legs and tugged on his waistband, urging Xander to raise his ass enough for her to pull the pajama bottoms down his muscular thighs. Both dicks stood at full attention, but the one on top was harder, flushed dark, and an inch longer.

"Thandie—"

"Is this what you were hiding from me? Did you think I'd judge you?"

His chest moved in a deep breath. She had the sexiest man on the ship, maybe the sexiest man in all the Royal Navy, sprawled back naked on a couch in front of her, vulnerable and exposed. She stroked one of his cocks and held back a gleeful giggle when the other twitched in response, as if jealous of the attention she'd given its twin. "Maybe."

"You're not gonna get any alien hate from me." She might not have known what the hell to do with two dicks, since all of her plans had involved one, but she certainly wasn't going to look a gift horse in the mouth. Improvising, she wrapped one hand around each and sized them up. "Do they both...?"

"Fully functioning, I assure you."

Twice the fun for her.

Up and down, she found a casual rhythm while a low growl rumbled in Xander's chest. Now, the resemblance to his Lexar ancestry was unmistakable. She thought back to all the signs—enormous muscles, impressive height, the feral gleam she sometimes saw in his eyes, and the glow she'd chalked up to her imagination. Both of his cocks were girthy and plump, thickly veined and so hard in her hands. She tried to imagine both of them inside her and a hot flush swept over her.

Would both even fit at once?

Daunted, but not disgusted, Thandie leaned forward between his thighs and kissed the dark, smooth crown of his bottom cock. He shuddered and closed his eyes. The other received the same tender care, but then she took it a step further and drew him into her mouth. Xander sucked in a sharp breath. His hips bucked forward, then he fisted a handful of couch cushion.

His low groan was pure pleasure to her ears and all the encouragement she needed to continue. To return the favor. To spoil and delight him as he'd satisfied her on Athena.

"You don't have to do this."

"I want to. Completely selfless. Because it's what you did for me." He opened his mouth to respond, but she cut him off. "And because I *want* to," she repeated for emphasis. Then her mouth was on him again, his hips jerking.

It took her a moment, but she found a rhythm, using her mouth on one dick and her hands on the other. Then she swapped, ensuring both received equal treatment. At some point, Xander had taken hold of her hair and threaded his fingers through it.

She peeked up to find him watching her, eyes smoldering with desire. One lick, one stroke of her tongue against the throbbing underside, sent a shudder through his body. "Is it good?"

"Fuck yes."

Thandie sucked him into her mouth again and tested her limit, thrusting him deeper on each glide. He filled her mouth, stretching her lips around him, and then she hummed. Xander swore again. His hips pumped up and down, breaths ragged and muscles so tight every inch of definition stood out from his glorious eight-pack to his corded neck when his head fell back against the couch. She pushed past the ache in her jaw and refused to stop.

"Thandie, baby, I'm gonna blow." His voice was thick and husky with passion, little more than a sensual murmur.

"Perfect."

Preparing for his orgasm, she pressed his cocks together and took the tips of both into her mouth, uncertain if they'd come simultaneously. Xander swore under his breath and tensed, the hand in her hair tightening its grip.

One spurted before the other, the rush of it felt throbbing down the shaft until it exploded from the rounded tip and filled her mouth with the rich, salty taste of him. Xander's fingers tangled in her hair, hips thrusting wildly, erratically, his low groans rising louder as the spent cock pulsed its final drops. She let it slip out, aware that the lower cock remained hard.

And then she slipped it deeply into her mouth until it reached her throat and hummed.

His cry was absolute bliss conveyed in one word. Another spurt pulsed as he shouted her name, every muscle of his delicious frame seeming to tighten and ripple. She lapped up and swallowed each drop, until his second dick was as soft as the first. Thandie kissed both a last time and turned her face against his thigh.

"Fuck," Xander exhaled after a few moments passed. He still hadn't opened his eyes.

Laughing, she stroked his abs. "Feel better?"

"I'd be better if you were up here beside me."

Needing no further encouragement, she joined him on the couch. The minutes blurred together, lost in a series of slow and drugging kisses. Hands wandered and fingers explored, gliding over curves, muscles, and ticklish places. They were free to kiss without urgency or guilt, no patients awaiting his care and no marines relying on their vigilance.

Suddenly, he drew back and ran his fingers through her hair. After a few moments of enduring his silent study, heat rushed to her face. How could he make her feel so beautiful with only a look?

"What are you thinking about?"

"I was deciding whether to ask if you wanted to stay. I happen to be an excellent bedtime cuddler."

"You'd have to toss me out to get rid of me now."

"C'mere." He reached down and dragged Thandie to her feet by both hands, only to draw her close with both arms around her. She stepped into the embrace, placing her hands at his hips.

"I feel I should warn you. I'm a horrible bed hog." Her words were only half in jest.

"I'm not worried."

"Good." The warmth and humor suffused her voice with an inviting quality, chasing the fluttering moments of shyness and anxiety away.

With their sleeping arrangements made, Thandie stripped off her boots and coveralls. She joined him in only a camisole and panties, crawling beneath the tidy sheets and into his secure embrace. The bed fit them both with room to spare, much nicer than her enlisted bunk.

"That's pretty." Thandie said, gesturing toward a keepsake bottle on the nightstand. Pink sand glittered at the bottom of a water-filled globe, cushioning three pearlescent shells. The room's dim lighting glinted off several fine purple and ivory filaments floating inside. It resembled a marine feather duster. "Is that from Elora?"

Xander inhaled deeply. "It is."

"What is it?"

"Ask me again another day, and I'll tell you." He squeezed her tightly and pressed his lips against her brow. "Right now, I only want to enjoy having you here."

She sensed a sudden wave of nostalgia and sadness fluttering to the surface of his thoughts. And the last thing she wanted was to taint the sensual mood. Rather than give in to her curiosity, she dropped the subject and snuggled in closer.

There was plenty of time to learn all of Xander Vargas's secrets, because now that she had him, nothing would convince her to let go.

CHAPTER ELEVEN

THE SHIFT WAS NEVER GOING TO END. WHILE THERE had been a decrease in the number of crewmen needing medical services, it had also resulted in one hell of a boring day for the doctors who worked in the infirmary.

"Want one?" Kathleen asked Xander, leaning one hip against the desk. She held out a bag of assorted chocolates and candies that had already suffered a thorough rummaging from the medical technicians.

He grunted. "Who the hell ate all the Silk Classics?"

"Lil got to them before you. Maybe if you were socializing with the rest of us instead of hiding in your office, you would have gotten a few."

Xander growled under his breath and plucked out an acceptable substitute, turning his nose up at the ones with nuts.

"I've never met a man so bloody picky about his sweets."

"We have an hour of this bullshit left. I need sugar, and I'd *like* to get it without picking nuts out of my teeth in front of my next patient." He plucked a few more of his choice favorites from the bag, then groaned inwardly when Kathleen scooted her rear onto the corner of his desk.

"*If* you get a patient. It's been dead for you, too." She popped another candy into her mouth and watched him. "You know, I'm a practicing empath."

"So? You mentioned this to me before." Every other person on the street had some empathic ability these days, a positive side effect of humankind moving to the planet Albion a few generations ago. Most never took the time to hone their skills and develop some talent with the ability.

"You're excited about something. What's up, Xander? You're hiding in your office, anxious to leave when you're usually the last to go, and you're stuffing your face with candies—when they're serving fried chicken in the mess tonight. Your favorite."

"If you are reading my thoughts, I will punch you out of this ship's airlock. I'll explain later to Bishop about why he lost a physician." He avoided meeting her eyes and kicked the trash bin out from behind his desk. "I have a lot of things on my mind."

"Oh, touchy-touchy. You know I don't read thoughts. C'mon. Dish."

A quick glance to the left and to the right confirmed no one was within earshot. Their conversation would remain private. "I have a date."

"Ohhh?" Her eyebrows rose beneath her bangs. "Will you meet her for tea in the cafe? Or shall it be a make-out in the bio-farm? That's where all the kids are snogging these days."

"It's an online date," Xander quickly clarified. "I don't want... we aren't ready to meet in public here yet." Except he'd been an excited dumbass and forgotten to ask for her game handle. Xander sighed and considered phoning

Thandie back to ask, but her time on the clock wasn't as fluid. He had all the free time he needed between patients.

"I have to say, I'm curious about who's caught your eye. Pretty sure you're not going to tell me, though." Hart wrinkled her nose at him.

"You guessed correctly."

"Go on, then. Sod off and get out of here. Shift is almost up, and unless Viljoen rips someone's tech out of a socket, you won't be needed."

"You don't mind?" Xander hesitated, perched on the edge of his seat.

"I can handle things. Besides, the way your feelings are bouncing all over the place, you won't be focused anyway."

"Thanks, Kath."

He was halfway to his stateroom when his communicator beeped.

"Tactical room, Xander."

Ethan's terse voice cut off and Xander swore. A call like that meant now, not later. He turned about and headed directly for the briefing room as ordered. Viljoen arrived at the same time and didn't utter a word or acknowledge his sociable nod.

Ethan, Amelia, and Oshiro had already taken their seats. Their grim expressions told it all.

"We just received word from the *Glenn*. She's been on similar missions as ours in the Tersian Nebula." Ethan cut to the point without greeting them. "They discovered a mining settlement out there under the same circumstances as Athena. Only they arrived too late and the pirates left more bodies behind than they took."

"We forwarded several autopsy results to your personal medical rig, Doctor Vargas," Amelia informed him. "You'll find them to be of interest."

"Why is that?" Xander asked politely.

"The survivors from Athena said the pirates took everyone with cybernetic implants on the ship first and secured them. After that, they weeded through the rest. According to the personnel files, everyone taken either had an implant or was a technician involved in the manufacture of cybernetic parts."

"Right. So, we have pirates on a high-tech ship with their sights set on cyborgs."

"The bodies found by the *Glenn* had been… stripped." Amelia frowned and pulled up a file on the display. Over a dozen images flickered open, each more disturbing than the last.

"What the hell is all that?" Viljoen leaned forward to get a better look.

"Someone practiced cerebral augmentation on that man. Right here, I recognize it by the cyberware burns on the left temporal lobe." Xander stared at the frozen image hovering above their table. "Typically, we're allowed minimal interference with the brain."

The photos portrayed another story, one with opened skulls and blank, staring faces attached to motionless corpses, their bodies strewn over the ground like refuse. It wasn't ethical. It wasn't *right*.

"He is correct," Oshiro said. "Good eye, Xander. I didn't recognize the burns."

"Okay. It's clear that they're abducting experimental subjects, but why would they prefer to take cyborgs?" Viljoen asked, cutting in. "If they plan to do the work on them already…"

Experimental brain research could help millions, but the strict codes enacted by the Lexar forbade it. Of all the scientific advancements they'd made to their own race and to humankind, the brain was the one organ left untouched.

To the Lexar, the brain was sacred.

His brows notched, then he went back to another autopsy photograph to examine the placement of the scarring. "I've got it."

"Well, don't keep us in suspense," Viljoen said.

The four officers gave Xander their full attention. "When the steps are made to become a cyborg, often we install a small neurochip against the spinal cord just above C_1. It's a wireless conduit between the brain and the new cybernetic part. Practically every cyborg over the past twenty years should have one. Because it isn't actual brain augmentation, it's cool with the Lexar."

"You think they're after the chips?" Ethan asked. "Why not simply hijack a freighter with a shipment of them on the way to a medical installation?"

"No. About ten percent of the cyborg population rejects their chip. When that happens, they're downgraded to a less efficient, but very useful, model from early century. There's a firm that specializes in building more of the old tech to today's standards.

"You think they're hunting for cyborgs who have already undergone the trial?" Viljoen asked. "Christ. I didn't know it was so complicated."

"Choosing cybernetics isn't an easy decision. There was once a time when many died on the table, but we've gotten that down to less than a 0.01% chance." For a marine with a career, like Thandie, augmentation became absolutely necessary to remain in the military. Otherwise they faced medical discharge, all their effort and years of training gone to waste.

Viljoen grimaced. "I didn't know."

Xander shifted through the remaining images until he reached the report. "But there's more to it than that. They're also claiming registered psychics. I believe that whoever we're after has chosen to abduct them for illegal brain experimentation. A psychic's brain can accept a lot of punishment before it's absolutely exhausted beyond the point of regenerating."

"Why plant the seed when you can purchase a sapling? Only, in their case, they're stealing living human beings." The words chilled Xander as they left Oshiro's mouth. "But what do we plan to do about it?"

"Find them," Ethan said. "I have Shahid and Lockhart conducting a search of their own. In the meantime, we plan to visit the remaining outer-rim colonies, set them on alert. We'll conduct weapons training with their militias and local police forces to prepare them."

Amelia crossed her arms, lips in a flat, disapproving line. "Still, what is their goal? Can just anyone do this kind of work on a body? You went through years of training to get where you are."

"Takes a skilled neurosurgeon and a cyberneticist working in conjunction with each other," Xander replied. "Anything less is murder. You can't pick this up from an online video and practice it out."

Oshiro sighed. "I haven't seen butchery like this in forty years. The Lexar warned us, but we were arrogant and thought, with their technology, we could finally solve the mystery of the brain. I was fresh to neurosurgery then, but I remember the grim reports. Hundreds died during unnecessary cybernetic procedures."

"That's when the Lexar stepped in and threatened to dissolve the treaty between us," Ethan said. "Obviously, someone has decided to pick that research back up."

Amelia grunted in disgust. "Doesn't matter why, not right now. We can figure that out after we catch them."

They adjourned the meeting after discussing their next destination. Ethan hung back instead of filing from the room along with the others.

"Xander, a moment."

"Yes?" The door closed behind Oshiro, leaving the two men alone.

"We've been so busy that we haven't had a chance to really talk. Free time has been shite."

"That's because you've been busy flirting with virtual nymphs." Xander grinned uneasily. He had a niggling feeling about the reason behind this chat.

"We don't all have young women visiting our staterooms aboard the ship."

"How did you—?"

"No one told me anything. No one alive, anyway. I tried to ring you last night for a chat, but Jem insisted you were busy with a female friend. She screened me. *Me*. Do you plan to tell me who?"

"No."

"Fair enough." Ethan backed down easily. He always had a knack for knowing when to push and when to withdraw. "At any rate, that isn't why I asked you to hang back a moment. You're aware of the mission schedule, right?"

"You're worried about our next scheduled liberty dock."

"Yes. Will you be all right there?"

All right. Such a simple concept, but far from how he felt when he considered the rolling green and blue oceans stretched endlessly over Elora. The little aquatic planet held memories for him of his deceased wife. Ylona wouldn't want him to avoid her homeworld. She would want him to celebrate every moment as if she were there in spirit.

"I'll be fine," he responded slowly. "I'm looking forward to it. I miss her, but I promise going there isn't going to push me over the edge or anything."

"And your new friend? Is that a one-time dalliance or will you be sharing the time with her?" Ethan regarded him with brotherly concern.

"We're still working that out." Xander frowned. "I haven't told her about Ylona."

"Or about other things, I take it."

"No, she knows about my heritage. I figured one bombshell was enough to drop on her. Bringing up my dead wife didn't seem appropriate." Especially when she'd had a double handful of dick and was keen on exploring.

"Well, that's a step in the right direction. Anyway, we'll work out the schedule if your shore leave doesn't overlap."

"You don't have to do that, Ethan. No special favors."

"This isn't a special favor. Now get out of here. I'd ask you to join me in game tonight, but I have plans to visit Engineering and the Main Battery. When we run into those pirates again, I don't want history repeating itself."

"Don't terrorize them too much."

They parted ways and Xander hurried as fast as he dared down the passageway.

THE GAME ASKED him if he wanted to log into his last known position, or teleport to a new location. He chose the Gardens of Manhattan. Seconds later, the virtual world greeted him with a splash of colors and humming sensation. It came alive, bombarding him with natural green smells and birdsong.

Thandie had picked the location. Xander turned in a

circle, taking in the exotic sight surrounding him. New York City as a whole didn't appeal to him; it was too crowded and noisy. No wonder their past ancestors had looked to the stars for greener pastures.

He waited in an oasis within the chaotic city replica. Trees grew inside and soared up to the vaulted glass roof, water fell over rocks in a natural fountain, and flowers in every color sprouted up in neatly tended beds. It was beautiful and quiet, with only a small handful of other players occupying the large space.

A soft breeze whispered across his cheek and stirred through his hair. It carried the scent he associated with rain and thunderstorms, mingled with the green and floral fragrance of the room. The game provided the most realistic tastes and smells, rivaling anything from the physical world. It was no wonder that some people logged in and lost their lives to the virtual world. For a time, he had been one of them, throwing away his physical life to numb the pain of losing his wife.

"Oh, hello, Juan. Fancy meeting you here."

The use of his avatar's name drew Xander's gaze upward. Zephyr's ethereal form shimmered and coalesced into existence near a vented window. Pale blue and silver silks fluttered around her slender frame, accompanied by beautiful iridescent wings that vanished once she touched the ground. Her bare feet left slight indentations in the grass.

His cock jumped up and stiffened, thankfully concealed beneath heavy layers of mage battle robes. Months of gaming, and he still wasn't used to his avatar having only one. Maybe he could download a mod. "Get bored with England's zones?"

Zephyr smiled and shrugged. "I was after a certain

weapon drop in this area last time I played, so this is where I logged out."

"Did you get it?" Chatting with Zephyr became an acceptable distraction until Thandie arrived.

The sylph nodded eagerly, her face aglow with enthusiasm. She accessed her holographic interface and removed a longbow from her inventory. Living vines twined around its length. "A reward from the local dryads for defending them against some fire-happy warlocks. I can hit an imp at a hundred paces, easy."

"Nice." He glanced it over, then handed the weapon back, watching as it disappeared into her inventory. "I'm a little envious. I like bows."

"So, what brings you around here? I'm so used to seeing you with the other two."

"Eh... I didn't set up a time to play with them today. They're busy."

"Just taking in the view?" Zephyr's glance slid past him briefly, toward the sound of an opening door. Two people stepped out of the gardens into the room beyond. She sighed and glanced back.

"Yep. What about you? I usually see you with a gaggle of your nymphly cousins."

"True, but today I'm waiting for someone." She dropped down onto a nearby bench and swayed her feet from side to side, tapping her fingers against her thigh. The familiar gesture drew his gaze until she lifted her eyes and caught him staring. "Nymphs don't have a footwear slot. I sort of like it."

"Sorry, I didn't mean to stare. It's just that you remind me of someone I know." He paused to consider the absolute absurdity, then marveled over how dry his mouth felt in a digital videogame. "Thandie?"

Zephyr's lips parted in a silent "oh" of surprise. She hopped up and hastily tucked her long, silvery hair behind her delicately pointed ears. "Xander?"

"You're a sylph." He'd expected some hulking Inquisitor type character with a flaming sword of righteousness, or maybe even one of the tough-as-nails wizard avatars.

"So?"

"You're roleplaying the most feminine class in the game."

"What's wrong with that?" Thandie drew herself up defensively. If Xander had any doubts about her identity, that action ended them. "I'm supposed to be a tank because I shoot guns in real life?"

"No, I like it!" he quickly clarified, waving his hands. "It was just unexpected. I..." He snorted, overcome with a realization that made him quake with laughter. "We've been playing together all this time."

"You're playing a healer." Her lips quirked at the corners into a broad smile. "You're a doctor and you're playing one here, too."

"Stick with what you know."

"It suits you." She clasped her hands behind her back, toes wiggling in the grass. "I should have guessed. You like chastising me in-game as much as you do out there."

"Sorry. I guess I can't help it."

"So..." She stepped closer and took his hand. "Now you know I have a girly side. I like dresses and stuff like that."

"I haven't seen you in a dress yet. I mean, in the real world. Last time I saw you step off the ship on liberty, you were wearing pants and boots."

She glanced up shrewdly. "You've been paying attention to what I wear?"

Xander slid his arms around her narrow waist. "How

could I not? I notice *everything* about you." The real Thandie was an Amazon, and he preferred her dark hair and bronzed skin. Her true smile featured a slightly crooked tooth too minor for dental correction, but the sylph avatar lacked her flaws and the minor imperfections that made her lovable and real.

Not that his Lexar brain chemistry gave a fuck, because it recognized her no matter the form. Damn. He'd hoped to be able to look at her and have a discussion with a clear head.

Overcome by impulse, Xander dragged her close against him and kissed her with all of the passion he could muster. Thandie's softer lips and fragile frame molded against him, her every curve as authentic in digital form as it had felt as she lay beside him the previous night.

Her fingers crept slowly up his arms, coming to rest on his shoulders.

"Come on. Let's have some fun," he whispered against her lips.

They came to the mutual decision not to share the evening with their military friends, although Thandie sulked when Xander refused to reveal the identity of his two guild mates. He told her it would ruin the fun, especially after she erroneously guessed O'Reilly to be the player behind Ethan's character.

A sudden message popped up from Gareth as they stepped outside into the digital sunlight. *Hey, we're going to raid the banshee citadel in Avalon. Finally got about two dozen good players to pull it off. Wanna come along? Oh, and here's the 5000 gold I borrowed from you. Made it back like I promised. Thanks, mate.*

Xander paused to reply. "One sec. Message from a friend."

"No problem. Take your time."

Go without me, he sent to Gareth. *I'm going to do an event in NYC area.*

Yeah? I heard about that. It's only a stupid haunted house.

So?

Testy, this evening, aren't you? All right, I'll keep an eye out for anything you might want.

Xander shot a glance at Thandie. She had bent to interact with a few of the digital pixie NPCs—non-player characters designed to interact with the actual game players. The programmed creatures flitted around the garden, occasionally landing on players with friendly auras. "Sorry. Just a second."

"No rush," Thandie assured him.

Xander sighed and typed out another hasty message to Gareth. *I'm grouped with someone who has a high faction rating with Avalon. I'll hang out with you next time.*

That seemed to end it by satisfying Gareth's curiosity. For her patience, and because he simply wanted to do it, Xander kissed Thandie again at the conclusion of his messaging.

"Okay, all yours."

Supposedly, the game designers had done their research by pulling information and scenes from popular horror movies of the time. Between a burned man wearing double-razor gloves and a bulky zombie wearing a catcher's mask, Xander and Thandie ran more in one night than they'd ever run during military training. Fortunately, the sylph's natural ability to control the wind translated into a powerful haste spell. Xander practically flew down the poorly lit halls of the dilapidated house.

"Are there rewards for completing this?" he demanded,

once they stopped breathlessly in a quiet hallway. The realistic loss of stamina made him lean against her. "I don't know if I'm having legitimate fun or if I'm too terrified to believe otherwise."

It was definitely fun. With Thandie, he enjoyed an exhilarating freedom denied to him as a kid.

"I thought you liked all these old horror movies. Are you going to need a teddy bear tonight?" Her playful taunt accompanied a laugh. She gazed up and down the hallway warily. "We're almost to the top floor anyway. That's the goal."

"Almost," he repeated. "If another clown chases me through a room of dolls and torture devices, I'm holding you responsible," he teased lightheartedly.

"I will humbly accept my punishment." She reached over and took his hand.

The top and final floor featured a maze of spider webs they had to navigate. Xander had the final laugh upon the discovery that Thandie was fine with zombie clowns but absolutely petrified of tiny arachnids. He refused to let her quit and dragged her through.

Maybe they couldn't enjoy a traditional date away from the *Jemison*, but in a way, their virtual videogame had given the very thing they both needed: a night together away from their military responsibility.

JUST BEFORE LOGGING out of the game, Xander and Thandie had both agreed to risk another late-night visit to his stateroom. He removed his headset and reclined with his eyes closed while waiting.

Eventually, the door chime announced her arrival, and

he found her on the other side dressed in standard ship coveralls, with a mild case of bedhead. Xander fought back the urge to smooth down the dark strands at the nape of her neck.

"Sorry. I had to listen to Angela's chatter before I could slip out," she said after the door slid shut behind her.

"About?"

"Actually..." She laughed quietly and glanced up. "It was about you. You're sort of the dreamboat of the ship. I just nodded and said 'uh huh' and 'I guess' a lot."

"Yeah, I sort of gathered. I spent my first three days bogged down by frivolous medical requests before Oshiro caught wind of it and put out word that any unnecessary sick calls would be visiting him personally in his office."

"Yeah, see, I never heard the reasoning behind that. I just thought medical here ran a really tight ship. Made me nervous when I came in about my arm."

"From that, I gather this means your bunkmates don't know where you've gone to? Did they ask about last night?"

"No. I'm always taking off anyway since I'm a night owl. Besides, last night was personal and none of their business."

Xander smiled easily. "I found a good movie on Cineweb in their Classics section. It's only about 100 years old but recently remastered for the Holovision."

Thandie left her boots by the door and dropped her coveralls on the floor. The thin cotton shirt beneath was too flimsy to hide the dark circles of her areolas and her nipples were semi-stiff, plump outlines beneath the fabric. The camisole's matching floral shorts barely covered her cheeks.

God.

After gathering snacks for their movie night, Xander guided her to the bed, where they curled up beneath the sheets. The ancient flick portrayed an interesting mix of family values and romance filled with awkward sexual tension. The heroine's family became overprotective jerks as the story's main plot device, while the young lover floundered and failed in every effort to please them.

Story of his life. Before Ylona, he'd dated Hannah for years prior to popping the question. Her father, an admiral in the military, recognized the Lexar blood in Xander and hated him on sight, and he had no doubt that her parents popped a bottle of expensive champagne to celebrate the end of the relationship.

"I've always wondered if this sort of behavior is common in real families."

"What behavior? Boyfriends sleeping in separate rooms before marriage?" Thandie laughed, and the huff of breath feathered across Xander's cheek. Her closeness would have weakened his knees if they were standing. "My folks did when my brother's fiancée came to visit for the first time after the engagement. Not that it mattered much, since I remember hearing them in the middle of the night. They hit it off. It was like love at first sight for them." She chuckled.

"That must have been nice."

"Have you ever felt like that for someone or am I the first?"

While he had half expected the question, it still took him by surprise. Hannah had been the woman he was expected to date, a trophy for her to claim, and the ideal woman aboard the *Glenn*. But he'd never felt truly attracted to her—and once he confessed to being part-Lexar, she'd asked him to undergo surgery to correct his condition.

And he'd almost done it. He'd almost been desperate enough for her affection to change the one truly unique and different thing about his physiology that connected him to his father's people.

Days before the surgery, barely a few weeks before their scheduled wedding date, Xander had backed down and ended the engagement. Then he'd taken some leave time and met Ylona while drinking himself into a stupor. While she'd been beautiful inside and out, he'd never felt the Mating Frenzy with her. Their love had been something different, transcending sexual attraction and lust.

And he didn't know how to bring it up without ruining the mood. It felt wrong to think of her now while another woman's lips pressed intimately against his throat, but in that moment, he also realized one thing—Ylona would have approved of Thandie.

Elorans didn't believe in Heaven, Hell, or any traditional afterlife, but they believed a surviving loved one deserved the chance for happiness. And Xander wanted so badly to be happy again.

Silence reigned until the credits rolled. Thandie raised her head from his shoulder and met his gaze. "Xander?"

"Hm?"

"It's okay not to answer. I wasn't trying to be nosy."

He tightened the arm wrapped around her. "Stay tonight?"

Her soft sigh of relief brushed his cheek. "Sure. I don't have assignment tomorrow."

"I do, but I think I can swing something." Xander tugged her into the bed alongside him and arranged the blankets over them. "Our chief medical officer sort of loves me, and I think, this time, I don't mind using a connection or two."

"Doctor Oshiro seems nice." Thandie nestled in closer, one leg drawing up over his. After a moment, she seemed to reconsider and stretched her leg out. Xander caught her by the thigh and pulled the limb back up.

"Known him since I was a scrawny kid. The Royal Navy denied me the first time I tried to get in." He chuckled against her dark hair at the memory of his younger self. "I didn't make the weight requirement. I'd just shot up about a foot over the summer and didn't eat enough to put weight on, too. There I was, barely fucking sixteen and six-foot-five already. And still growing. I don't know what made him do it, but he wrote me a waiver and took me home with him. He even told them he'd have me meeting all the regs by the time they shipped me to boot."

"I have a hard time imagining you as scrawny." Her trailing kisses ended at his chin. "You grew up nice. Look how far you've come, fixing up folk like me."

"Yeah... Doc had a huge impact on me. I knew then that I wanted to be a doctor, but I didn't think I'd get accepted into school. I guess for a kid who missed getting his certs, I must have scored really big on more than just my entrance exam. The commodore was on the review team."

"And now you serve with both men who helped shape your life."

"Yep."

"It must be nice, having role models and friends like that. I haven't dealt with Commodore Bishop at all, but I hear good things. Usually, my sort doesn't run into him unless we're in trouble or getting an award. Tends to be better that way."

If only she knew she'd raided with him in the game against the warlock landlord. "Mm. He's not a bad guy. Just has to set that impression around the rest of you. You should see him during liberty."

"No, no, I get that." She chuckled softly and turned her

head to nuzzle his throat. "He kidnaps officers and forces them to have a good time."

"I had a horrible time," he muttered. "Some little tart from logistics tried to rub her tits in my face."

"Torturous."

"In this day and age, there's no excuse for obviously false tits."

Snickers turned to full-blown laughter. "Oh, you mean, um, Keita. I was on the Armstrong with her six years back when she first joined up. The girls were *much* smaller then, yes."

"She should have paid a few more quid to get it done right. Yours, on the other hand..." He cupped one breast in his palm and brushed his thumb back and forth across her nipple. The stiffened peak stood out against her top. "Yours are perfect."

The soft hitch in Thandie's breath sent his pulse racing. He leaned in close, but she raised a single finger and set it against his lips. Xander went still.

"We don't have to rush," she said in a soft voice. "I know I was eager before—"

Xander stiffened. "It's all right. No need to explain."

"Hey, no, it's not like that." She pushed up on one elbow and looked down at him. "I am not put off by your differences, trust me. But I'm not sure how to, uh... I need time to work up to two dicks. I'm trying to figure out how to make that physically work."

The tension in his chest eased. Able to breathe again, Xander nodded and tried to view the situation through her eyes. "I guess when you put it that way, it makes sense. I'm not going to rush you. I don't want you to *ever* feel pressured to have sex with me. Okay? Let's agree on that now before we take this anywhere else. I'm happy to wait."

"Well, I don't want to keep you waiting too long. Hell, *I* don't want to wait too long." Her cheeks flushed. "I downloaded half-Lexar porn once. It's... hot. I just never thought I'd be in the position to experience it myself."

He blinked. "I didn't even know that was a thing."

"It's not exactly easy to find. I was really determined and had just moved out of my parents' house to join the Royal Navy, so the galactic web was a fresh new place full of unmonitored, forbidden mysteries."

He chuckled. "Well, guess we both hit the jackpot then. I can be at ease, and you don't need to search the web anymore for obscure porn. There's something else I need to tell you before we go any further with this."

"Pretty sure nothing can be more shocking than two penises, so let's have it."

Xander laughed again despite the serious matter. "What else do you know about the Lexar when it comes to sex?"

"Not much, really. They don't exactly spill their secrets to us."

"Lexar males sometimes go into a sort of, hell, a rut, I guess you could say. They meet a woman and they can't focus on anything else but them. They'd do anything to protect her. To claim her as their own."

He watched her face as his words sank in. Thandie's golden eyes widened and her lips parted. "You're..."

"The first time I ever experienced the Mating Frenzy, you were on my exam table, and it took all of my concentration not to humiliate myself."

"Is that why I'm here? Because you got hit by genetics?"

He shook his head. "No. It's why I tried so hard to resist you. I didn't want some genetic sexual urge to be why I got to know you. But everywhere I turned, there you were, like fate had intervened, and when we did get to know one another, I realized I didn't want to be without you."

"Wow."

"I'm sorry, that was a bit much, wasn't it?" Fuck. What if he scared her away? He bit his tongue and held the rest in.

"I just didn't realize... I mean, I know you mentioned it before, but I thought you were exaggerating."

"Sweetie, I was so anxious to see you again this evening that Kathleen spent most of our shift making fun of me."

"I, uh, ran into her this morning. In your bathroom."

He tilted his head back to look at her. "You didn't lock the door?"

Thandie giggled and turned her face against his arm. "Sorry. I'm not used to locking doors. We still use a shared space in the enlisted section. A bunch of women fighting over three showers."

"The bint didn't even tell me. She played it dumb the entire time she questioned me."

"Well, we didn't talk or anything. She sort of blinked at me a few times then backed out again mumbling about not seeing anything."

"Of course not. That isn't her style. She must have expected me to offer it up to her."

"That was nice of her." Light pecks traveled up his shoulder and neck, little kisses that wormed their way into his heart and filled him with warmth.

"I'm glad you're here," Xander said impulsively. "I mean it, Thandie. I enjoy when we're together. It's about more than your beauty...and, uh, how much the alien half of my genes really wants to dick you. I admire your strength and your perseverance, the work that got you here on the *Jemison*."

"I like you, too. And…" Her gaze dropped downward then back up to his face. "Not just because you have two really impressive cocks, though that's definitely a bonus."

"A bonus, eh?"

"Uh huh. Definitely a two-for-one deal. I'm just not ready to turn in my coupon yet."

CHAPTER TWELVE

After a quiet two weeks of dating in supposed secret, Xander invited Thandie to join him for tea at a small cafe-slash-pub tucked beside the crew lounge. The invitation took her by surprise, but at the same time, brought an instant gratification. Hiding wasn't her strong suit.

And neither was deciding what to fucking wear on a date with a hot guy, because the last seven years of her life had been fatigues and boots. The time preceding that was lace dresses, petticoats, and corsets—the life of a virginal southern belle from Tallulah.

If her parents knew how much she'd cut loose after leaving their home, they'd be appalled.

Thandie spent the hour prior to their scheduled meeting tearing through what little wardrobe she'd acquired over the years of military life. Most of her purchases landed in a military storage container somewhere on Albion with her name on it, but she stuffed the rest into a small trunk beside her rack.

Elizabeth glanced up from her book. "What *are* you doing?"

"Failing at 'Woman 101,' apparently. I need to look nice for a date, but not too nice."

"Please tell me you didn't say yes to O'Reilly. Jean-Claude is such a bore."

"No, not with him. Someone else from medical."

"Really?" Elizabeth's brows drew together. "Who? That freckled ginger in the pharmacy? He's a bit of a cutie, even if he does lisp."

"Um, no. I'm actually meeting Doctor Vargas." Since it was going to get around anyway, she figured she should be the one to tell her friend. Elizabeth stared at her as if she'd grown two heads.

"No fucking way."

"It's true. We've been seeing each other on the sly."

Elizabeth hurled a pillow from their little futon at her. "I can't believe you didn't tell me. How long?"

"Since Athena."

A second pillow flew through the air. "That's been *weeks!* Oh my God, tell me everything. Is the sex good? He's gotta be hung, right?"

"We haven't had sex yet, but I *can* say that he is very well endowed. And that's *all* I'm gonna say about it."

"Oh God, I'll never be able to look at him the same way in medical again. I can't fantasize if you're dating him. You've ruined it."

"Sorry." She laughed and pulled out a long skirt. Elizabeth helped her put together an acceptable outfit that fit the shipboard dress code. The commodore allowed them to dress out of uniform during their non-duty hours, as long as they met professional standards. Jem had even locked Saskia in their room once when she'd tried to head out in cut-off shorts and a tank top.

"Should I put on—"

"No makeup unless you want to. We make fun of the corpsmen in medical who shellac on the bloody foundation prior to shift. I don't think he cares for it."

"Right. Good, I'm crap with it anyway. It makes me feel like a clown."

She headed out with ten minutes to spare, wearing a calf-length swing skirt and a fitted, off the shoulder ivory sweater—the maximum amount of skin their commanding officer allowed if they weren't in PT gear. Xander met her at the lounge door.

"You look…"

"Different? I know it's not a dress, but I don't have any ship-appropriate ones."

Xander leaned in and kissed her cheek. "I was going to say you look great. Ready to go public?"

"No time like the present."

The tranquil atmosphere allowed them to slip in unnoticed, though it lasted mere seconds before the first whispers and elbow nudges began. Xander took her hand and led her over to the counter.

A small menu rotated each month, featuring baked goods, various coffee flavors, and an assortment of teas from across the galaxy. The cafe also stocked a limited amount of wine, beer, and spirits, from which all crewmen were allowed a two-drink allotment every 24 hours.

The young woman behind the counter had to be sixteen or seventeen, likely some officer's daughter. Thandie couldn't be bothered to learn everyone's relatives yet. "What will it be?"

"It's harvest season, which means pumpkin everything. I'll take a pumpkin cheesecake and a spiced hard cider, please," Thandie said. Once harvest season arrived in Bromwicham, the *Jemison*'s homeport, the monthly supply ships inundated them with squash and other fresh goods.

"I'll take a muffin and an Eloran whiskey."

Once they both scanned their identchips, they collected their order and moved to an empty table near the viewport.

More stares fixed on them. Xander took the attention in stride, ignoring the lookie-loos in favor of biting into his pumpkin seed muffin.

"Are they really so shocked to see you with someone?" she asked.

"Pretend they're not there. That's what I'm doing. People have spotted you in the corridor outside of my room, so you'd think the news would be well spread by now."

"The news that Hottie Vargas is currently off the market?"

"Very much off the market and completely happy with that."

"Me, too." Thandie leaned in and stole a bite of his snack.

He offered the rest to her. "If it wasn't so late, I'd get a pumpkin pie latte. You want the rest of this? I'm getting a slice of cake instead."

"Ask for a decaf."

"Then it isn't coffee. It's just dirty water masquerading as coffee."

Thandie nearly choked on the cider she sipped to wash down his muffin. "Right. If I ever bring you coffee to medical, it won't be decaf." She took the muffin and nibbled it thoughtfully. "I told Elizabeth Fairchild today. We share a room. My other bunkmate is across the room staring daggers at us. I'm guessing I'll be getting the silent treatment for a while, which, frankly, I am perfectly content with. Can't wait."

Xander glanced. "Ah. Daksha Bains. I heard she's pro human-human. I'm surprised she'd even show me an ounce of interest unless it was all some diabolic plot to reclaim me for our race. Of course, the joke would be on her."

She swallowed down a bite of cheesecake and considered her next words. "You're talking about the alien you used to date, right?"

"You heard?"

"She and a couple others were pretty quick with the dish on you when I first arrived, after my appointment with you. Said a cousin or someone like that served with you and that you dumped your fiancée for an alien."

"There's only a hair of truth to that rumor."

"You don't have to talk about it."

"No, I've been meaning to." He leaned close, voice barely a whisper. "I *was* engaged to a human once, but when she learned about my true nature, she wasn't as accepting as you."

Thandie reached across the table and laid her hand over his. "Her loss."

"She wanted me to have a surgery. I considered it. I scheduled an appointment."

Thandie blinked at him across the table, a flash of rage sending heat to her face. "That *bitch*." When a marine at an adjacent table glanced at them, she lowered her voice. "Sorry."

He put on an uncertain smile and continued in his low voice. "I backed out at the last minute, a few days before I was supposed to go under the knife. Told her I couldn't do it, said we were done. About a week after we split, I met Ylona while drinking at a bar in Pacifica Cove. We crossed paths again about seven months later when our ship docked on Elora. Hannah just assumed her to be at the source of our breakup all along. Too convenient, she said."

"The Elorans are very pretty…"

"They are," he agreed.

"She must have been special."

Xander nodded quietly at first. "Special enough for me to marry."

"Oh…" That tidbit had somehow missed the rumor rounds.

"I just want you to understand that I don't have a thing for aliens, as the gossip claims. I had a thing for *her*. I didn't care that she was an alien. Like you said, there's more to a relationship than sex."

"If you were married, what happened to make you two part ways?"

"She died."

Thandie took Xander's hand for a supportive squeeze. "I'm sorry, Xander."

"No, it's quite all right. I… well, it's about time that I… So, okay. I'm getting a slice of cake and a latte. You want anything else?"

"I'm good. I don't see how you stuff yourself with sweets and look this great. I should count myself lucky."

"When I'm not dragged into a raid in Spellbound, I spend the rest of my free time exercising at the gym."

"I'll have to challenge you to pull-ups one day."

"You're on." He grinned at her and strolled to the counter to make his next order.

And then she stole a piece of his pumpkin pound cake, too.

"Are you one of those girls who will never order anything of her own, but picks meager bites belonging to everyone else?

"Hey, I got myself a cheesecake, but you're putting tempting, delicious things in my path. I caved. But I promise to eat a full meal and not peck like a bird if you ever take me out."

"When I take you out," he corrected her. "We're coming up on our next port soon."

"You, me, and a beach? Sounds like heaven."

THEIR DATE ENDED with an affectionate kiss that Xander willingly initiated. Before leaving the area, he bought a mug of Ethan's favorite Earl Grey, made to his preferences.

A quick trip to the bio-farm for a treat to sweeten the pot. Ethan had a weakness for the gene-spliced chapples grown in the bio-farm. The juicy fruits had a delicious cherry-flavored center within their crisp apple flesh.

Una won't care if I take just one... Technically, they were supposed to visit her for a Harvest Badge, but Xander only planned to pluck one. *I'll have Jem let her know in the morning.* Sure, Una wouldn't recognize a single missing apple from her beloved tree, but it was the polite thing to do.

"Oh shit! Rank coming!"

Several shadowed figures darted off and a group of over a half dozen men and women quickly scattered down the different paths. Xander raised a brow and proceeded forward and down the darkened path leading to the rear of the bio-farm's starboard side. There, Una, the farm's Chief Botanist, kept a 500-gallon tank filled to the brim with organic trash. The evening's dinner leftovers from all three mess halls and the civilian deck glistened wetly. The lid was off and a pair of legs angled out of the steamy slop pile. A hand clutched at the rim beside a long rubber oxygen line passed along the floor for air exchange.

Xander scanned to the left to follow the hose. A young man in evening dress attire, perhaps hoping to go unseen, crouched beside the source of the oxygen line. His fingers were on a bold yellow sign announcing their unfortunate captive's plight. Busted, he leapt up and snapped to attention.

"Sir!"

"Name and rank."

"Corporal Danyl Speirs, sir."

Xander sighed and set the lidded mug of tea on the nearby bench. "Who's in the compost?"

"Etherington, sir," the young man admitted.

"Assault of an officer is a dischargeable offense, but you're the only one who didn't flee when I approached. Why's that?"

"I'm not prone to cowardice, sir. I'm willin' to face disciplinary measures for my part. I know what I did was wrong."

Etherington remained in the compost muck during their discussion. Under normal circumstances, Xander would have hauled the officer out first before resuming the conversation, but something bothered him about Etherington's predicament.

"How'd you catch him?" Xander asked the young man.

The freckle-faced kid rubbed the back of his neck and cleared his throat awkwardly. "Well..."

"It's okay, you can tell me."

"With his pants around his ankles, sir."

Holding back his snicker became an exercise in control. "What? I need details, Speirs. Start from the beginning."

"I won't name names."

Xander raised one brow. Years of practice with his subordinates gave him the edge required to keep a strict poker face. "It's admirable that you're protecting your mates. Tell me why you did it. I want the honest truth from you and only that. Don't sugarcoat it and don't feed me a load of bullshit you believe I want to hear."

"To be frank, sir, we all got tired of his demeaning attitude. I mean, I know we're enlisted, but that doesn't make us lazy or stupid. A bunch of us got together and found a rank-tagger to lure him to the bio-farm. She did it happily."

Ah. Xander maintained his stern countenance despite the desire to double over with laughter. "You're dismissed."

The corporal stared at him. "I'm dismissed?"

"Yeah. Go on, get out of here. I didn't see a thing. Everyone was gone when I arrived."

After Corporal Speirs was long out of sight, Xander tugged Etherington's booted foot and freed him from the greasy mire. Once he'd set his feet to solid ground, the younger officer spit out the mouthpiece to the oxygen line and wiped a lump of mashed potato and gravy from his face. Partially decomposed food and fresh compost offerings clung to his uniform and stuck in his hair.

"Christ, about time. Thank you, Comman—"

"You're out of regulation there, Lieutenant."

"What? You can't possibly be serious."

"I'm very serious. Your uniform looks like shit. Your boots aren't shined."

Etherington gaped, like a fish out of water. His mouth opened and closed several times, but no sound emerged.

"Well?" Xander crossed his arms over his chest.

"A group of enlisted assholes tossed me in the bin, and you're mad about my uniform?"

"Your situational awareness must be shit for a group of enlisted men to get the better of you."

Etherington flushed red, fury in his eyes. "Be careful, Commander, and choose your next words wisely. My father *will* hear about this."

"Hear what? That you were ganked while an enlisted girl slobbed your knob? Ah, yes, that's precisely what I'd want my father to know."

Etherington's face went beet red. "I was assaulted!"

"Excuses. I didn't witness an assault."

"I—"

Xander arched a brow and Etherington fell silent, showing the first signs of good judgement.

"Shall I add insubordination to the report to your department head? Now get out of here and clean yourself up. You're a disgrace to the uniform looking like that."

"Yes, sir."

After the soiled lieutenant was out of sight, Xander exhaled a relieved sigh. "Jem, delete all data pertaining to this incident." He had lucked out; a smarter officer would have demanded Jem to replay the event.

"I cannot do that, Xander."

"Can't or won't? Use your judgment in this instance, Jem. From what you've observed aboard this ship, would you say that the lieutenant deserved his punishment?" No one deserved humiliation on a daily basis, and maybe now that Etherington had had a taste of his own medicine, he wouldn't be so quick to abuse his subordinates.

The program remained silent for a moment. Her final answer brought a grin to his face. "I am able to perform a security upgrade at the risk of losing pertinent data related to the last half hour in the bio-farm."

"Please do."

Chuckling, Xander resumed his mission and took the lift to the bridge, carrying with him the hope to bribe the ship's commanding officer for a small and insignificant favor.

"Do you have a moment, Ethan?" He decided to keep the news of Etherington's humiliation to himself, wary of bringing trouble on the heads of the participating servicemen and women.

Ethan glanced away from his console and groaned when Xander presented him with the chapple. "Are you finally deciding to use our friendship to your advantage?"

"Apt assumption to make. Yes. Here's your tea. I made it just for you. Milk and honey, as you like it." Xander set the hot mug in the cozy armchair's cup holder.

"You never ask anything, so tell me, what is it that you want?" Ethan warily accepted his bribes.

"I have a friend out in this sector," Xander promptly said. "Doctor Mathias Campbell retired from the Navy last year. He's a good man and he's the only board licensed physician on his planet."

"The *planet*?" Ethan repeated.

"Kantarn has three colonies within a hundred miles of one another. One is practically a city now, or so I'm told. The council is planning to apply to New Cambridge in hopes of opening a doctoral college with his help. He's also the man who helped me with the research for my theory on neurocybernetics."

"All right. This'll delay our arrival to Elora by a fortnight, but we can swing it. Navigator Agosti, set our coordinates to Kantarn."

"Aye aye, Commodore."

"Thanks, mate. I appreciate it. I've tried contacting him by message twice this week, and..."

"No response?"

"Nothing," Xander replied.

"We'll be there in five days. Tell Kruger I said hello. Brilliant choice by the way, mate."

Xander grinned at him. "Of course I will. We enjoyed tea together, so I won't be seeing her again until tomorrow. I plan to return to the medical bay to resume reading the medical histories on the psychics who were taken. There's something odd about them that I want to evaluate further, but I just can't make it click."

"Keep me posted."

CHAPTER THIRTEEN

The *Jemison*'s bio-farm remained open 24 hours a day, all 365 days of the standard galactic year. While its primary purpose provided nutritious food to the ship's crew, the ship's civilian botanist had developed one additional perk to the system—Zen Time.

Each member of the crew received two hours of private time per season. Some pooled their hours for group yoga classes or friendly cookouts, but most people spent the personal time for private picnics and dates with a loved one.

When she'd seen a cancellation on the schedule, it hadn't been difficult to convince Xander to go halfsies with her on the two-hour slot. And he looked so damned good in his jeans and fitted t-shirt, the latter stretched over his defined muscles. Ever since jeans had cycled back into fashion again, the ladies of the *Jemison* had counted themselves fortunate, because nothing else in the galaxy seemed to showcase a tight male ass the way denim could.

"Did you bring me out here to snog in the trees?"

Thandie laughed and leaned her cheek against his arm. "Well, we can kiss if you want, but I came out here for some sunshine and delicious food since Elora has been put off for a bit."

"Sorry about that. Kind of my fault."

"I forgive you, but only if you help me fill a basket." Thandie tugged him down a path. They plucked a bounty of blackberries and raspberries in one basket, then packed the second with fresh strawberries, always eating as many as they picked.

"Are we going to eat all of this, or do you intend to drag me into the lounge to bake a pie, too?" he griped.

"Half goes to Una for the galleys, and I was going to greedily hoard the rest. Why? Do you bake?"

"I've burned a pie or two in my time. My cakes are better."

"*You* bake cakes?"

"With real buttercream frosting."

"Obviously we need a kitchen date next time."

"Ha. If I can't talk one of the chefs out of a couple of steaks in the mess, I'll make a pick-up at our next port and cook you dinner. I'm glad you pulled me in here... thanks for that."

"After all the work you've been doing, I thought a break would be nice."

"I know, and I appreciate it. It's just that I'm worried. The more we learn about all these abductions, the more disturbing the pattern becomes. Cyborgs, psychics, and kids."

Thandie raised a brow. "How has your investigation been going?

"Awful. I notified Mathias that I'd like his opinion on a theory I've developed about the recent abductions, and he hasn't uttered a word. There are no reports about Kantarn going under fire from pirates, so I can't fathom any justification for his failure to respond. Something must have happened."

"Could he be busy? I mean, you get real focused on your work sometimes. I figured it was just a doctor thing. Or maybe an officer thing. Lopez says Lieutenant Shahid is always forgetting dates."

He shook his head. "If it were only a matter of days, I could buy that, but I've been trying to reach him for weeks. There's also a high concentration of abandoned colonies near Kantarn. Doubtful that's a coincidence, either. If pirates aren't already assessing their worth, they will be soon. I'm afraid we'll arrive to find the entire colony in shambles or an attack in progress."

Thandie attempted to soothe his concerns. "United Command would have reported that when the *Jemison* altered her course for Kantarn."

Xander sighed. "You're right."

"We'll get it solved, but for now we have two hours alone. You're *supposed* to relax during Zen Time."

"I *am* relaxed. It's difficult to feel anything but relaxed when I'm with you. These past few weeks have meant more to me than you can ever know, hon."

They spread out a blanket on an open patch of clover and grass and settled down with their basket. Thandie straddled his lap and wrapped both arms around his neck before peppering his jaw with kisses. "No more business talk or I'll be forced to distract you."

He leaned back on one palm and raised an incredulous brow. "Yeah? And how are you going to do that?"

Thandie heard the challenge in his voice, a practical dare for her to do something—anything ballsy enough to distract him from the woes of his investigative search and worry for a friend. Impulsively, she unfastened the top two buttons of her blouse and tugged her bra down until both breasts spilled out into the cool, fan-generated breeze designed to simulate an autumn afternoon on Albion.

Xander quieted, thoroughly distracted by her tits.

Success.

The tips beaded tight, sensitive to the open air. With him fully captivated by her breasts, she unfastened the remaining buttons and shrugged out of it, bra following.

"Distracted yet?"

He circled his thumb over her left nipple then played with the right, stroking, rubbing, and tweaking both until they were as hard as pebbles between his fingers. "Maybe. Not sure. You may have to remove more things."

Removing her skirt came next, leaving her in only sheer black lace panties.

Xander made a low growl that resonated through his chest. "You have no idea how much I want you right now."

"I think I do." She stroked her hand over the hard bulge in his pants. "And I want you just as much. I just..."

"You don't have to take them both. When you're ready, that is."

"Wouldn't that be awkward for you?"

He shook his head. "No, not really. To be perfectly honest with you I've never... I've never actually had the opportunity to use both at once. Human bodies aren't the same as the Lexar. Their women are kinda, uh, designed to match."

Thandie leaned back to look at him. "*Really?*"

"A set to match their twin dicks."

She tugged his belt. "Take them out."

"What? *Now?*"

"Why not? We're alone and no one is going to bother us

for at least another hour." She followed his jawline until she reached his ear and nibbled. "Or is an hour not enough?"

Xander loosened his belt so fast she giggled. "It's definitely enough to get a damned start."

Then her heart leapt in her throat a little once he slid both semi-hard cocks out. She touched the one on top and curled her fingers around it, smoothing up and down with a few testing strokes. "Promises, promises."

Her gentle touches and teasing kisses transitioned into something more. Before she knew it, they'd both stripped down and sprawled across the blanket with their arms and legs entwined.

Gentle, explorative kisses became deep and needy. She stroked his dicks until both were hard as marble in her hands, but it wasn't enough. The ache building between her thighs demanded more than his fingers and tongue.

"Fuck. I didn't bring—I didn't realize we'd need—"

Thandie touched her index finger to his lips. "I get yearly shots in medical. Do you trust me?"

He nuzzled her bare breasts, then skimmed his lips against the tip of one plump mound, trembling with barely contained need. "I've seen your records. I know you're clean."

"If you trust me, I trust you."

He answered by grazing one nipple with his teeth, sending ripples of sensation throbbing in her core. She squirmed and rubbed against the hard cock settled between her thighs, finding the ideal angle to stimulate and tease her clit until she was dying to know the feel of him.

He groaned and guided her movement, one of her cheeks in each of his huge palms, until they were both wet with each other, her slickness over his top shaft, the tip of both cocks glossy when she glanced down. She sighed and trailed her fingers through his hair.

"How should we...?"

Xander twisted and tucked her beneath him on the blanket, sprawling her out like a banquet. Then, shamelessly, he spread her thighs obscenely wide. For a moment, he did nothing more than look at her, his gaze roaming over her body. The raw desire she saw shimmering there made her feel beautiful. Powerful. Like he was lost in her spell.

"You're perfect," he whispered.

How did she respond to that? Without words, she reached out for him. Xander bowed down over her, kisses starting at her breasts and working their way up to her throat while he reached between their bodies and adjusted himself. Both silken cockheads bumped against her in turn and all Thandie could do was lift her hips from the blanket in a desperate plea.

Xander groaned, gliding back and forth against the wet cleft of her. Her back arched as he sank the upper dick in, little by little, an unbearable tease that ended when he withdrew and began anew with the lower cock instead, as if he couldn't decide which he wanted to use.

And since they were both so wondrously thick, it didn't matter to her which he preferred, as long as he kept her filled with one of them. Anxious, Thandie locked one heel behind his ass and dragged until he gave another inch, the delicious stretch sending shivers up her spine.

He laughed, low and husky against her throat, the sound wrapped in a moan. "Impatient, sweetheart?"

"You're killing me."

"Good things come to those who wait."

"Awful man."

Then he thrust, and her complaints died in her throat,

the length filling her so completely her fingers curled into his shoulders. She nearly climaxed right then, gasping against his lips. Still slick with her, the fat underbelly of his upper cock bumped against her clit, sending little sparks of bliss coursing through her.

Heaven.

Xander found a steady rhythm, each stroke delivering twice the pleasure. Thandie writhed against the blanket, her toes curling tight.

"You feel amazing."

"So do you." Amazing didn't feel like enough to describe how he felt. She reached between their bodies with one hand and took hold of his upper dick. The breath hissed between Xander's teeth when she ran her thumb around his swollen cockhead.

As though her touch spurred him on, Xander quickened his pace. He swapped again, withdrawing one dick in exchange for the other, and a part of her, a desperate part of her filled with the urgency to come, almost told him to hell with it—to use both at once. The blanket that had been beneath them bunched up under her back, mostly soft grass and clover under her bare skin.

Thandie wrapped her arms around his neck, sailing away on an ocean of sheer bliss, so close to climax she could feel it settling in her limbs, tensing in her core, tightening every muscle with impending release. And it had to be doubly intense for him with his two cocks.

"So fucking close. Gonna be... gonna be real messy, baby."

"Don't care."

He shifted above her, making a final swap, his bottom dick once more plunged deep within her while the top slid against her swollen clit. It was enough to send her over the edge, thrusting her into sheer bliss, her body impossibly tight before the tension snapped and release shuddered through her limbs.

The only word on her lips was his name.

A hot jet of Xander's seed spurted against her abdomen, the next shot reaching her breasts. The rest was inside her, bathing her inner walls. Thandie didn't care, floating on cresting waves that took her to new heights of ecstasy.

Just when she started to come down from one orgasm, another began. Every time Xander moved, riding through the clenching pulses of her pussy for his own pleasure, her core shuddered around him anew.

Xander groaned, the sound deep and long. His hips stilled and he sank down atop her with his face against her throat. Thandie managed one soothing stroke down his spine with her fingertips before her arms fell to her sides against the cool grass. They stayed like that for a long time, until their racing heartbeats slowed and their breaths evened out.

"Are you sure you're not an empath?" His question came suddenly, interrupting the silence.

She laughed and shook her head. "Nah, I tested too low on those entrance exams they do, but it does run intermittently in my family. Why?"

"You always seem to know what to say... Or what I need. It's like you're too good to be true. I spend half of our time together expecting to wake up."

"Funny, I think the same thing about you sometimes."

Xander lifted his head to look at her, but all Thandie could think about was kissing him again. She drew him down and took her time until at last they separated and he sprawled beside her on his back.

"Think we can convince Jem to turn on the weather

cycle?" She grinned and traced one finger down Xander's sticky chest. "We could both use the cleanup."

"Never hurts to ask."

A bounty of misty rain fell from above, showering them at once. "The bio-farm is due for a simulated storm."

Thandie laughed. "Thanks, Jem." When the rainfall intensified, she took Xander's hand in hers and urged him to join her, as there were few things more satisfying after a sweaty round of lovemaking than a naked dash through the rain.

CHAPTER FOURTEEN

The *Jemison* reached Kantarn's system five days later, but a meteor storm delayed their arrival to the planet itself by another twenty-four hours. Even then, they were given the runaround for landing clearance. The whole situation only solidified Xander's gut feeling that something was wrong.

After Ethan threw his weight around, they were permitted into the planetary atmosphere and directed to a landing space outside the town.

The plan was to allow Xander to go down and reconnect with his former comrade while Ethan coordinated with the planet's governor and council. He wanted them prepared in the event of a pirate attack, since Kantarn had all the qualities of the other colonies that had gone dark already: secluded, small, and connected to the cybernetics trade.

"Well, don't you clean up nice," Thandie commented as she neatly knotted Xander's tie. She smoothed her fingers down his chest and smiled up at him. "You look good in the dress uniform."

"Thanks. Where'd you learn to do this?"

"My dad," she replied. "He wore a tie every day and I was fascinated. He always told me I didn't need to learn it, since women on my planet are only allowed to wear dresses."

"I've never visited Tallulah. Really? Dresses *all* the time?"

"Really," she confirmed with a big grin on her face. "I guess that's why I always wear pants and boots to shore leave. Makes me feel like a rebel."

"True rebels wear lace lingerie. Just thought I should tell you."

Thandie swatted him playfully and leaned up for a kiss. "I hope everything is okay with your friend."

"Me too."

Xander exited the ship's airlock and descended the ramp into a village occupied by antisocial townsfolk. They hurried away and avoided him, parting like the Red Sea.

"Hello? Excuse me, young miss?" A woman reluctantly paused and spared him a glance. Xander continued gratefully. "I'd like directions to Doctor Campbell's facilities."

After she gave directions, Xander made the mile walk across the township toward the colonial medical center. Its stylish exterior conflicted with the rest of the modest town.

Campbell must have put some of his own money into the center, the man known for random acts of kindness. Smiling, Xander strode inside the pristine lobby and up to reception.

"Good afternoon, I'm Doctor Xander Vargas. Please let Doctor Campbell know I've arrived."

"Do you have an appointment?"

"No, but I'm an old friend. He asked me to drop by whenever I was in the sector, so here I am."

The woman skimmed her fingertips over a floating hologram pad. The thin glass glowed orange beneath her touch. "Doctor Campbell is currently in a delicate procedure."

The hairs on the back of his neck prickled. "I'll wait."

Xander sat in a chair nearby and became embroiled in a bitter staring contest that lasted for a half hour before the receptionist caved and tapped a few buttons on her monitor.

"Doctor Campbell, you have an eager visitor from the Royal Navy here to see you at your earliest convenience." She paused, presumably to listen to Campbell respond from the other end of the link. "He claims to be Doctor Xander Vargas. Yes, I will inform him."

Xander pretended to hold interest in the news feed scrolling across the wall instead of jumping to his feet.

"Doctor Campbell will be out shortly," the receptionist relayed with a cool smile on her plastic face. Everything from the flawless arch of her immaculate eyebrows to her sculpted chin and nose advertised Campbell's work. He'd always had a fantastic talent for reconstructive and cosmetic surgery, which he'd put to work on scarred marines.

"Thank you."

At ease again, Xander settled back until loud footsteps announced his friend's arrival. Doctor Campbell had always been a heavy man, but his time out of the Navy had added weight to his already bulky frame, especially around his middle.

"Xander, you should have called ahead," he said, offering his hand. Perspiration dotted his brow along his hairline.

"I did. Or I tried, anyway." Xander put on a smile and shook Mathias's hand. "Since we passed this way along our route to the next port, I wanted to stop in and say hello, as you *asked*." He added a touch of passive-aggressive emphasis to get his point across.

"So I did..." his voice trailed off and he cleared his throat. "I wish I could show you around, Xan, I really do."

"The *Jemison* will be here a day, at least. I can return tomorrow if that's better. I'm really looking forward to seeing your work."

"I'm afraid that won't be possible."

Xander frowned. "Anything I can do to help take the load off while I'm here, Mathias?"

"That's kind, but unnecessary. The fact is, I'm heading off to the neighboring colonies tomorrow to see private clients, so I really do need to get back to my packing. Don't want to forget anything."

"Do you need a hand?"

"No, no. I have it covered, thanks. Next time, all right, chap?"

"Next time," Xander agreed, cheeks aching from the stiff smile he forced himself to maintain.

"I TELL YOU, IT WAS DODGY." Xander shrugged out of his jacket and tossed it over Ethan's chair. "The whole place gave me the fucking creeps."

"Lieutenant Shahid stepped off ship for a time and returned with some troubling observations." Ethan rubbed his chin. "Lockhart, too."

If the two most powerful psychics on the ship had the same vibes, then something was amiss.

"Something's not right, Ethan. Campbell has always had a bad poker face and that hasn't changed. I had the distinct impression he was hiding something. We aren't wanted here, and my war buddy asked me to leave. He had no interest in showing me his greatest life's work, when half a year ago he couldn't wait for me to see."

"So what are you asking?"

"Send a small team back in with me."

"Granted. If they don't want us here, they'll just have to sod off and accept that we're the ones with the firearms."

Ethan typically believed in allowing colonies to handle their own affairs. For him to take such a heavy-handed approach could mean only a single thing.

"I take it the governor blew you off, eh?"

"Fucker told me to mind my own business."

Xander barked out a laugh. "I wish I'd been there to see it."

"As there is a true possibility of danger, I've contacted United Command and received authority from Admiral Novak to take prompt action. In case this goes tits up, I wanted our arses covered."

"Fair enough. I'll grab Viljoen and tell him to assemble the team."

"Excellent."

In less than an hour, the assault team was assembled onboard the shuttle and on their way to the hospital landing pad while Ethan went to make a diplomatic connection with the planet's governing body. Xander checked his weapon and gave everyone a quick brief on the lobby layout.

"This is a medical center. I don't want a single civilian casualty once we're inside. Watch your aim and use non-lethal rounds unless otherwise ordered."

"Sir, I'm getting a warning from the center denying us landing privileges," Lopez called from the front. After the events on Athena, he'd taken Rogers's place as pilot, then

Gareth had volunteered to fill the gap as the team communications expert.

Viljoen snorted. "Land anyway. We have United Command behind us on this."

"Got it."

The shuttle doors opened before they touched down and Thandie took up her usual position, her rifle at the ready. She scanned the area with her eagle vision then gave the all clear when no one came out to challenge them.

"All right team, move out." Viljoen stepped onto the ground first. "DuPrie, when we get inside I want you to monitor the main entrance. Ears open. I'm sure they'll have some things to say."

"Yes, sir." She went camo and moved alongside them.

Inside, the same receptionist greeted them with a phony smile. "I'm afraid Doctor Campbell is—"

"We aren't here to see him," Xander cut her off, stepping up to the desk. "This is a matter of military business now. Buzz us in."

"I can't—"

"We won't tell you again."

Her pale gaze darted to the various weapons, then she tapped a button and the security doors flashed green. Three guards met them halfway down the hall.

"Gentlemen, stand down." Viljoen grinned at the men. "Unless you want a piece of this for obstructing justice, move out of our way."

Part of Xander hoped they'd put up a fight. They backed down, instead, sending one another uncertain glances and communicating with their eyes. He had a bad feeling, and it was echoed by Gareth when they turned into the next corridor.

"Something doesn't feel right here, Commander."

"What do you mean, Lockhart?" Viljoen asked in a low tone.

"I can't put a finger to it. It's just like... *everyone* in the village is hiding something." Gareth shook his head and cast a wary glance around the sterile interior. "And... the background noise is excessive. Too much of it for so small a place and what they have listed on their patient registry." He raised both hands to his temples and shut his watery eyes, clearly afflicted with one of his migraines.

Xander touched him on the shoulder. "We'll keep an eye out. Are you going to be okay here?"

"I'm fine, Doc. Which way is his office?"

Xander gestured down the hall. "It should be down this way. He always liked to be back by the labs."

"You didn't meet him in his office before?" Thandie asked.

"No, and that was another tip off. He made me wait in the lobby and came out to me."

Six rooms lined the hall, but Xander spotted a sleeping patient in only one of them. Nothing indicated any surgical or time-consuming procedures had recently taken place.

"Hold up a minute. It's this way." Gareth stopped by a door marked as a restricted area. "I know the office is down the hall, but... this ominous feeling, it's coming through here."

Viljoen led the squad through the door and down a single staircase that emptied into a green-lit corridor. They passed a room housing a mechanical rig as lavish as Xander's surgical theater on the ship.

"There's blood on the floor," Thandie muttered, moving ahead.

"Kruger!" Viljoen knocked the smaller marine to the floor and threw up his arm to block the security laser aimed at her back. The beam cut through his armor and seared his skin, filling the hall with the smell of burning hair and skin. Thandie rolled to her back on the floor and took out the machinery with two well-placed shots.

"Are you okay?" Xander asked quietly while helping Thandie up from the floor. His heart galloped in his chest with the force of a stampeding herd of wargs. Her appreciative smile eased the anxiety and instinctive urge to sweep her protectively into his arms.

"I'm okay. Commander Viljoen took the hit." Her gold eyes flicked toward the commander. She winced. A distinct line had been cut through his forearm vambrace.

"Here, let me look." Fairchild moved to the injured commander's side and inspected the wound. "It's not deep and it's cauterized, at least. Nothing a little nanogel can't cure."

"Can we expect more tricks like this?" Thandie asked, supporting Viljoen's arm while Fairchild wrapped the injury. "Thank you, Commander." He grunted something unintelligible.

Gareth searched the wall for an access panel and hooked his computer in. He studied the projected holographic screen beamed from his wrist device. "It was operated remotely. Someone clearly doesn't want us snooping around."

"Obviously," Viljoen muttered.

"I can try and hack into the system," Gareth offered. "If we're lucky, I can gain all remote control, or at least lock out any other consoles like this."

Xander's fingers tightened into a fist at his side. "Do it."

They lurked behind him in the chilly hall while Gareth toiled at the device. A few seconds later, a series of gentle clicks echoed down the hall.

"Done. I've disabled all the doors and security. There shouldn't be another surprise like this. The room at the end is the only one in use."

Viljoen stormed ahead. "Let's go say hello, then."

Frosted glass on the door blocked their view of the room within. Viljoen put his hand on the knob, made a silent count to three then slammed the portal open. Chang, gun out and extended, rushed through first with Abernathy a step behind him. Viljoen followed with the rest of the marines and then Xander and his medics.

"Oh my god..." The nightmarish scene scorched itself into his mind and turned his stomach.

It wasn't a medical laboratory; it was a chop shop. Fairchild turned green in the face and Gareth backed out of the room entirely. As a psychic, the pain must have been excruciating for him to feel.

A cold corpse lay on the examination table. The young man, barely out of his teens, showed extensive cybernetic modification, but most of the components had been removed, leaving yawning holes in their place. A shallow pan of pink-tinged solution lay to the side of the corpse on a metal tray, filled with gore-covered cybernetics. Three more bodies were laid out on tables at the back of the room, connected to life-support machines.

Mathias Campbell stripped off his bloody gloves and discarded them into a bin. Wise enough to understand the gravity of the situation, and that his guards wouldn't be coming to his aid, he stepped away from the table with his hands raised in a gesture of surrender.

"Xander, I wish you had listened. You should have gone."

He didn't think, he acted. Xander crossed the room and caught Campbell across the face with his fist. Cartilage cracked and blood splattered from the man's hooked nose.

"You were supposed to help people. You took an oath to do no harm!" Xander raged, punctuating the harsh words by striking Campbell in the mouth. The force cracked a tooth and scraped Xander's knuckles, but twice wasn't enough, and he quickly had to follow suit with a third. No amount of physical violence seemed large enough to wipe away Campbell's evil.

The other marines stood back and said nothing.

"What do you have to say for yourself?" Xander demanded. "Why would you do this to your own patients? To anyone? Answer me!" He slammed his fist into Campbell's mouth again then shook the heavyset doctor—no, the *monster*. A doctor was a person who healed; Xander held a killer in his hands.

"It all seemed so right. The research will save countless lives. You don't understand, Xander. They have power. They promised to help us—"

"How in the bloody fuck is this help!?" Xander raised his fist but the other man shrank back and screamed.

"Don't hit me again, no wait, wait! I can give you information. I can tell you anything."

"You're going to do that anyway, whether you want to or not," Gareth spoke up quietly from the doorway. "You pathetic bastard."

"They brought research and medical necessities that we needed. We were forgotten by the UNE and left on our own here! Your government abandoned us."

"Of course they brought medical research, they experimented on innocent civilians."

"I didn't know... I didn't know, Xander. Please. You must believe me." Campbell sagged in Xander's powerful grip. Bloodied spittle trickled from his mouth. "They brought prisoners at first. Murderers. I thought... I was doing what we talked about! I thought we would make new discoveries to advance science. To help people with debilitating brain injuries."

"And then what happened?" Thandie asked. She pointed toward the young man on the table. "He doesn't look like a murderer or a prisoner to me."

"They blackmailed me. I didn't have a choice! I would have lost my license if I didn't continue."

Xander shook him again. "That's your excuse? Nothing justifies this depravity. Who's this mysterious *they*, Campbell?"

"They're close—" Campbell's facial muscles tightened and twitched. He arched his back and stiffened without warning.

"Campbell?"

"Oh, shit," Viljoen swore.

The man didn't respond. A shake began over one side of his body and then the convulsion gradually spread. The doctor collapsed to the floor and seized, his arms locked against his body until he finally stilled.

Thandie touched Xander's arm and wordlessly drew him back. His limbs shook, indignation and fury taking firm hold.

He squeezed her hand to signal he was all right, and then he knelt beside the corpse to run his bioscanner over Campbell's head. "Someone cooked his brain remotely."

The hydraulic laboratory door sealed shut with a sudden slam, its lock clicking into place. Above them, small nozzles that resembled a fire extinguishing system began to emit a barely audible hiss.

"Masks!" Fairchild called the warning, prompting them all to don their rebreather masks.

"DuPrie. What's happening?" Viljoen asked over the comm.

"I killed the receptionist. She began punching a bunch of buttons at her desk. I believe she fried your friend's noggin and sealed you in."

Xander swore. Wherever his skin was bare and uncovered by his suit, he felt heat and warmth. "What about the guards?"

"I had to put them down, too. What do I do?" Panic filled her voice. "Christ, I can see you on her monitor. What's happening in there?"

"She's gassing the room. Can you unlock the doors?"

"This is a little foreign to me, but I'll try."

As precious seconds ticked by, the gas flow picked up at an exponential speed, flooding the room until a heavy, burning cloud filled the air.

"I can't find anything!" DuPrie cried.

"Goddammit." Viljoen turned to Gareth. "Lockhart, can't you do anything?"

"I'm trying!" Gareth found the nearest console and jacked in with his personal rig. A brilliant green user interface expanded to surround him, alive with flashing symbols and numbers.

Clueless about hacking and overrides, Xander stood by as helplessly as the others.

"Gareth, hurry!" Fairchild cried. "It's burning!"

"Doin' the best I can. I'm in the system, lass. Just a moment."

The lock released with a noisy click. Once the door flew open, their team spilled into the hall, eager to be away from the unknown gas. A desperate decontamination began, each of them stripping from their hard suits down to their undergarments for Fairchild and Xander to spray them with a neutralizing compound. He went last.

He could take it. Their fragile human skin couldn't last.

Most of the victims had been children and teenagers. Xander sat at his desk reviewing the files they'd pulled from the medical center and swallowed down his disgust. Everything he'd known about Mathias had been wrong, because only a monster could do the vile acts performed in that lab.

"United Command is sending two more ships," Ethan said from the doorway.

Xander spun his chair around and blinked at him. "How long have you been standing there?"

"Long enough to know you need to stop drinking coffee and get some sleep."

"I can't. I tried sleeping and..." Xander grimaced and ran his hands through his hair. None of those kids had been any older than he was when he'd run away from home, desperate to escape his aunt's abusive boyfriend. The guy had known Xander was a Lexar half-breed and spent his every day punishing him for being an alien mutt. "I just can't sleep."

"All right, then. What have you got so far?"

Xander brought up his research in 3-D for Ethan's perusal. "He was playing around with concepts I never even conceived. See this? Nanofiber filaments spread through the frontal lobe."

"Why so many children?" Ethan asked.

"The preadolescent psychic brain is incredibly malleable and plastic, and neurosurgeons once believed they could recover from many more traumas than an adult. We had a theory once, but we dismissed it... I thought—I *never* imagined he could do this."

"He was a real dick, but someone commissioned this shit. I just finished with Admiral Novak. They want us on the job of tracking down the source of it and who's responsible for the laboratory. You up for that, mate?"

"There are few things lower than harming a child. I'd do it without orders." He closed his eyes and tilted his head back to breathe. His heart pounded frightfully fast and the world around him shimmered. He blinked through his blurry vision and inhaled a few deep breaths.

"Hey, we'll get whoever's behind this."

"I hope so."

A week later, reinforcements arrived, but by then, the *Jemison*'s crew had whipped the details out of most of the so-called villagers. They were all employees and actors hired by a faceless corporation no one could name. Financial records and evidence dug up by their ship's tech team revealed some had been paid to do Campbell's bidding and to occasionally fly off the planet to abduct more victims.

Most of the original inhabitants of the settlement were long gone, used as experimental fodder in Campbell's grand scheme. A probe determined that the two outlying colonies had no idea about the atrocities committed in their sister community.

Many families received closure at last and mourned the loss of their own children—those whose care they had entrusted to Doctor Campbell, their sole medical provider. Records showed six months of questionable deaths and illnesses.

The combat squad discovered three dozen victims in a prison block beneath the clinic and surmised that those dirty and malnourished survivors were next in line to visit the table. Half of them originated from Athena. Five survivors turned out to be the only remaining colonists from the lunar colony of Loki 4.

Xander's investigations made him heartsick. The total number of experiments in the system painted a gruesome portrait spanning back well over a year. Campbell kept meticulous notes, but he failed to include his employer's identity.

They were still out there, and he intended to find them, no matter what.

CHAPTER FIFTEEN

Almost three weeks overdue, the *Jemison* arrived at her next port practically running on fumes. Engineering hadn't discovered the fuel leak until it was almost too late, and the department looked forward to receiving help from the technical experts on Elora's local military space station.

Elora had no actual spacecraft docks on the surface. Instead, a UNE space station hung in synchronized orbit around the planet and shuttles traveled between it and a few key landing pads.

The tiny shuttleport occupied a carved mountainside cliff. Since water covered 93% of the planet's surface, creative engineering utilized land space to the maximum potential without disrupting the natural flora.

If not for Ethan and Thandie teaming up to get Xander off the ship, he would have remained in his office poring through data. But he'd promised his girl a vacation paradise, and nothing could make him go back on his word.

He just needed time to adjust. To re-center himself.

Step by step, the tension left him as he walked along the

shore of a pink sand beach, miles of it contrasting the turquoise waters.

He hadn't visited Elora in nearly three years, not since Ylona left her birth planet in favor of dwelling in a human settlement on Albion. With him. She'd moved with him into a home in Gloucester, lavishly tailored to her unique aquatic needs. During the funeral, he couldn't bear to face her parents, too consumed with his own guilt. Deep down, a small part of him still expected to see them waiting to greet him on the beach.

Time dwindled and people passed him as they headed on their way, but Xander remained where he was, his gaze held to the horizon.

"Ready for sunshine, frozen drinks, and snorkeling?"

Xander nearly startled out of his boots. He jumped and swung his gaze around to focus on Thandie. "Huh? Yeah. Yeah, I'm ready."

Her dress became the distraction he needed. The rich teal color stood out bright against her bronzed skin. The thin straps hung from her toned shoulders and the corset-laced bodice amped her breasts up to "I need to tittyfuck you *now*" levels of appealing.

"Finally, a dress."

"You've seen me in dresses before."

"True, but each one is prettier than the last."

Her eyes lit up, and she twirled, letting the skirts flare around her calves. "You like?"

"I do. Very much."

Without a rush to reach their lodgings, they took a romantic stroll along a rambling path parallel to the tropical coastline. Their walk cleared his head and allowed him the chance to relax. Ethan had been right to insist. Not only for himself, but for Thandie's sake, as well. She deserved the R&R just as much.

Thandie tilted her face upward, her delighted expression bathed in sunlight. "I know the lamps in the bio-farm and medical are supposed to mimic this, but nothing beats the real thing. I could sit out here for hours just soaking it up."

"It was like this at home in Paradiso. I remember the sun always seemed to be shining, and the summer rain made for the best time of the year. As a child, I'd just stand in it."

"Back on Tallulah, I used to run out and play in the puddles during a rainstorm, but that usually ended with a day or three in bed afterward."

"You're more than welcome to dance in the rain now." He paused to kiss her beneath a flowering tree with purple and golden leaves. "Are we going to come back to swim after check-in?"

"Not right away if I can help it. I don't really want to share you." Her eyes twinkled. "The nude sunbathers are already out in force."

"C'mon, our room should be ready by now."

Pacifica Cove maintained only two surface structures, a shuttle dock near the beach and a domed entrance to the city, accessible by following a long pier onto the ocean. The structure at the end was only the tip of the proverbial iceberg, the rest of the city concealed beneath the waves. They made their way to the city entrance, passing a few of their shipmates, some tourists, and the Elorans who walked among the sunbathers passing out sea flower garlands with their webbed fingers.

The Elorans, as far as Xander was concerned, were a beautiful people. He'd always thought that even before meeting Ylona. While humanoid in shape, their basic physiology differed from the humans who lived at peace with them. Most had skin ranging in hue from pale blue to deep violet, their dewy flesh velvety soft, like old world seals. Identical gill slits glistened on each side of their throats, and their large, dark eyes gleamed beneath the sun.

When they reached the pier, an Eloran approached with a big welcoming smile on his aquiline face. He offered out a lei made of orange blossoms, pink shells, and braided greenery.

Thandie's smile turned magical and stirred Xander somewhere deep down in his soul. "Thank you." She bowed her head to accept the gift.

Another Eloran arrived with a garland for Xander, as well. He dipped down to accept it. "Thank you."

Their kind hosts only smiled back, revealing all of their sharp little teeth. Elorans lacked the capability for human speech, instead communicating with one another through a series of sounds and inhuman vocalizations that carried beneath the water. Among their own kind or close friends, they conveyed deeper meanings and thoughts through physical contact.

The first settlers had come to the world as a scientific expedition full of oceanographers and their families. The native Elorans, curious and unafraid, had come out to greet them.

But it hadn't gone well.

The human race had tried to colonize the planet despite the native population. That's when the Lexar had stepped in and enforced their sovereignty. Despite the year-long war that had raged through space, and humanity's eventual surrender, the Elorans had still welcomed them to the planet.

It marked the very first interspecies friendship in human history, and Pacifica Cove was born.

After checking in on the establishment's upper level, they took the scenic stairwell to the ocean floor. Thandie flitted from one window to the next along the way, bright-eyed wonder on her face as she pointed out one ocean creature after another. An enormous jellyfish skated by, gelatinous tendrils gliding behind it with luminous bulbs at each tip. It glittered in shades of vermillion, orange, and black.

"I take it you've never visited the Cove before?"

"No, my friends always wanted to stay in Atlantica for the slot machines and gaming tables, so I never came down this way." The northern hemisphere settlement provided an abundance of eye-catching activities for visitors who preferred parties over relaxation, a literal den of sin tucked away in the chilly waters.

"There's a marauder crab." A dog-sized, soft-shelled crab worked diligently at hollowing a colorful lump of coral. "They wear pieces of coral for protection but they're known for evicting other creatures from inhabited structures and prefer that over an empty dwelling."

"Seems like more work. Why would they rather fight for one?" Thandie crouched beside the glass for a closer look at the muddy brown crustacean. It froze, completely aware of her attention.

"No clue," Xander admitted. "Maybe the theft makes the house more appealing."

Without warning, the crab lunged and struck the glass with one claw.

"Shit!" Thandie startled and fell on her rump, fingers instinctively flying for a non-existent holster left behind on the ship. Weapons were highly restricted on Elora, disdained by the peaceful natives, so only a small number of human security personnel kept arms locked in strategic points for emergency purposes.

Chuckling, Xander offered both hands to Thandie and pulled her back to her feet and into his arms. "I considered warning you, but that's the best part."

"I was right about you at our very first meeting," she grumbled as she smoothed her dress back into place. "Sadist."

Xander grinned. "They're one of Elora's intelligent lifeforms and loathe to be seen naked. Come on. Our room is this way."

"I will get you back for this." Fingers entwined with his, Thandie cast a last glance back at the crab, then nudged Xander to continue down the hall.

"I think he liked your dress," he teased.

"Ha! Well, if he wants it he'll have to fight you for the honors."

Their playful banter helped Xander to brace himself for the next wave of nostalgia. It struck as he led Thandie down the familiar corridors. He'd met Ylona at Neptune's Garden, the only high-class restaurant in the city, where she served meals to lonely diners who declined a table to sit at the bar. At the time, Xander was one of those lonely men, too embarrassed to take a table for one, and absolutely bewildered that the lovely Eloran had seen his heartache and wanted to comfort him.

Ylona had touched him ever so gently and conveyed all of her concern in a single mental caress of her mind against his thoughts. They chatted for hours after the end of her shift. She'd been his best friend.

Now the honor belonged to Thandie, because a day didn't go by that he didn't need to hear her voice or see her in passing.

"We're here." He let them into a room at the end of the hall and sent Thandie ahead of him while he kicked off his shoes.

She gasped, hand clutched to her chest. The room was a normal suite with a stretch of plush, wine-hued carpet and a bed bigger than his home planet, but one wall had been replaced entirely with glass.

Light from above the ocean surface shimmered in fantastical patterns over the king-sized bed, while multi-colored fish swam in school formations, undulating their slender bodies in the underwater paradise.

"It's lovely, isn't it?" He gazed at the graceful creatures. Coral formations created privacy screens for the room's occupants and provided homes to bottom-feeding creatures. He dropped his overnight bag and crouched near the glass to watch a scuttling sea-spider pursuing an emerald feather worm. A larger shrimp-like crustacean struck from within the hollow coral and caught the spider with its many segmented pincers. Its double pairs of eyestalks watched them through the glass.

"The fish, yes. That thing... not so much." Thandie knelt down beside him to watch. "Is it going to attack the glass, too?"

"No, he won't do anything to threaten you. You're too large. Come on. You have to admit, it's sort of beautiful, even if it is nightmare fuel. They'll let you hand feed them in certain areas."

"As much as I enjoy our lab sessions, I'd really rather not lose another limb."

"You're not a particularly brave Royal Marine," Xander teased.

Thandie shot him a dirty look.

"I'm only joking. You'll see plenty of them once you're

snorkeling off the coast." He moved to the in-room bar where a bottle of wine waited in an ice sculpture carved to resemble a crashing wave.

"I'd really like that. Gosh, this room is gorgeous. You didn't spend a lot, did you?"

Xander grinned and shrugged before popping the cork. "Don't worry about what I spent. It was worth it to have time alone with you. Private time that isn't set to a schedule."

While he poured, Thandie snuck behind him and wrapped one arm around his waist. Her cheek pressed against his shoulder blade, breasts a firm presence at his back. Her body heat soaked through his thin t-shirt, a comfort in the cool underwater hotel room. He almost overfilled the first glass.

Whiffs of peach and subtle oak enticed him to sneak a sip. Sweet, effervescent bubbles tickled across his taste buds, and then Thandie slid her other arm around to steal the glass from his hand.

"Since you're the guest, our next destination is up to you, my dear. What would you like to do? Dinner? Dancing?" With three nights promised to them, Xander had no desire to waste a moment of their leave from the ship. In his head, he planned dozens of possible activities, from waterskiing on the coast to hiking in the jungle terrain.

"Xander?"

"Hm?"

The palm that had been flat against his stomach slid lower and cupped him tenderly. Both cocks, especially the ill-behaved upper one, were almost always in a state of near-arousal when she was near. One stroke was all it took to firm them the rest of the way.

She traced one out, then the other, sizing them up with her thumb and index finger. "I love how fast that happens."

"Keep doing that, and you won't be seeing anything but the ceiling. Maybe the pillow, if I'm generous."

Thandie's breath hitched audibly. "That a threat or a promise?"

He took the glass from her other hand and set it aside before spinning her around for a kiss. Thandie melted against him, both arms circling around his neck and shoulders. She surrendered to his hungry exploration, molding her body against his, rubbing against his dual lengths.

He turned his mouth away from hers and nipped her earlobe. "Get this dress off before I rip it off."

Indecision warred on her face, as if she were considering letting him tear it from her body.

"Too late."

As much as he loved the pretty turquoise gown, he'd buy her a thousand more just like it. Xander grasped the front of the bodice and ripped, shredding material and baring her breasts. She hadn't worn a bra beneath the tight bodice.

"Xander!"

He dipped his head down to her breasts and claimed one. "Warned you," he muttered. She wore only panties and those were coral pink with dainty scalloped edges that contrasted the tough warrior woman he'd come to love.

Love. God, he loved her.

"Your turn." Thandie's right hand fisted in his shirt and yanked, tearing the cotton like tissue. If anything, her dominant display made him even more desperate to have her.

Xander growled a low sound of animal lust and moved closer, grabbing her by both hips and yanking her in against him. He kissed her, tongue licking into her mouth, the taste of her as sweet as the wine they'd shared.

She fumbled with his belt and shoved his slacks down. Both cocks sprang free, hard and eager to meet her anxious fingers. Her touch was fire to his blood, and the way she looked at them both—not in horror or disgust, but raw fascination and lust—sent a surge of pride pulsing straight to both cocks.

"I want all of you, Xander."

"You have me."

"No, I mean..." She curled her fist around both dicks at once, pressing them close together. They were flushed dark and red, throbbing with need, but he loved the contrast of their skin tones together, her smaller fingers wrapped around his dicks. "I want *all* of you inside me."

Raw, primal lust rose within him. Another growl rumbled in his chest. Part of him demanded instant satisfaction—to dive in and take what she offered. What little of his sense that remained cautioned him to go slow.

"If we're going to try this, I don't want to hurt you."

"You won't."

Lifting her up in his arms, he stepped from his pants and shorts in the few quick strides to the bed. He tossed her in the middle of it and lowered to one knee between her spread thighs. A single tug was all it took to rip her panties from her body. Like the dress, he'd buy her a hundred more. Right now, he needed her free and bared to him.

While watching her face, he dove in and claimed her pussy with his mouth. He stroked with his tongue, thrusting it in and out the way he'd use one of his cocks. Her rewarding gasp fueled him. Thandie grabbed a fistful of the sheets in her right hand, a handful of his hair in her left.

Suppressing the alien instinct boiling inside him, he slid

into a pose of worship between her gorgeous thighs and loved the sweet, tight core of her, laving it with attention.

Her hips raised from the bed. "God, Xander. Make love to me, *please*. I can't take... can't take any more of this teasing. I want to feel you inside me."

"Not teasing," he murmured against her folds, before a playful lick divided them again and he found her clit, sucking it. Hard. Her thighs trembled, fingers curling against his dark hair. "If I'm going to fuck you with both cocks, baby, I want you wet enough to take them."

She shivered with delight. "I'm so wet you could probably fuck me with four."

He laughed and worked his way up her body until his warm breath feathered against her throat. "As tight as you are? I doubt it."

Taking the lower cock in his fist, he slid in, finding her as wet and wonderfully tight as she'd been every other time she'd dared to sneak into his stateroom for the night. He sank full hilt, the upper cock sliding against her swollen clit, and watched her face, the way her breath shuddered and her lips parted.

He paused after the next backstroke, only the tip inside of her, and brought down his other cock. Thandie watched him, golden eyes bright and eager. Using every bit of self-control he possessed, he introduced his second cock into her body's embrace and eased forward.

Tight. Way too fucking tight. He grunted and dipped his brow to her shoulder, muscles straining and sweat beading on his temples.

Her heel pressed in against his ass, all the indication he needed to continue. Her safety and well-being warred against his innate, animal urges, alien genes filling him with raw desire. With each rock of his hips, he drove deeper, until the snug fit left them both gasping, clinging to each other, moaning together in bliss and shared ecstasy.

She was his. At last. Exactly the way things were meant to be.

ONE OF XANDER'S cocks alone was deliciously thick. She'd known from the start what to expect and even planned it out in her head during many nights alone in her rack, imagination running wild as she pumped three or four fingers into her body. But all the practice in the world couldn't prepare her for the sheer girth of him.

He stretched her to capacity, and it burned so good that the merging of sensations startled her. Pleasantly surprised, she locked both legs around his waist. "Don't stop, Xan, please." She gazed up at him, saw his jaw clenched and the corded muscles of his throat standing out taut.

How it must have killed him to go slow and steady, fearing he'd hurt her.

If she was a female Lexar, he'd have no such qualms.

No worries of hurting her.

Thandie nudged him with her heel again and raised her hips. "Please. I can take it. Give me all of it."

Something about him being seated to the hilt, with each inch of both dicks buried inside her, stimulated every single nerve ending and set her ablaze with sensation.

Xander nodded tightly and sucked in a sharp breath between his teeth on the first backstroke. Then he plunged forward anew. He was grinding against her clit, stroking her inside and out. Moving again introduced her to a whole new plane of rapture, a world where two dicks would always be better than one.

Their moans blended together, sharing the same breaths, and all the finesse he'd displayed during prior sessions together evaporated, becoming something raw and primal. Urgent.

Confident.

One strong hand grasped beneath her thigh and hooked her calf over his shoulder. Then he thrust again, rocking her against the sheets.

For a moment, she could only lie there beneath him in awe of his beauty, of how his muscles shone in the dim lighting, of the way his magnificent abs flexed and tightened on each forward stroke. Then farther down, she saw where they were joined, slick and gleaming, the thick root of his upper dick all she saw exposed as it plunged in and out. A jubilant cry left her lips.

Tension wound inside her body, orgasm fast approaching but lingering just beyond reach. Xander leaned over her and nipped her left breast, the little bite of pain enough to send her cresting over the precipice. And still he didn't stop, unrelenting and powerful with a desperate urgency to his rhythm until the moment he stiffened, too, and she felt the throbbing pulse of both cocks releasing at once.

Stars burst behind her eyes and her entire world condensed down to him. To the feel of his hot skin against hers, the pleasure coursing through every limb, and the sweet sound of her name on his lips. That low, feral groan was everything she'd needed to hear.

Nothing would ever compare.

"You okay?" He stroked a damp curl from her brow, his soft voice pulling her back to the moment.

"Uh huh."

"Just uh huh?" His breath tickled across her closed eyes.

She wanted to smack him for the tease but her uncooperative body refused to move. Instead she made another pleased groan and waited for her heart to stop racing.

Then Xander moved, and the sparks started all over again, delicious aftershocks causing her to clench around him in erratic flutters.

He swore. "Fuck." And the cocks that had been so soft and sated a moment ago twitched.

"Again," she whispered, finally opening her eyes. Later, she'd question why the hell she wasn't sore, deciding to simply appreciate her blessings as they came. Rolling him onto his back, they remained locked together while she rocked astride his lean hips. "Let's do it again."

Afterward, when neither of them could do more than lie in a sweaty sprawl across the enormous bed, she wondered at her good fortune, because Xander was like a dream come to life. Not only the sex—though it had ruined her for all other men—but everything about him.

"Hey, Thandie?"

"Hmm...yeah?"

"I'm glad you're my patient."

Her communicator buzzed with an incoming personal message. Thandie glanced toward it, too drowsy to crawl off her mountain of cuddly, affectionate man to fetch the device on the floor. "Sora, play that message."

It lit green, then a synthesized robot voice said, "Playing your recent voice message from Saskia DuPrie. *Thandie, there's one hell of a party jumping off at Atlantica Gulf right now. You're missing out! Bring your man and come hang with us.*"

Xander chuckled against her hair. "Wanna go?"

"Nope. Got all the party I need right here."

CHAPTER SIXTEEN

"It's not that I don't appreciate whatever miracle happened last night," Thandie said the next morning as she tried to choose between swimsuits for their snorkeling tour, "but why am I not sore?"

"Huh?" Xander had already stretched across the sofa in his trunks, content with watching her shimmy in and out of one suit after the next. He tore his gaze away from her bare ass and blinked. "What now?"

"I kind of expected to feel like I've been reamed by an elephant, but I actually feel great. Not complaining or anything, but I'm curious."

Xander laughed. "Oh. I guess I inherited that part from my Lexar father."

"Besides two amazing dicks? Magic?"

"Do you really want to know? I warn you, you may not like what you learn."

She twisted around and stared at him. "Okay, now I really have to know. Spill."

"I don't know the specifics, since it isn't my exact field of study, but the Lexar have a sort of healing enzyme in their semen. My best guess is it has something to do with how, uh, strong they are. Their mating frenzies are almost beastial. I tried to take it easy on you, and it still almost got the best of me."

"That makes sense, in a weird way. Nothing ominous about it, though."

"What if I told you that you're regularly exposed to refined Lexar semen?"

"I'd say yeah, because I have you."

"Something else. A particular gel component the UNE buys from the Lexar."

A sinking, awful feeling settled in Thandie's stomach. "You're not saying..."

"Let's just say if our nanogel shipment is ever delayed during an emergency, our medical department will have a fresh supply on tap. It just may, ah, take a moment to fulfill the demand."

She hurled her swimsuit at him. "You are awful!"

He just grinned back. "Go with the two-piece. Your tits look amazing in it."

"Aren't you worried people will look?"

"Not really. They've been in my mouth, and no one else gets to touch them."

After she wiggled into the sexy sunflower-print triangle bikini and a matching bottom that barely covered her ass, they went out for an Eloran-led snorkel tour.

Their guide was so beautiful Thandie found herself as mesmerized by the slender alien as she was the schools of glittering fish swimming around them. So far, she'd noticed no two Elorans had the same pattern on their skin, always different colors, stripes, or marbled patches.

During the two-hour tour, she swam alongside a two-headed shark that glowed orange as lava, visited an underwater grotto with living crystal flowers, and tentatively handfed one of the creepy aquatic spiders cruising around the magnificent reefs.

A little after the end of the tour, after dragging on coverup shorts and a t-shirt, she wanted nothing more than to return for another two hours.

"I'll schedule a second tour for tomorrow, if you're serious."

"I'd love that. Unless you have something else in mind," she said.

"Well, there are a few places I'd love to show you on the island." He tugged her against him and leaned down for a kiss. "Places no one else knows about."

"Sounds like a date."

"Great. You ready to meet up with Gareth and the rest of the assault team for some parasailing?"

Thandie lifted to her toes and kissed his cheek. "Since I have to share you, fine, but tonight you're all mine."

At the dawn of the next day, Xander took Thandie on a private hike through the rainforest.

More than a dozen paths led away from the beach, winding into the overgrown thickets and tropical flora. Three miles of trekking through the lush growth was enough distance to escape civilization, and afterward, the landscape treated adventurous visitors to a host of natural wonders. Waterfalls, quick-flowing rivers, and cenote caverns were only some of the other sights Xander had found over the years.

And he shared all of them with Thandie, though the

sixteen-mile round-trip excursion into the wilds claimed most of the morning and afternoon.

They celebrated their return to civilization with dinner at a beachside cafe. Cuddled side by side on a wide hammock, they shared a colorful salad of local fruits and a plate of double-tail prawns stuffed with marauder crabmeat.

"Want to head back to the room or do you have enough energy to wander the market?"

Thandie tilted her face up to look at him. "Shopping, definitely. If I don't send some souvenirs home to my sister I'll never hear the end of it."

Hand in hand, they strolled down the beach to the seaside bazaar. Every time a UNE ship made port, the locals set up colorful stands to peddle their wares. Because the Elorans had no need for money, they preferred to barter for physical objects over galactic currency.

"Oooh! These are pretty."

Thandie beelined to a table covered in small figurines carved from crystalline ocean rocks and opaline shells. The aqua-skinned Eloran behind the table smiled, spread her webbed fingers, and invited them to touch and admire her wares.

"Look, it's one of those crabs." One of the statuettes depicted a vain crustacean holding a piece of fan shaped coral in one claw.

"As ugly as the little blighters are on the outside, their interior polishes like mother of pearl. This was carved from the inside of a marauder's bottom shell," Xander explained, much to the Eloran woman's surprise. She clapped giddily and nodded, sending her sleek strands of green-and-pink-striped hair bouncing over her shoulders.

"Really?" Thandie's eyebrows hiked upwards. "They're

all so pretty, and one would be a nice reminder of our visit, even if you did laugh at me."

"Your little shriek was adorable. Well worth the two seconds you glowered at me."

Rewarding him first with a kiss, she shooed him off to look around while she bartered for the keepsake. A wandering pace through the stalls lightened his pockets and wallet, exchanged for his favorite soap and a few local sweets. By the time he caught back up with Thandie, she was carrying a new woven basket full of her own purchases.

Xander peered down at her collection of goodies. "I can see that you're an impulse shopper."

"What? Okay, so I want my own seasilk sheets," she fussed. "Yours spoiled me."

Xander grinned. "And all of that?" He gestured to the polished coral trinkets, bracelets, and glittering shells. Bright jewels shone from the surface of a unique hair comb crafted from a coral shrimp's tail.

"The bracelets are for my sister," she defended. "Well... most of them, anyways. And... oh fine, I'll put some of it back."

"Ignore me, I'm only taking the piss out of you again. Enjoy the time away from the ship and buy what you want." Otherwise, he'd be forced to return and purchase the very things she removed from her basket.

"Honest, I'm being good. I didn't even try to stuff in the dress that I saw. I had no idea the Elorans wore such pretty silk."

"They don't. Elorans only began to wear clothing when the first human settlers came. They do it for our modesty. Get the dress. You'll regret leaving it once we're gone if you don't."

The crisp ocean breeze was alive in the air, infusing

every woven article with the smell of the saltwater. Lingering traces of it clung to Thandie's skin, along with the fragrance of a native citrus she'd dabbed against her throat. Xander breathed it in and set his cheek against the top of her head.

Once Thandie made her final purchase of the evening, she returned to him with the dress in question, an airy, semi-translucent fabric fashioned into a strapless, knee length dress. Multiple layers of the gold and green material fluttered into an asymmetrical gauzy hemline against her thighs when she held it up for his approval.

"It'll look great on you," Xander said.

"You don't think it's too short?"

"Nope."

"My dad would call it scandalous and my brother would challenge you to a duel for failing to rein me in," Thandie told him.

"I take it that your region of Tallulah is rather..." A war of humor versus horror raged in him. What the hell kind of family was he about to get attached to?

"Old-fashioned? Yeah. Some of the newer cities, like Viljoen's hometown, aren't quite so traditional."

"I see. And they've reinstated dueling. That's always grand."

Thandie chuckled. "It's not as bad as some places."

"I suppose you've brought this up for a reason and I'm to be accompanying you home during leave?"

"Oh..." Her gaze dropped and she tucked a lock of hair behind her ear. "Xander, I left home to escape all that sort of stuff. I wouldn't drag you there unless you wanted to go."

He placed a hand on her hip and turned her to face him. "Do you want me to go home with you?"

"I think my sister would like you."

"I'm not asking whether your sister or family would like me. Do *you* want me to go home with you?" Xander smoothed a disobedient lock of hair away from her brow.

"Yeah, maybe one day. We can talk about it when all this colony stuff is over."

"Fair enough."

Her smile brightened. "Good. Now, c'mon, I'm ready for our little private bubble again."

They made their way back to the room and set their purchases aside. Thandie flopped down on the bed with a relieved groan.

"I didn't think it was possible, but you've worn me out with your outdoor escapades."

"Are you so certain of that?" Xander asked. The moment he approached, she scooted away and dashed to the adjoining bathroom. "The hell?"

Her voice reached him through the door. "I need a minute!"

"All right."

While Thandie peed, Xander undressed to his shorts and caught up on messages. Gareth wasn't happy about his online girlfriend monitoring his virtual time. He'd logged on once, only for her to demand to know why he was video gaming during a supposed vacation.

Xander snorted back a laugh and replied. *Sounds like a good woman. Take her advice and enjoy the downtime. We have mere days here to enjoy the sunlight and fresh air.*

The messages passed back and forth for a while, but Thandie never emerged from the bathroom. Then the bathtub faucet turned on, and water splashed against tile.

"Seriously, Thandie? Do I get to join you, or—"

The bathroom door opened to frame his gorgeous *naked* girlfriend in a sensual pose. Candles glowed behind her on the sink and rim of the tub. Hints of sunlight from the world above shimmered blue ripples against the walls and floor through two portholes.

"You definitely get to join me."

His communicator beeped with incoming messages from Gareth, but his friend would have to wait. He put down the device and stepped inside the bathroom, dropping his shorts to the floor.

"So, um. I kinda had some practice while trying to figure out how we could have sex with both of your dicks at once... As much as I loved having both in the same hole, I kinda figured..." Her shy smile widened, then she nodded to the bathroom vanity, where a bottle with a photo of an Eloran aloe plant waited. "If you want to try, I will."

He stepped forward, closer to her, nudging her. "What kinda practice?"

She nibbled her lower lip and gazed up at him. "I bought a toy online..."

Both cocks twitched. Xander rubbed them against her bare mound, and when she spread her thighs farther apart, he pushed his hips forward and nudged the slick warmth of her bald slit. He loved the little runway strip left after the waxing. "And you didn't tell me?"

"I was... a little embarrassed." Then the tip of one cock notched against her clit, hitting it just right, and she jolted in place, wiggling closer before wrapping her arms around his neck. She pulled him down to meet her mouth, the demanding and assertive minx he'd come to love.

How was it that every time they kissed, it was like the first time?

Xander thrust his tongue into her mouth the way he wanted to plunge into her body, rocking his hips and grinding against the softness of her, Thandie's every moan like magic. She reached down between them and stroked both of his dicks, gliding her fingers up and down the thick shafts.

Then she took the bottle from the sink with her other hand, flipped up the cap, and smoothed a liberal amount of cool gel over both steel-hard lengths, sliding her fists up and down until they glistened.

"I'm ready for you," she murmured against the corner of his mouth. "Take what's yours."

Hefting Thandie onto the edge of the sink placed her at the ideal height, with her legs splayed wide and one bent at the knee, curving around him. By the time he prepared her with his finger, she was wet and panting, rubbing against him and glistening from her own natural moisture. Her nipples stood out so perky and firm, he dipped his head and took one in his mouth, skating his teeth over the sensitive, pebbled tip before curling his tongue around it and sucking.

"Xander... Please."

"Please what?" He barely gritted it out.

She licked her fingers, then stroked her own clit, inspiring an ache in his balls so real he thrust forward, taking her in a single stroke with one dick. "Yes!"

He groaned with her. "You're insatiable." By the time he prepared her other entrance, so was he. Delirious with need, he slipped his lower cock into her ass and almost convulsed from the grip of her. Almost came right then. While having both of his dicks together in her sweet pussy had been phenomenal, gliding each into its own sheath paralyzed him with pleasure.

Thandie's breath hitched. "No more than you."

"You like this?" Xander trailed his lips down her throat. Her fingers tangled in his hair, then she jerked his mouth to hers again.

"I *love* it."

He fucked her with long, deep strokes, sliding out until only the tips remained, and thrusting home again, hilting so deep a small squeal escaped her. He'd have bruises on his left shoulder from the tight grip of her cybernetic hand squeezing him.

And fuck if that wasn't hot, that he drove her to the point of forgetting her own strength.

With each rock of his hips, he carried them higher along the path to ecstasy, because nothing else in the world could ever be better or more precious than granting the ultimate pleasure to his bondmate—his beloved. She deserved nothing less.

Drawing back once, he glanced down at the wet connection between them, her body so full of him she was stretched tight. "Look at us."

And she did. Her clit was so exposed and hard above his dick, he licked one finger and teased the tender jewel, rubbing and circling it until those tight muscles clamped down.

When she spasmed around him, pleasure barreled down Xander's spine and put him on the edge, the sexy look in her eyes and way she moaned his name everything he needed. All he'd ever want. Shuddering, he climaxed on the next thrust, filling both holes with his seed. The whole while, she milked him with the sweetest tremors.

Afterward, they shared the bath before tumbling into the bed again and crawling beneath the sheets. Limbs twined and drowsy snuggles carried Xander to sleep until a persistent beep from his messenger pulled him from pleasant dreams. A digital clock nearby claimed it was morning again.

Half-asleep, he swept the device off the floor, only to stare at the screen and swallow back his conflicted feelings.

"What is it?" Thandie mumbled. "Ship recall?"

"No, nothing like that. It's Ylona's mother. She wants to meet me for breakfast."

Thandie blinked blearily and pushed up on her elbows. "Then you should go."

"Are you sure? I don't want to leave you up here alone."

"Yeah. Go. I'm going to sleep in to recover."

He grinned and leaned down. "Worn out from the hike or the fun?"

"Both. That was amazing." She chuckled and fell back against the sheets with her eyes closed. "Enjoy your breakfast."

Xander leaned down and kissed her nose. "I promise I'll make it up to you."

THE MEETING TOOK place in the underwater restaurant attached to Xander's hotel. Elaborate decor sculpted from unique marble, pearl, and other precious metals displayed the best features of Eloran and human design. They were a friendly culture, and while they prohibited the desecration of their beautiful world, the natives had aided the humans in the construction of their own underwater colonies, protected by glass domes. The two cities, Pacifica Cove and Atlantica Gulf, were proof that the two species could peacefully coexist.

Xander traveled down two flights of stairs and crossed the hotel grounds until he reached the restaurant. He passed several Elorans on the way, as the hotel employed both species in its staff. Some waved to him in passing. He may not have remembered them, but recognition was visible in their pale, slender faces. He smiled courteously in passing and waved.

Ylara didn't waste a precious second. She threw herself into Xander's arms and hugged him tight, catching him by surprise with her affection. Deep down, he'd always feared she would blame him for Ylona's death.

She smelled like the ocean. Like Ylona. Her daughter had resembled her greatly in life, from skin the color of a twilit sky down to the sleek strands of bicolored, purple and ivory hair spilling down her back. A thin, frayed skirt of seaweed and kelp covered her lower half, adorned by beaded embellishments, pearls, and tiny shells that glittered in the candlelight.

Eventually, Ylara leaned back and held him at arm's length with her hands on his shoulders. She stood eye to eye with Xander, as the Elorans were a tall race, with builds varying by their climate preference. The Elorans of Pacific Cove, like Ylona and her mother, possessed aquiline features and graceful, elongated limbs. Their cold-water counterparts were much shorter and stockier, carrying an abundance of insulating fat beneath thicker arctic fur. Xander once joked with his wife and showed her photos of Earth's extinct manatees.

You look well, Ylara said to him, her voice a mere whisper that slid through his mind. He had never quite come to understand how it worked—whether she knew the language, or if the magic of her psychic prowess translated it for her.

"As do you."

I did not think you would come.

"I'm sorry. Coming back, it's been hard in a way."

I understand.

"Well then... shall we?" Xander asked nervously. He offered an arm and escorted her toward the hostess who led them to a small table where they settled near the window view to the ocean.

Ylara took his right hand in her left. *I tried many times to contact you, Xander. You have become a stranger.*

He ducked his head, too ashamed to meet her gaze, and studied the menu instead. Sensing his discomfort, Ylara leaned across the table and touched his cheek with her other hand to guide his attention back to her huge, midnight blue eyes. *I am not upset with you. We have missed you. Most of all, we have wanted to know if you are well.*

"I am."

You hide something from me.

The Eloran matron took both of his hands in hers. Xander's fingers trembled between her webbed digits.

With no idea what to say, he blurted out exactly what was on his mind. "How could you possibly want to see me again when Ylona is dead because of *me*? I killed her, Ylara. Me. If I hadn't deployed again, she'd be alive now."

She had no words, but Xander experienced the full range of her emotions. Sorrow, loss, and compassion—but no condemnation.

We never blamed you. There are many worlds in this galaxy, each one filled with its own dangers. Ylona knew this when she left our home, but you were worth the risk to her. You showed her a world beyond Elora, Xander. There is no shame in that. Oron and I lived for our daughter's stories of Albion and your people. He will be disappointed that their hunt cost him the opportunity to reconnect with you. You are missed dearly.

"She told you stories?"

Many. She told us she once answered your door for the postman without the pretty clothes you bought for her.

Xander chuckled. "She frequently forgot. I would find her in the garden without a stitch on. Our neighbors were scandalized."

They chatted for hours over a few local delicacies, as was Eloran custom when reuniting with a friend. Eventually, he remembered to check his watch, amazed at how quickly the morning had flown by.

"Christ. Where did the time go? I should get back, Ylara. I... Someone is waiting for me."

She perked and a big smile spread over her face. Eloran smiles were disconcerting for some humans, but Xander had long grown used to them. *You have taken a new bondmate?*

"I have," he answered slowly, uncertain despite Ylara's delighted expression. "Her name is Thandie."

Will you allow me to meet her?

Xander stared across the table. He blinked a few times. "You really want to?"

Of course. She must be truly wonderful if she has earned your heart.

"She is exceptional."

May I meet her?

The sincerity of the request took Xander aback. "I... well, yes, of course you may."

He paid the bill and offered Ylara an arm. Before they made it out of the restaurant, his comm went off in alert mode. Xander groaned and checked the message scrolling across the display.

Trouble?

"It's an emergency recall from the *Jemison*. Something's happened."

The same message passed over the city's announcement system. "All hands, return to the *Jemison* immediately."

"I'm sorry, Ylara. I have to go."

She raised her hand to his jaw and smiled. *Keep safe and return to us soon. We have never stopped loving you, Xander. You will always be my son.*

He took her kind words with him and rushed to his room.

CHAPTER SEVENTEEN

Decontamination burned sometimes. Thandie's eyes still stung when she emerged to a world of orderly chaos. Enlisted personnel ran back and forth, accepting their new commands and preparing the *Jemison* for takeoff on short-notice.

"All combat personnel, report to your supervisors," the XO announced over the public channel.

Thandie pushed her way through the heavy crowd and quickly visited her berth to change into uniform. Afterward, she descended to the armory and found the rest of the squad had already gathered in the adjacent shuttle bay.

Their nervous faces revealed what she had already guessed—they were all still in the dark.

"You know anything about what's going on?" Saskia dropped down in the seat beside Thandie. "Did your boyfriend say what's up?"

"Not a thing. He was clueless when we packed up the room together."

Elizabeth glanced around, then leaned in close and

lowered her voice. "About Doctor Vargas... I heard some nasty rumors when we were boarding the shuttle."

Saskia blinked at her. "Like what?"

"Well, Daksha told everyone on the deck that his lust for xenophilia must not have ended, and that he broke off your relationship."

"*What?*"

"I guess she saw him cozying up with an Eloran. I'm letting you know before someone blindsides you with bullshit."

And Thandie fucking loved her for it. She sighed, letting her shoulders drop. "Thank you for letting me know. I appreciate it."

"No prob—"

Viljoen strode in and called them to attention. "Listen up! The *Jemison* received a distress call from one of our own in this very system. We will arrive at the coordinates in fifteen hours. I want all of you back here, rested, geared up, and ready to go in twelve."

"Aye, Commander."

"Kruger and Abernathy, I want you both in the armory for the next hour making sure everything is good to go. DuPrie, make sure Lackley has things in hand on the cannon. Lopez, get the pre-flights done on the shuttles. The rest of you, report to your bunks. We can't afford for anyone to be less than their best."

Everyone dispatched as ordered. Thandie stepped into the armory and started pulling down the first pair of weapons to check. Preparation for missions involved a full inventory check on all squad weapons and gear. Thandie and Abernathy had the dubious honor of guaranteeing that everything was in working order.

"Any idea who he meant?" Abernathy asked across the workbench.

"No. From the sound of it, I'm guessing they received a Royal Marine distress code."

"Huh. That doesn't make much sense. We're the only ship in the system right now."

"Who knows. Maybe someone in a personal craft."

A deep line creased Abernathy's brow. "I dunno. They wouldn't recall everyone for something as basic as engine failure. I'm betting the pirates are involved."

"In that case, I hope this is our chance to finally blast them into dust."

Thandie finished the first set and moved to the next locker. She set down Saskia's shotgun and pistols on the table and began her check. The weapons, as expected, were in perfect, well-maintained condition.

"Hey, I'm going to go check in with Saskia a minute. One of her clips is missing. I bet she left it in her vest again."

Abernathy waved her off, focused on the rifle in front of him. "Bring back some coffee, would you? This is gonna take longer than an hour if Viljoen wants it done right."

"Yeah, sure thing."

With the ship on high alert and everyone at their stations, the passageways were empty and eerily quiet. Thandie made her way through the ship to the Main Battery and stepped inside. As expected, the room teemed with offensive specialists and technicians charged with the maintenance of the ship's guns.

"Where's Saskia?" Thandie swept her gaze around the room. Lackley was squeezed between two power panels adjusting a series of resistors.

"She stepped out to get some coffee," Lackley replied.

"The cannon is off by two millimeters and I have no clue how it happened. I just calibrated this damn thing."

"Okay, thanks. I'll go see if I can catch her. You want me to send her back with anything else?" Thandie asked.

"More coffee."

"Popular request today. I'll let her know," Thandie laughed and stepped out of the enclosed space.

"Jem, can you please locate—"

The entire ship shuddered. Thandie stumbled to the right and hit her shoulder against the wall.

"Breach detected on level 3. Breach detected on level 3," Jem announced over the ship's system. Alarms blared and red lights flashed from the wall panels.

Another explosion rocked the ship and nearly threw her off balance again. The floor beneath Thandie's feet vibrated with the hum of energy.

"All hands to the shuttle bay. The *Jemison* is currently under at—" The sensual female voice abruptly stopped mid-sentence and died. The emergency lights flickered.

"What the hell is going on?"

Thandie continued forward with one hand braced on the wall. Without power, she didn't bother making her way to the nearest lift. Instead, she climbed down an access shaft with only emergency lights guiding her. Another quake shuddered through the ship and the shaft went pitch black. The explosion knocked Thandie's grip loose and she fell several feet before she snagged the rungs with her bionic arm and caught herself. The alarms dimmed in comparison to her beating pulse. She clung tightly to the ladder and waited for her trembling limbs to still before continuing down.

When she crawled out of the access shaft into the

hangar, Thandie stumbled over a motionless shape on the floor. A shape with a bullet hole between his wide-open brown eyes, beneath neatly gelled black hair.

"Oh my God, Lopez." He hadn't been dead for long, his skin still warm beneath her touch. "Kruger to Medical. I have a man down in the hangar—" Thandie cut herself off. Something moved in the corner of her vision, something familiar and colorful. To her, the vibrancy of Saskia's genetic ability always looked like dozens of multihued sparkles.

Thandie slowly stood.

"Saskia. I know you're there. I *can* see you."

The splicer dropped her camouflage and stepped out of the shadows. She held a gun aimed at Thandie's unprotected chest "Toss your communicator here."

Weaponless, Thandie did as instructed. She pulled her comm from her wrist and tossed it. The slim band skidded across the floor and hit Saskia's boot. The woman promptly crushed it beneath her heel.

"I didn't want it to come to this, Thandie. No one else has to die. Step back and walk away. Let me leave in peace." Saskia's calm tone chilled Thandie and ran icy fingers down her nape.

"You killed Lopez. *Why?*"

"He locked me out of the bloody shuttles. I could have been far away from here by now, but it's taken me every second to unjam what he did."

She swallowed back the forming lump in her throat. A nearby console glowed with a combination of green and red lights. The shuttles were still offline, and Saskia must have been trying to override it.

"Did you also take the engines and A.I. offline?"

"A necessary price to guarantee my freedom from this farce. A Commodore whose chief concern is his cock, and a government that doesn't care about the people beyond its closest borders. I found a new cause to serve, Thandie. You can come with me."

Thandie stiffened. "Excuse me?"

"Come with me," she said again. This time she lowered her gun to her side. "You'll have the best cyberneticists at your disposal. Modifications the bloody Lexar won't allow because of their stupid religious hang-ups. Think about your future and come with me."

Behind her, one of the shuttles began its startup routine. The engine hummed to life.

"That's treason."

"So? It's a small price to pay. What did they teach us at United Command? Sometimes, a little sacrifice is required for the greater good. Don't you have a little sister in brain cancer treatment? She could benefit from their research," Saskia pleaded to her. "They could have fixed her by now and allowed her to live a normal life."

"No... Xander said—"

Saskia shook her head. "Don't make me laugh. Vargas is a brilliant tool, but he won't take the steps needed to further his work. Any intellectual knows you have to crack a few eggs to make an omelette."

"Saskia, you sabotaged the ship and now we're under attack."

"They came for me, and the moment you allow me to leave, the attack will end. Don't force me to kill you, too. You're the perfect candidate, Thandie. Don't you understand that we're working for a cause willing to improve this galaxy?"

"They're murderers, Saskia! You saw with your own eyes what they've done. They're abducting innocent children and subjecting them to torture. If you're with them, I'm not letting you get on that shuttle."

"So be it." Saskia lifted her arm and leveled her weapon at Thandie's heart.

CHAPTER EIGHTEEN

When Xander arrived at the medical bay, technicians had already received their assignments from Kathleen. They rushed to and from the stockroom to gather necessary supplies and made portable first aid kits. O'Reilly arrived out of breath, bearing an armload of nanite core gel. As the base of almost all medicinal products that went into the field, it served as the binding glue for bio-stitches and anti-toxins.

Xander's hands began to cramp, so he stopped to sweep his fingers through his hair in frustration. A visceral headache pounded behind his eyes, but too much work remained to take a break. "Hand me another pack, O'Reilly. We'll need about..."

"I've kept count, sir. We require one for every man aboard the ship and five for every medic. This marks ninety-three."

"Xander, can you tell us what we're walking into?" Hart finally demanded.

As the leader of the medical department, Oshiro had another task ahead of him. It became Xander's duty to lead preparations for deploying their combat medics into a possible battle situation. And he didn't believe in leaving his men in the dark. "All right," he agreed quietly. All eyes fell upon him. "I don't think there's any harm in telling you what's happening. Due to the severity of the situation, it's to the benefit of everyone to remain completely aware. We have a possible hostage situation involving a marine thought to be killed in action."

"Who?" Davis asked curiously.

"Kaiden Lockhart sent a Royal Marine distress signal to his brother while we were on Elora."

Kathleen raised both brows. "No shit?"

"Three hours ago, Jem picked up an emergency distress signal from him and patched it to Chief Lockhart. He confirmed its authenticity. We're looking at the recovery of a man who has been missing for five years and subjected to the unknown. We need to be on our game."

She shook her head in pity and resumed her work at the station. "You have a thousand doses of nanomorphone left in quantity, Xander. You're getting low."

"What do we have as a substitute?"

Before she could answer, a quake tore through the *Jemison* and tossed bottles of antibiotics onto the floor. One shattered and the others rolled out of sight beneath the table.

"Shit," Xander swore under his breath. "What was that?"

"Breach detected on level 3," the ship's artificial voice announced. "Breach detected on level 3."

"Level 3 is engineering," Xander muttered.

"All hands to the shuttle bay. The *Jemison* is currently under at—"

The glowing nimbus of color surrounding the PA system speaker dimmed and sparked out.

"Jem?" Kathleen called out.

"And now we've lost the main ship console," Davis said. Her brow furrowed in concern. The lights flickered and died, but the backup generator activated and restored power to the medical wing.

"Never mind that. I think Jem tried to warn us of an attack," Xander said.

Gareth skidded into medical. His flushed face glistened with perspiration. "The lifts dropped offline. I can try to get them goin' again with the access panel in here."

"Do it," Kathleen said. She abandoned the lobby workstation and left it open for his use. "Fairchild, take O'Reilly and get down to engineering. They're bound to have injuries."

"You'll have to use the maintenance hatches," Gareth called over. He pried off the wall panel and pulled out his datagram to access the electrical module. A dozen red and green lights winked on and off, indicating a disturbance in the system. "It's goin' to take me a few moments to get this sorted."

"Got it!" The two medics grabbed emergency kits and headed out.

What if it was planned? The terrifying revelation crossed Xander's thoughts, running his blood cold with fear. "Gareth, do you think this is connected to our mission objective?"

"I hope to God it isn't. Kai's counting on us, and I'll tear anyone apart who stands in my way. If... if that really is my brother out there sending a distress signal, we *have* to retrieve him."

Xander set a hand on his shoulder. "We will. Calm down and do your job. Focus."

Gareth nodded. "Thanks. I'm just... after thinking he was dead for all this time, for him to send our special code... It's got to mean that it's him, doesn't it?"

"We'll find out. Viljoen will have the assault squad ready for the retrieval by the time we arrive."

Xander's personal communicator shrieked to life. "Kruger to Medical. I have a man down in the hangar—" Thandie's voice cut off abruptly before she could complete her message.

"What happened? Did communications drop?" Fear made Xander's lungs squeeze like a vice constricting his ribcage. *Not Thandie. Maybe her link dropped. Maybe systems are down across the board.* His breath shook and his heart rate increased despite his attempt to maintain focus. Oshiro had taught him methods to remain under control, but for a moment they failed him. He was terrified of losing her.

"Shit," Gareth swore. He left the panel and crossed to the medical terminal. "No, comms are still up and running, but Thandie's is inactive. I can't get a link to it."

Xander lingered behind his friend, practically lurking over Gareth's shoulder. "We need those lifts back up. I can't evac wounded without them." Or reach the hangar to Thandie.

"I'm doing everything I fucking can, Xander. Let me breathe! I know you're worried about her, but I can't rush this."

Given a man with a gut wound, Xander knew exactly what to do to save his life. Place him in front of an open series of connectors and power couplings, and he was all thumbs. He grabbed emergency gear while Gareth feverishly worked at the panel.

When the green light above the lift in their hallway blinked on, Gareth slammed the access panel shut. "Done."

"Kathleen, report to Bishop and let him know the lifts are up and we have an issue down in the shuttle bay."

The two men arrived on the lower decks within a minute, stepping off the lift as the *Jemison* rocked beneath another assault.

"Shit. Looks like the pirates." Gareth directed Xander's attention to one of the small viewports in the hull. "I recognize the build... That's the flagship of the Black Jackals. Where the hell did they receive those kinds of upgrades?"

"What do you mean?" Xander asked.

"That's a bloody military cannon."

"Probably scavenged off a ship..."

"Face facts, Xander. If they scavenged a military cannon off a ship, that means one of ours was lost in battle. Have you heard reports to that effect?" the man asked grimly.

"I know. We'll consider those ramifications later. Right now, we need to get to Thandie."

The passageway took them directly to the hangar. The double doors remained dark and unresponsive, but that was the least of Xander's worries. The sight through the window chilled him.

"What in the hell is going on in there? Why is Sassy holding a gun on Thandie?" Gareth asked in bewilderment. "Christ, that's a body on the floor!"

"Thandie!" Xander banged on the glass.

His arrival drew Saskia's attention to the viewing portal. Thandie capitalized on the distraction and charged. The two women struggled for control of the weapon until Thandie struck Saskia's wrist, forcing her to drop it. The weapon discharged the moment it struck the floor. Sparks exploded off the nearest shuttle and left a charred, circular dent in the metal.

Xander held his breath, a helpless observer to the chaos beyond the unbreakable partition.

Gareth swore. "We're locked out."

"Can you hack into it?"

"Already on it," Gareth muttered from the dataport beside the door. "With the ship offline…"

The two women exchanged blows, matching strikes and kicks. As a cyborg, Thandie had strength on her side, but Saskia weaved in and out of the fight to avoid her opponent's powerful right hook, always coming back with two punches of her own.

Blood trickled in a crimson river down Thandie's chin. She shrugged it off and maintained her guard.

"Gareth, what's taking so long?"

"Workin' as fast as I can, I swear to you. I have to get into the wiring to disable the magnetic locks." His expression of intense concentration dissuaded Xander from questioning him further.

Xander's pulse thundered between his ears, blood racing through his veins. A year and a half ago, he'd been completely helpless when news reached him of the ECF *Orlando* suffering losses during a meteor storm. When he had learned that the water supply lines burst and that his wife's H_2O tank had drained on the floor during transport, life had barely been worth living afterward. Despite all efforts by the flight attendants to keep her moist and comfortable, despite other passengers donating their glasses of refreshment, she had suffered an excruciating death—and he hadn't been there to help her.

He'd never considered himself a praying man, especially not to the Lexar's gods, but he hoped anyone listening heard his pleas.

Not Thandie, too.

Gareth growled and swore at the panel, while Xander paced in a circle, raking his hands through his hair.

Then Thandie's cry of pain reached him through the shatterproof glass, and all control he'd carefully maintained for the past year since the *Glenn* came apart. Xander slammed his fist into the thick pane. Pain spiked up through his wrist but he ignored it and struck again. And again.

A crack fractured through the window.

Thandie hit the floor and rolled in a desperate bid to get away from her attacker. Saskia got ahold of the gun and fired.

"No!"

Glass shattered beneath his next strike. He barreled through the opening and sped across the hangar.

Xander collided with Saskia. Something pinched his bicep, and the gun flew from her hand.

Then his entire world became red rage and fury. He hit her again, and again, slamming and shaking Saskia against the floor. Hands took him by the shoulders and arms, desperately pulling at him. Voices shouted, barely penetrating the haze of fury.

"Xander!"

"Doc, Doc, you gotta stop! You're killing her!"

"Vargas, let up, man!"

Faceless, familiar voices broke through the fog, though he recognized Viljoen on one side of him and Gareth on the other, both trying with little effect to pull him off. Other hands joined their efforts.

"He's not budging!"

"Commander Vargas, you're killing her."

Abernathy grabbed him around the arm, and Viljoen tried to pry his fingers loose from Saskia's throat. She wasn't moving anymore, though he felt her weak and thready pulse beneath his thumb and knew an ounce of pressure would be all it would take.

Then the cool touch of familiar hands framed his face, and he glanced up to see Thandie crouched in front of him. "Xander, *stop*. It's done. She can't hurt me anymore."

The rage receded and he came back to his senses, but his hands continued to shake long after he dropped Saskia to the hangar deck and rose to sweep Thandie into his arms.

Saskia gasped in a starved breath and huddled against the floor. Medical swarmed into the hangar as Viljoen took charge, barking out orders for restraints on Saskia and medical attention to Xander and Thandie.

All he wanted, all he needed, was her arms around him. Aware of her injuries, he hugged her close and buried his face against the top of her hair, just breathing her in.

Thandie pulled back and looked up at him. "Did she get you? When the gun went off, I swear my heart stopped."

"I'm fine. She only grazed me." He'd barely felt the bullet or even registered he was shot until he noticed blood trickling down his arm.

Full lighting returned online. "The ship has returned to online status. All services will resume shortly. Please standby," Jem's calm voice announced shipwide.

"C'mere. Let me look at you." Xander led Thandie aside to check her over. One of the medical teams arrived but he waved them off. Sometimes, Xander preferred to do the work over delegating authority to anyone else. Thandie was worth that time.

"She broke your nose." Saskia had also gashed

Thandie's forehead, but it was nothing a few nanites couldn't set right. He drew his penlight and swiftly assessed her for lingering effects from the fight. "Pupillary reflex looks fine... how's your head?"

"She killed Lopez," Thandie whispered instead.

"I know, Thandie. But how are *you*?"

"Maybe I should ask you that."

"I told you, my arm is nothing."

"I'm not talking about your arm."

He drew in a deep breath and closed his eyes. "I'm good now. I lost control, and I'll answer for that, but I'm in my right mind again."

Thandie kissed his forehead and whispered, "Thank you for rescuing me."

"Anytime." He released his pent-up breath, opened his eyes, and smiled at her.

"Hart to Vargas. We need you in medical. Creswell lost footing in a maintenance shaft and jammed an abductor cable in his left cyberleg during the fall. I'd wrench it back in, but I'm likely to fubar the entire thing. We need you."

Xander paused. He turned his face toward the link pinned to his lab coat. "We have injuries in the shuttle bay, Hart."

"Go. I'll be okay," Thandie smiled fleetingly and squeezed his hand. "Creswell needs you. Elizabeth can stitch me up."

"I'll check in on you when I'm done, I promise."

Leaving Thandie in a state of need hurt him to his soul, but he trusted her care to his medical team and made his way back to the ward. With systems back online, the *Jemison* engaged engines and began evasive maneuvers. Xander had felt uneasy with the previous stillness of the ship and took reassurance from the familiar thrum of power coursing beneath his feet.

They may have rooted out and neutralized the traitor in their midst, but they still had one hell of a firefight ahead of them with the enemy.

And the enemy had military tech.

Xander and the other doctors had their hands full with injuries ranging from mild bruises to second-degree burns. Realigning Creswell's damaged cybernetics hadn't taken more than ten minutes, before he moved on to the other crewmen hurt during the explosion in engineering.

"I can't believe they're still attacking us."

Xander glanced up from his work, occupied with applying a neat line of bio-stitches to a marine's injured scalp. "Stay away from that viewport, Kath. It's small, but if movies have shown me anything, it's that we should never leave a blasted thing to chance."

A few other members of the medical team nervously shot glances at the translucent portal to the world beyond their ship. Occasional bursts of cannon fire lit the open void of space like a thousand stars all combusting at once.

"Agreed," Oshiro said from the mouth of the corridor that led into their open lounge. He and Davis approached from the examination rooms.

Kathleen reluctantly stepped away from the small window. "How's our traitor?"

"Properly secured under an armed guard in the treatment room," he replied.

"Hogwash is what it is. The bint hobbled our ship,

killed one of our men, and now we've got to play nice with her?" Davis demanded.

O'Reilly snorted. "After the beating Doctor Vargas gave her, no one's playing nice with her. You can't interrogate corpses."

Fairchild nodded in agreement. "You weren't there to see it. Haven't seen a fight like that since a gorilla alpha male put a smaller primate in his place at a zoo. She's bloody fortunate Thandie is a better woman than her. I'd have let him snap her goddamned neck after what she did to Lopez."

Xander waited for the condemnation and distrusting stares. None came, and he relaxed, all of his clenched muscles untensing. News on a ship spread like wildfire. Saskia's arrival under guard in medical had started an entire slew of rumors and accusations. It didn't take long for the story of her betrayal to make the rounds.

Xander shook his head. "Trust me. She won't find anything nice about what happens to her next, once our ship is in the clear."

"Yeah? What's happening, Commander? What can you tell us?" Fairchild asked eagerly.

"Yeah. About that. I don't actually know what's happening next. With the commodore on the bridge directing the battle, I'm honestly in the dark, too."

Their expressions deflated. Just as Xander opened his mouth to apologize for his lack of information, Jem's voice blasted over the public channels, "Red alert status has ended."

Kathleen sagged in relief against him. He leaned against her in return. "Thank God. I've never been in an actual battle before. That was terrifying. And *now* I'm going to the viewport."

She and Davis fought over it. The result of their squabble was that both women ended up cheek to cheek, peering through the small window into the outside world. The *Jemison* used its tractor beam to anchor and draw the deactivated enemy ship toward them.

Oshiro joined them and placed a hand on each woman's shoulders. "They'll board the ship now. We must be prepared for more injuries."

A doctor's work was never finished.

CHAPTER NINETEEN

Rendered completely harmless, Saskia lay upon an examination table with nothing more than a sheet covering her. Medical staff had secured her with restraints.

Xander slanted his gaze to Ethan. "How long do you suppose she's been on their side?"

"Impossible to tell." The man crossed his arms against his chest. "I want to throttle the little bitch for what she's done, but you already beat me to it."

Xander grimaced. "I know I lost it, and I'm—"

"Don't you dare apologize. Anyway, we're waiting for Nisrine to begin the interrogation."

"Is she up for it?"

Ethan nodded. "She's eager to have answers for what happened, and she wants justice for Lopez. I won't deny her that."

"Hopefully, we will receive answers for this travesty," Oshiro said. The older man shook his head and quietly observed.

"How's Kruger?" Ethan asked suddenly. "She's earned herself a promotion as far as I'm concerned."

"Lil patched her up and sedated her to ensure she got some rest before we arrive for the mission. She insisted on going down and is fit for duty, if that's what you're asking," Xander said.

"No, I simply meant—"

The doors hissed open and cut Ethan off, heralding the arrival of their intelligence officer. Nisrine approached with her chin held high despite her red and puffy eyes.

"Are you sure that you're good for this, love?" Ethan searched her weary face.

"I am. May I begin?"

Ethan gestured toward Saskia. She hadn't said a word since she was detained, though they'd made numerous attempts to question her. Nisrine stepped over to the bed and looked down at Saskia's battered face without any pity.

"As you won't willingly give over the information we seek, it appears that I shall have to retrieve it all myself." Nisrine made a show of pushing her sleeves up and reached for Saskia's head.

Their prisoner struggled against her restraints. "You can't do this to me. There are bloody laws prohibiting—"

"You seem to forget something, DuPrie. You're a traitor and this is my ship. A good man is dead because of you," Ethan spoke out in an even voice. "You won't receive an ounce of pity from us. Begin when you're ready, Nisrine."

"This will not hurt *me* a bit. I cannot say the same for you." Nisrine lowered both hands to Saskia's head and cradled her face, anchoring her head in place.

They all knew when the real work began once Saskia's terrified shrieks began to reverberate through the room. She thrashed on the examination table and her pupils dilated as her memories were rifled through.

The use of telepathic abilities lacked pretty physical

effects to mark Nisrine's progress; she didn't glow, shimmer, or appear any different while invading Saskia's mind. Instead, they were treated to the spectacle of the psychic victim convulsing and screaming while Nisrine calmly leaned over her without loosening her grip. "Good. I hope it hurts a lot."

Ethan dropped his voice low and whispered to Xander, "She isn't killing her, is she?"

"I don't believe so. Of course, there's always a risk of brain death whenever a psychic goes into an unwilling mind like this."

His friend grunted, then cleared his throat. "Anything useful from her, Lieutenant?"

"Yes. She is the one who took Kaiden Lockhart," Nisrine reported. "There is a clear memory here of stalking him during his patrol. Attacking. She dropped his body for others to pick up."

"That means she's worked for the enemy at least five years. Perhaps six," Xander said.

"What about the people directing her movements. Who are they? Who's responsible for this treachery?" Ethan asked.

"This woman," Nisrine spat the word with vehemence, as if she had another description in mind. "She informed Jarvis Crane of patrol routes, allowing him to keep ahead of United Command."

Ethan hissed out a breath between his teeth. "That bloody tosser wasn't even on board the ship we captured. Bastard must have fled prior to the assault, but we do have his second mate's corpse. What else do you see?"

"She reported to the leader of her cell, Doctor Mathias Campbell, and she killed him when you were too close. She is the one who attempted to gas you on Kantarn."

Xander deflated a little more with each revelation. How long had Matthias been part of their scheme?

Better yet, who had he worked for?

Ethan clapped a hand to his shoulder. "Is that it, Nisrine? There has to be someone higher."

"Nothing. Her mind is particularly resilient when it comes to identifying her superiors. Either she remains unaware of their identities or she has been conditioned to conceal them. I can continue to delve deeper, but it may kill her this time." Nisrine's hardened gaze remained on the woman in her hold.

"Do it."

"Do we want to risk losing her?" Xander spoke up suddenly to his friend. "I want the information as badly as you do, but..."

"I know. Do no harm," Ethan muttered.

"Nisrine is one of the best in her field when it comes to retrieving mental data. If she is unable to do it safely, no other psychic can," Oshiro said. "But the possibility of loss is great. We are not the ASR, Ethan. Please. Let us have a traitor to release to the prison ship when it arrives."

"Fine," Ethan agreed. He waved a hand. "Get her to the brig in a paper gown only. I want two armed female officers by her cell at all times."

Saskia's history as a highly trained and deadly field operative meant Ethan didn't plan to leave anything to chance. Xander didn't blame him. He'd watched Saskia pick a lock with her fingertip once.

Once Nisrine released their prisoner, Kathleen moved in and guided the quaking psychic away.

"Doctor Hart gave her an injection to destabilize her abilities. She won't be going camo any time soon, either, but we colored her arms with medical dye just in case," Xander said.

"Brilliant. All right, I have to go write some reports. I hate this bloody part of my job."

Xander sympathized. Losing a member of the crew was never easy and he could only imagine the deeper loss Ethan felt as the commanding officer. He clapped his friend on the shoulder.

"We'll get who did this, Ethan."

"Yes. We will." Ethan drew in a deep breath. "Go on now and check your bird."

"She's asleep, remember? There's too much work to do, and too many injured."

"No, you are going to rest. I need you fresh for this mission, Xander. Check on Kruger to ease your worries, then hit your rack. That's an order. I'll see you in ten hours."

"Ten hours. We'll get our guy back."

If they made it in time.

CHAPTER TWENTY

Midori resembled an emerald marble hanging in space, a moonless planet covered in dense jungle, with very little visible surface water. Xander stared out the viewport and frowned. Beside him, Viljoen wore a matching expression.

"I thought the UNE decided against colonizing this place. Something about dangerous wildlife," Viljoen said.

"Yeah, well, looks like somebody decided to risk it despite the oversized reptiles."

"We're coming up on our target," the pilot called back. "Single structure ten klicks ahead."

"Good. Land us on the rooftop. You know the drill, everyone. We are going to sweep through this position and lock down everyone inside. Let's make this clean and quick and find our man."

Viljoen stood and opened the side door, then Thandie slid smoothly into place with her rifle at the ready to cover their landing. They touched down on the empty rooftop without any resistance.

The moment Viljoen kicked open the roof access

door, the squad spilled into the facility as a cohesive unit. They had a single mission: to safely retrieve their lost comrade. Kaiden Lockhart had to be somewhere in the building.

Abernathy and Thandie took point as the team swept through the building, while Xander and his medics brought up the rear. No opposition came forward, the upper hallways silent. The tingling sense of unease followed them down to the main floor. The group left the stairwell and came across two uniformed guards.

"Weapons down and hands up!" Viljoen bellowed.

Both guards threw up their hands, weapons tumbling from their fingers.

"Don't shoot!"

"We didn't do anything. Please don't shoot."

"Holy shit. Royal Navy? What's going on?" another confused voice shouted from the lobby.

Three more security officers emerged from a surveillance room. Once they saw the guns leveled at them, they also put up their hands.

"Any one of you wanna tell us what happened here?" Viljoen asked.

The guards all exchanged glances, then one cleared his throat and stepped forward. "We wish we knew. The scientists packed up in a hurry. First, they put out an alert about some experiment escaping the laboratory, then they had us out there searching in the jungle, but wouldn't tell us shit about it."

"Did they reclaim their experiment?" Xander asked.

The spokesman shook his head. "Not that we know of. They said the tracking equipment was shot to hell. Apparently, their science project killed a few men in the lower levels. Next thing we know, they're loading up on the shuttles. Took off without us. Until you showed up we were trying to figure out how to get a signal off-planet."

Expendable. Xander's jaw tightened.

The guards voluntarily confined themselves to an empty office. Viljoen left two marines to keep watch and then led the rest of the squad to the lower levels.

The subterranean rooms reminded Xander of Kantarn. They passed empty surgical suites and cybernetic labs. Further ahead, two bodies lay sprawled across the floor.

"This must be the security they were talking about." Thandie crouched by the nearest corpse. "Their armor is better—cutting-edge tech. The holsters are even specialized."

Viljoen whistled. "I know the model that belongs in there. I'd put money on it that the main level guards are non-essential staff, and these were their loyal security squad members."

Xander joined Thandie and looked over the two bodies. "Both had their necks snapped."

"Got a third body in this next room," Abernathy called over. "His uniform has been stripped. My guess is that our guy took him out first and snagged his uniform, then came up on these two without raising an alarm."

"I'll be damned," Viljoen muttered, impressed.

"Kaiden was always one of the best operatives on any ship. Maybe... I want to try something. If the body hasn't been dead for long, maybe I can see this guy's last sight," Gareth said.

"Go for it," Xander encouraged him.

Gareth swapped positions with Thandie and took a deep breath. With both hands against the cheeks of the corpse, he turned the security guard's face toward the ceiling and leaned above him to make direct eye contact. He jerked back and toppled on his ass.

"It was Kaiden. He's really *alive*."

Xander leaned down and pulled Gareth up to his feet again. "Then let's find him."

"You don't get it, Xander. I *saw* him. Right in front of me."

"You're going to see him for real in a second, man. Keep it together."

Once Gareth gathered his wits, Davis pointed out a trail of carnage for them to follow. It led to a locked door requiring a security clearance.

Gareth viewed the map briefly. "It's the only way out of here," he muttered.

"Can you hack it?" Thandie asked.

"Sure I can," Gareth knelt beside one of the fallen bodies and hefted the corpse to his feet. He scanned the cybernetic clearance chip installed in the guy's wrist. "Or I can swipe this and get out faster."

The door led outside, letting out on a steep slope covered in dense vegetation.

"Keep sharp, everyone. Local wildlife isn't friendly," Viljoen warned.

The tracks were easy to follow at first, heavy footsteps leading deeper into the jungle. Wind rustled through the trees and insect chirps echoed through the humid air.

"Shit, I lost the trail," Thandie said. She twisted around and searched the ground, but the increasingly thick growth obscured the ground.

"Here!" Davis cried. Her call came from the edge of a narrow stream. "Someone came through this way barefoot. You can see a heel indent in the soil. The ground is still soft."

"Good catch, Davis. Where'd you learn to track?" Viljoen eyed her thoughtfully.

"My dad used to take me hunting before I joined up with the navy. Showed me a lot of things," Davis replied. "He went this way. No wonder no one found him... It's thick. Poor bloke's probably scratched to bloody hell."

"And scared," Xander remarked for Gareth's sake. "Set your handguns to non-lethal rounds. He's armed and we don't want to give him any reason to fire at us before he recognizes our colors."

Gareth shot him an appreciative look, which he returned with a smile. Their path took the group deeper into the jungle, where the ground squelched beneath their feet and became boggy from the atmosphere's excessive rain patterns.

Davis gestured to some broken ferns. "There. He tripped over that root and fell down on one knee here. Heavy bastard, isn't he?"

A shot glanced off the helmet protecting Xander's head. Every marine ducked and moved into defensive positions with their guns drawn.

Before anyone could shout a command, Gareth dove into the thick foliage, pushing forward while calling his brother's name.

Sweeping heavy branches out of his path, Xander broke through the thick growth a second later, to find Gareth in a standoff with his twin, the two identical in features but not in builds—Kaiden was enormous and muscled. His head had also been shaved, revealing the scar tissue on his scalp from multiple surgeries.

The gun shook slightly in Kaiden's hand as he backed away from the approaching marines.

"No one move. Give him a moment. Put your weapons away," Xander ordered. "You too, Viljoen."

Viljoen grunted but followed the command. The others did, too.

"Kaiden, I'm your brother. I'd never do anything to hurt you."

"Prove this isn't another test. Tell me something only Gareth would know."

"When we were six, you shoved another kid face down in the mud for knocking my ice cream cone out of my hand. Da' was upset about the trouble it caused, but mum praised us behind his back and said we should always count on each other."

Kaiden's hand wavered. Seconds ticked by, but the handgun didn't lower. "I can't trust that. I can't trust any of you. They've been in my head... they know everything. This is all a lie. You only want to drag me back to that room."

"Read my thoughts. You'll see the truth."

The expression on Kaiden's face transformed from terror and distrust to the bleakest desolation Xander had ever seen. "I can't," he whispered. "They took it from me."

Gareth stopped in his tracks, and the placid mask he wore for the sake of his brother finally cracked. "Big brother, let me help you. Please put down the gun."

Kaiden shook his head again and took another step backward. "They like to play games. You're not real."

"They're gone," Xander spoke up gently. He stepped forward slowly with Gareth, only to pause when Kaiden's muscles stiffened. The tension spread down his arm to his trembling hand. "How do you feel about leaving this place, Kaiden? Would you like to see the *Jemison* again?"

"I'd like to go home. I want to return to the *Jemison* again," Kaiden admitted. His gaze flicked back and forth, giving him a close resemblance to a trapped animal. He tracked their movements, missing nothing, always watchful and alert.

"What do you have to lose?" Xander asked softly. He grazed Gareth's hand with his knuckles. *I'm going to distract him so that the rest of you can take him down, mate. Tell Fairchild to sedate him. Have Thandie and Viljoen secure him.*

He'll shoot you. He's a caged animal right now, Xander. Don't do it.

I won't allow him to strike anything vital. Their mental conversation occurred in the span of a second.

Gareth reached back and touched Thandie, who touched Viljoen, and one by one the others made subtle contact, creating a chain of telepathic thought to coordinate the operation. Once it seemed they were all on the same wavelength, Xander made his move and lurched forward.

"No!" Kaiden squeezed the trigger with the barrel already trained on Xander. The impact shattered a protective plate of his combat armor and punched down to the bone. He stumbled and dropped to one knee while the others rushed in according to the plan.

Thandie pitted the strength of her cybernetic arm against Kaiden's weight to pin him down from one side. Viljoen and Chang took him from the right and practically laid their bodies across his torso to secure him to the ground. He bucked wildly and drove one of his knees into Viljoen's side. The commander grunted out in pain.

"Now, Fairchild!" Viljoen ordered.

Gritting through the pain, Xander sat heavily on the ground and fetched two additional tranquilizers from his personal medipack. His instincts were rarely wrong, and his intuition told him one dose wasn't going to be enough.

Fairchild dove in and jabbed the auto-ejecting tranquilizer against the outer aspect of Kaiden's thigh. As she slammed it home, it cracked and the needle snapped.

"No good!" Fairchild reported. "He's got cybernetic muscle weave beneath his skin."

"Catch!" Xander hurled the second toward her. "Inject it into the jugular!"

Kaiden threw an elbow back into Chang's face, shattering the demolition-grade plasteel faceplate. "I won't go back there!"

Thandie jerked back. "Holy shit! Cybernetic arms, too!"

Kaiden's larger size and superior reach granted him the advantage in the fight, but Thandie moved faster and with more flexibility. She threw her weight against him and wrapped her arms and legs around him in a full-body hold.

"Stick him already, dammit!" Thandie cried.

"Viljoen, secure him from the right," Xander barked out, leaping in with Fairchild and jabbing with the third injector. "Kruger has it handled on her side."

The injector pumped Kaiden with milky fluid, and then the true fight began. He buried the soles of his feet against the ground and shoved.

"Hold him until it works!" Fairchild screamed.

Between the combined efforts of the marines and the potent mix of sedatives, the fight slowly drained from Kaiden Lockhart. He feebly pushed and shoved until his eyes rolled back and his jaw became slack.

None of them dared to move.

"Is he out for good?" Thandie grunted, wedged halfway beneath the heavy man. She tried to shove him off but barely managed to nudge him an inch. "How the hell much can one guy weigh?"

Viljoen helped pull her out. "Damn, he's strong as an ox."

"Sort of glad you put us through the ringer on the mats, Commander. Longest ground tussle of my life," Chang complained. The man sagged against a tree while Davis tended to his bleeding face. Jagged shards from his shattered faceplate were embedded in his cheeks.

With the worst over, Xander began his own field dressing. Applying it one-handed took more skill than he anticipated.

"Here, let me help."

"I've got it. Kruger, you see to Kaiden."

Thandie ignored him and pulled the shredded remnants of his shoulder piece, revealing the dark blood soaking the uniform beneath it. "Let me help you, your hand is shaking. Here, I can—"

"I said I fucking have it."

She flinched and dropped her hands. "As you say, sir."

He regretted his tone immediately and tried to cast aside his feelings; he needed an obedient marine, not a lover right now. Cool logic didn't change the way his stomach twisted in turmoil, and Xander knew if their positions were reversed, he'd have done the same thing.

CHAPTER TWENTY-ONE

Thandie reclined on her bunk and gazed up at the ceiling above her. A poster collage of her favorite family photos decorated the formerly bland gray surface.

"Sergeant Thandie Kruger, you have a new message from Commander Xander Vargas," Jem said.

Thandie jerked her attention toward the speaker aperture located in the corner of the room. "Go ahead and play it, Jem," she replied to the ship A.I.

"Report to my office in medical, Sergeant Kruger. Now."

Shit.

"Uh-oh," Angela muttered. "What did you *do?*"

Thandie ignored her bunkmate and hastily slipped back into her uniform, heart pounding. She had a solid guess what he wanted to talk to her about. Before heading out, she dampened her fingers and ran them through her hair to tame the disheveled strands.

Xander's office door took on an intimidating presence, one she steeled herself against with both palms pressed over the cool surface. Once her racing heart calmed, she knocked.

"Come in."

Thandie stepped inside, muscles tense. She closed the door behind her and stood at attention in front of Xander's desk. She focused on a spot over his shoulder because she couldn't meet his dispassionate gray eyes.

"You wanted to see me, sir?"

"Would you like to tell me what you were doing down there, and why you disobeyed my order?"

"I saw our medical officer bleeding out and struggling to treat himself." It came out before she could tame her tongue. Xander wasn't amused.

"I must be mistaken. I wasn't aware of your medical training, Sergeant Kruger."

Thandie opened her mouth to speak but quickly snapped it shut. She swallowed back her protest, stomach churning. It wasn't the first time she'd been subjected to a reprimand or stern words from a ranking crewman, but it cut deeper coming from him.

"It's recently become apparent to me that we've surpassed the point of maintaining a professional relationship. There's also no room on our squad for a marine who can't follow my orders."

His words carried the same effect as dousing her with a bucket of ice water. She was numbed initially, and then furious, the anger sweeping through her until the heat of it reached the top of her ears. "Permission to speak freely, sir."

He nodded and leaned back in the seat.

"With all due respect, *sir*, but if you have a problem with me being on this team, then *you* need to deal with it. Yes, I tried to help you instead of tending to Kaiden, but my actions hurt no one and pulling rank on me like this is crap."

"Is that all?"

She swallowed back another bitter retort and nodded. "Yes, sir."

"You're dismissed, Sergeant. We'll speak later outside the office."

Thandie snapped to attention, turned about-face, and strode out without another word. She didn't trust herself, even if she had the breath to speak. Without looking, it felt as if every eye in medical followed her on the way out.

She made it out the department's door before the first tears slipped down her cheeks. The path ahead of her became the least of her worries, right up until she sped around a corner and bounced into a solid wall of chest. The most muscled chest she'd ever seen in an officer's uniform.

"Kruger?"

Kill me, now. Please. Running into the CO, literally, seemed like the worst sort of luck on top of a day gone so horribly wrong.

Her face warmed to a feverish temperature. "I'm so s-sorry. I should have been paying attention."

"Toss the formalities into the rubbish for a moment. Now, what's wrong? What have I missed?"

Thandie shook her head, wishing she had a hole to crawl away into. If it was possible to die from shame, she'd be a stone-cold corpse at his feet.

"It's n-nothing, sir."

"We'll have a jaunt through the bio-farm, then. Come on. I'm told by one of my officers that it's the cool place where all of the kids like to snog these days. Let's go have ourselves an eyeful."

Commodore Bishop left her little choice in the matter. His hand settled on her back between her shoulder blades, guiding her down the passageway.

He even offered her a handkerchief. The gentlemanly gesture caught her by surprise.

"Take your time."

His kindness opened the floodgates. Thandie couldn't stop her tears, so she focused on not blubbering—on controlling her breathing and pulling it back in like a proper marine.

"Are you feeling better now?" Once she nodded, he continued. "The poor sod didn't dress you down in front of the rest of medical, did he?"

"Doctor Vargas called me to his office, sir, to address my insubordination. He was right to."

"I read his report. Sounds to me like he was being obstinate. Doctors are like that, you know."

She hesitated to say anything, so opted for silence.

"Look, Kruger, I've seen your record. I know you're an exemplary marine. That's why I requested you for assignment on the *Jemison*. That hasn't changed."

"Thank you, sir."

"Thank yourself. And don't let this hiccup throw you off your game." He punched in something on his personal display. A subtle beep from her badge indicated a change in her duty status. "Go clean up and relax for the day. I'll handle our mutual friend."

"Thank you, sir, but you don't need to do that. I didn't mean to trouble you." Thandie offered the handkerchief back to him.

"Keep it. I've got a thousand of them for the enlisted." The commodore strode away.

Thandie remained beneath the trees a few minutes longer, wondering if she'd be forced to choose between the team she loved and the man she treasured.

CHAPTER TWENTY-TWO

Xander loathed invasive neuro procedures, but he'd learned to do them for epileptics and to cure other brain abnormalities during his surgical residency. Arms and legs were basic performance modifications, but none of those were potentially life-threatening issues. If he botched a job by misplacing a cybernetic leg's nerve connection to the hip socket, no one died. He simply opened the patient's incisions and tried again.

The human brain required absolute precision. Doctors relied on virtual enhancements, droid-assisted surgery, nanobots, and software protocols to perform necessary neurosurgeries. For that reason, and that reason alone, he had no intention of physically delving into Kaiden Lockhart's skull. An hour of exploration with the NORI machine told him everything he needed to know and confirmed that the blueprints in Campbell's database referred to Kaiden.

Fairchild dabbed Xander's brow with a cloth while he made the incisions with his surgical laser. Anxiety beaded his forehead with sweat, almost to the point of distraction.

One wrong move could activate Kaiden's internal defenses and instantaneously counteract the sedatives in his bloodstream.

"Never seen anything like this," Xander muttered as he opened a window into the cyborg's chest. The layer of synthetic skin peeled away to reveal Kaiden's metal-plated bone structure. Plasteel-laced bone guarded his interior organs, most of which appeared to be improved or replaced by machinery.

"As you can see, they've augmented roughly 60% of his skeletal structure with a reinforced periosteum. Both arms are prosthetic with reinforced shoulder joints."

Davis took her position at the opposite side and assisted with holding the small incision open. Kaiden's sternum split open down the middle once unbolted and pried apart, designed for easy access.

"Overhead lights: swivel fifteen degrees starboard, thirty degrees downward," Xander commanded the surgical theater's artificial intelligence. "God, would you look at this, Oshiro." The micro-camera on his tools projected a live-time feed on the monitor to the doctor observing on the other side of the glass. "His heart has a complex filter to separate the cybernetic lipids from his bloodstream. You see, humans need blood, but blood clots in cybernetic parts. Causes blockages. Kaiden doesn't have to worry about that."

Or plenty of other things, Xander realized. The boy was an anomaly, constructed piece by piece to such a degree that more machine existed than man. At the very least, the ratio was close.

"According to the notes from Campbell's files, they added a failsafe. If I remove it now, that's one less concern to trouble us later," Xander muttered.

"His vitals are steady. The suspended microparticles

seem to be holding the sedatives in his system," Lil reported from the side of the room. Her sole job was to keep Kaiden under.

"All right, I'm going in."

A series of leads connected to Kaiden's heart, wiring him like a ticking time bomb. First, Xander snipped the signal relay. Someone out in the galaxy held Kaiden's life in their hands, and Xander would be damned if they ended it now. Second, he cut the feed from the electrical current along with its backup supply to be absolutely safe. Xander performed the operation as dictated by the manual until the cardioverter was no longer a threat to Kaiden's life. He dropped the device into the metal tray O'Reilly held.

If he hadn't gotten his hunch about Campbell, saving Kaiden wouldn't have been possible without floundering in the dark. It took less time to close him up than it did to open him. In ten minutes, Bio-sutures and medical grade glue restored him to near-perfect condition. Their patient was none the wiser, but his medical staff only relaxed once they returned him to observation status.

"Do you have that thing cleaned up, O'Reilly?"

"Right here, sir."

The round device looked like any other pacemaker at first glance. They worked off a kinetic power source, converting movement from the beating heart itself to keep their charge. This one had been heavily modified to release a lethal shock.

Xander set it beneath a magnifying scope and brought the display up for everyone to observe. The enhanced image revealed small details the human eye alone would miss. A small series of numbers were etched into a chip on the cardioverter next to a faded pictogram. Oshiro magnified the image further.

"It looks as though they tried to acid wash the serial away."

"Yeah, but they couldn't all the way without compromising the integrity of the chip itself. This logo looks vaguely familiar, too."

Oshiro stepped over and laid his hand on Xander's back. "Go and rest. You will need fresh eyes to solve this, Xander, and you have been running on fumes."

"But—"

"No excuses. Kaiden is safe now. O'Reilly can take this down to Intel and let them research it while I keep an eye on our patient."

Xander sighed. "Take it directly to Lieutenant Shahid, O'Reilly. No one else. Ask her to please find out all she can about it and its manufacturers."

"Will do, sir."

While Kaiden remained in hibernation under Oshiro's watchful eye, Xander retreated to his office and tended to his own needs after pulling up a chair to a small mirror. He removed his scrub top and peered down at the jagged line of staples across the front of his shoulder. Sloppiest work he'd ever done on himself, and he didn't know whether he had Thandie to blame for the distraction, or if his hand had shaken as much as she claimed.

Ethan stepped in and took one look at him. "That looks like shite. Did you let a local monkey stitch you up?"

Xander grunted and continued to pluck the staples from his skin. "It's not that bad. The bloody tosser fired a shatter round at me. It was a piece of armor that punctured my skin—not the bullet." He dropped the final staple into the tray and sagged in his seat. It would heal on its own in a couple days.

"Ah, I see."

The simple words carried more than one meaning. Xander sighed. "What do you want, Ethan? Kaiden is stable, and I'll be back to work as soon as I finish this. I actually planned to call you down once I reviewed the surgical exam."

"You work too hard, but in this instance, I understand. Still, that's not why I've come. I wanted to see if you were serious about this request. A reassessment is a bit dramatic, isn't it?"

Xander paused with his back to his friend. Ethan knew how to read him as well as Oshiro did, and that meant he had to keep it cool. "Are you officially questioning my judgment, Commodore?"

"Maybe. Or perhaps I'm simply trying to get a better handle on what happened."

"I am merely reporting that I have entered into a personal relationship with a marine on my squad. I can't have a member of our team playing favorites, nor can I be accused of doing the same."

"Of course not, but did anyone play favorites today?"

Xander stiffened. "I gave a very clear order to attend to the man we landed to rescue. She ignored it."

"According to Viljoen's report, Thandie is the one who pinned him down after he shot you. Seems like he was well attended." Ethan spread his hands. "Look, Xander, I know how hard onboard relationships can be. Why the hell do you think I avoid entanglements?"

"Yes, and then you behave like a randy, ill-bred canine the moment we disembark from our ship. Not to mention your online behavior."

Ethan grimaced. "As we're having a personal discussion and not an official one, I'll accept that. Anyway, this is about more than avoiding preferential treatment. If it had been anyone else on the team, would you be requesting a transfer?" When he didn't respond, the commodore continued. "Let's say I humored your request. If I put her on the boarding team, are you going to be useful, or are you going to be pacing the medical wards like a caged drake? I refuse to waste her talents in the armory."

"Maybe I've decided to end it and follow my commanding officer's lead, you bloody hypocrite."

"Oh, of course. End it and make the woman cry. Then you'll be in your cot doing the same bloody thing by midnight, you wanker. Once this mission is complete, I'll support whatever you choose... but I want you to know this, Xander: your Eloran is gone, but you've got a fine woman right here who cares as deeply. Don't ruin it. Don't chase her away because you haven't the slightest clue about how to handle a shred of authority. You, most of all, know how much you deserve happiness."

Groaning, Xander ran his fingers through his hair and leaned forward against the table. "I hate when you talk sensibly. Go diddle one of your online playmates and leave me be."

"I'll enjoy some downtime once you and the Lockharts are settled. How is he?"

"I successfully removed the device from his heart, and intel has their hands on it. He burns through sedatives like nothing I've ever seen, though. Lil had to keep a constant stream going to hold him under for the surgery."

"Damn."

"C'mon. I'll take you to him since you're here."

Xander led the way to the patient's room. Kaiden lay upon a hospital bed in a simple gown. His blank, emotionless stare focused on the wall opposite the bed while Gareth sat beside him.

"Gareth?"

The conscious twin scrubbed at his face with the heel of his palm to dry away the moisture on his cheeks. "Oshiro let me in a minute ago after they finished the cleanup. I had to see him in case he wakes up. You know?"

Xander waved him off. "No need to explain, believe me. But would you come into the office with us for a minute? I'd like to review the results of the examination and surgery with you both. I promise, if he shows any sign of waking, we'll come right back."

Once Oshiro joined them, Xander began a video replaying the exploratory surgery and his findings, transforming his office into a macabre picture show.

"Using the intel retrieved from Campbell's system, I managed to locate and disable a kill switch sutured into Kaiden's heart. It can't threaten him now, but it was the least of his troubles. He also has extensive brain modifications. I've never operated on anything this complex in all of my studies. I don't even know how he survived brain wiring to this extent. Hell, I'm still trying to piece together how some of these parts work. All right, look there."

"The amygdala?"

Xander nodded to Oshiro. "Yes. I believe that could be to blame for his bland affect. They installed a chip—"

"Speak English, Doc. Please," Gareth pleaded, cutting in.

"The amygdala is the... you could call it the control center for human emotions," Oshiro explained.

"And many other things," Xander confirmed. "Memory, aggression, our sexual orientation. Everything that makes us a feeling human being resides there."

"So they've done something to Kaiden's... amygdala."

"Yes. Until we can rule out any remote control and

compulsion, we'll have to maintain strict IV sedation, Gareth. I don't like doing it, but it's the only way."

"Will he be... himself again?"

Glancing at the video again, Xander rubbed his chin thoughtfully. "I think so. I can't access the interior braincore software without the override code to the chip. If I try, I run the risk of frying his brain."

Gareth's expression fell and all signs of hope evaporated from his face. "So... you're saying that my brother's going to be a vegetable for the rest of his life because we're missing a bit of code?"

"Far from it. We have the best intelligence agents in the United Empire tracking down information," Ethan assured him.

"Thank you, sir. I just... How are we going to find anything?"

"Tech like this came from somewhere, Gareth. Nisrine has the fail-safe device I removed from Kaiden's heart. She's tracking down all leads on the logo etched into it."

"Thank you, Xander. All of you. I... I couldn't even bear to write home to Mum. I can't tell her about this until I have good news."

"Now you do. Tell her we've found her boy and that the doctors have sworn to do everything in their power to help him recover."

JEM AWAKENED Xander when it seemed he had just laid down to sleep.

"Lieutenant Shahid requests a conference at your earliest convenience to discuss recent findings regarding Kaiden Lockhart."

"How long has it been?"

"Her request came an hour ago, but I determined six hours was insufficient rest and allowed you to remain asleep."

Xander groaned and rolled to his back.

A quick shower and a fresh change of uniform later, he made his way up to the restricted halls where the intelligence and operation departments were housed. Jem provided a dim trail of blinking lights to Xander's destination.

"Please come in." Nisrine smiled when he entered. "Did you get enough rest?"

"A few hours, yeah. Thanks." Xander crossed to the desk and practically collapsed into a chair. "What have you found?"

"The first logo actually led me to Hephaestus Tek. You'll recall them from Athena. The base of the device was their design."

"But this has been modified." He plucked up the small piece of tech from a glass dish.

"Yes. And from that, I picked up images and impressions of its makers."

She swept her hands over the desk to send the other screens away, then manipulated one to a larger size. A gold and black icon dominated the upper left corner, depicting a double helix within an upraised robotic arm. She swiped down and zoomed in on a small picture of a researcher in pristine white scrubs. "This is what I saw. Only they wore tight hoods too, to cover their hair and necks."

"DNAturals." Xander read. "Wait, I recognize the name. They pioneered the nanobot technology for vein restructuring. Like what Sergeant Kruger has equipped in her arm."

"Yes, and they have developed other technology for the UNE, as well."

"Do you think it's an inside job? We know about DuPrie and Campbell, but are there many others above their rank who were working with them? How far could this possibly go?"

"I will not know until I sift through their financial records. If you and Doctor Oshiro are willing, I would appreciate a list of equipment and tools required to maintain such cybernetics. As well as any other unique requirements pertinent to these operations."

"Absolutely. What will you do with it, though?"

"I will attempt to narrow down which facility we should be looking at." She called up another screen. "DNAturals works exclusively from two planets in this system. Their main facility is on Saphiris 5, while they have a secondary research laboratory on Azura."

"Saphiris 5 is on the edge of the system, isn't it? Those are days apart, so if we hit the wrong one, the other will be tipped off."

"Exactly so."

Xander rose from his seat. "Then I'll get you that information within the hour."

"Commander—"

"Xander, remember?"

Nisrine bowed her head. "Xander, there was something else I picked up while handling that. Something that disturbs me."

"What is it?"

"I felt pain. Kaiden was awake, I think, for many of their procedures. *Aware*," she clarified with particular emphasis.

"That's common for a craniotomy. In order to safely

navigate the brain, you need your patient to be able to respond to you."

"Yes, I know, but they did much more. I received the impression they kept Kaiden awake for more than what was necessary."

Xander stiffened. "You mean he felt it. They didn't sedate him?"

"I believe so." She looked away and folded her hands together. "They wanted him awake during the limb replacements. Someone missed a nerve connection during the first surgical procedure, which cost them time and money to correct."

"We never conduct nerve grafts while a patient is awake. It's too painful a procedure."

Disgust twisted his belly into a cold, hard knot, and then an overactive imagination pieced together a detailed portrait of Kaiden's five years in captivity. Pain. Torture. Madness. If some part of him did remain alive beneath their programming, they faced a large chance of discovering he was no longer the man Gareth and Ethan remembered. He would be lucky to have a shred of sanity left.

CHAPTER TWENTY-THREE

With the final hours approaching before their arrival at Azura, Thandie spent a hectic shift in the armory conditioning gear for the team. She was the last to gear up and head out into the hangar.

Most members of the Alpha team had already loaded onto the shuttle. They'd only received orders an hour ago from Commodore Bishop, the man deciding to launch a ground mission investigating a laboratory belonging to DNAturals without authorization from United Command.

Saskia had proven moles could be anywhere, and their mission objective was too important to risk. According to Lieutenant Shahid and the commodore, they only had one chance to get it right. She'd done her part, and now they had to do theirs.

Viljoen cleared his throat from behind her. "Sergeant Kruger, a word."

"Yes, Commander?" She looked up from her pack, tense and ready to accept the next twist life threw at her.

"I heard you're considering a transfer to the boarding

team. Is there anything I can do to convince you to remain with us? It'd suck to see you go."

Word must have traveled fast. All she'd done was ask her direct supervisor about his experiences on the boarding team. "I don't have much of a choice in the matter."

The easygoing smile dropped from his face. "What's going on?"

"Kruger!" Xander barked out from the hangar's entrance.

Thandie's spine stiffened. Viljoen glanced past her shoulder then back down to her apprehensive face. A supportive pat on her arm accompanied a quietly muttered, "Shrug it off." He moved past her toward the shuttle.

"Kruger," Xander called again. "A moment, please."

She turned around to address him. "Commander Vargas, how may I help you, sir?"

Xander wore his scrubs. During the mission briefing, Viljoen told them Doctor Matthews planned to fill in the medic position during the mission, since Xander would be staying behind to care for Kaiden.

"Don't 'sir' me right now, all right? I know you're upset at me for being an ass, and I deserve it."

"This isn't the best time—"

"I know, but I couldn't let you go down there without apologizing."

The tightness in her chest eased. "I'm sorry, too."

Pinched worry lines across Xander's brow smoothed out. "Good. Now then, let me do a quick final check on your arm."

"Of course."

Thandie shrugged off her tactical coat and offered her right arm. He palpated tenderly along the nerves beneath her synthetic skin.

"How's that feel? Any discomfort?" he asked.

Xander's touch was no different than the very first day they'd met in his examination room, covering her skin with goosebumps.

"No. Everything's been tip-top since you fixed my wrist the last time."

Satisfied, he released her cybernetic limb. Her overactive and hopeful imagination felt him caress the back of her hand ever so gently before ending contact. "Give them hell." The conflict showed on his features. Maybe he wouldn't say it, but what she wanted more than anything at that moment was to hear her first name from his lips. Not a title. Not her surname. Thandie. "Take care down there, Thandie."

"Kruger, time to buckle up!" Viljoen called over.

Thandie glanced toward the shuttle and licked her lips, unwilling to part from his company without one kiss. She dared it, standing on tiptoe and slinging her arm around Xander's shoulders without caring who witnessed it. That moment was theirs, a kiss before the mission to remind her of what she had to come back to. His arms circled her waist, and he surrendered to the moment, too, dragging her in tightly against him.

She had to break away first. "I have to report in. Good luck with Kaiden."

Xander grinned and fell back a step. "I'll be waiting for you."

Holding that moment in her heart, Thandie jogged to the shuttle.

"ARE YOU NERVOUS?" Viljoen asked.

"No." Thandie used the shuttle ride to clear her thoughts, knowing the slightest distraction could cause a disaster.

"You'll be fine." Viljoen clapped her shoulder with his heavy hand. "Go in hard on your last mission with us."

"With all due respect, sir, I figured you'd be glad to be rid of me."

Viljoen's mouth curved up in a half-smile. "It wasn't anything personal against you, Kruger."

"It sure seemed personal."

The man sighed and tilted his head back. "I guess in a way, it was. A few years back, when I was still new to being an officer, I had a young kid under me with a brand-new set of arms. Put every quid he'd received with his recruitment bonus toward them. Hell, I still remember the model. The P-69 LeadBuster. Supposedly impervious to every modern-day round."

Thandie winced, envisioning the worst outcome.

"Ran into a hot zone and that was the last we saw of him alive. We were up against a cell of terrorists with armor-shredding rounds." He paused. "Like the one that almost took out Vargas. Stupid, but brave, thing to do."

"The doctor can handle himself," Thandie said while keeping her gaze directed to the rifle sitting across her lap. "So, the kid with the arms. You think he did it because of the upgrades?"

"I think so. Yeah. I've seen a lot of recruits dive into battle thinking their upgrades will win them the fight."

"Well, if it makes you feel better, I didn't ask for mine."

"I know, and for what it's worth, I'm sorry for misjudging you, Kruger."

"I'm not sorry for hitting you in the balls."

"Good. I deserved it and needed to be taken down a peg. Vargas made sure I knew it, too."

Thandie shifted on the cold metal bench. Davis, Abernathy, and Chang occupied the seats in the rear of the shuttle. Their newest addition, Creswell, sat between O'Malley and Jefferson.

"We're entering the planet's atmosphere," their pilot shouted over one shoulder. He flicked a few buttons on the dash above his head and glanced back. His fresh-faced enthusiasm didn't lighten Thandie's spirits, but she made a valiant attempt to put on her brave face. "Requesting permission to land on the shuttleport at DNAturals."

It wasn't the same without Rogers or Lopez. Thandie mourned their respective losses. The former would return to the *Jemison* within a year, after his recovery, physical therapy, and adjustment to his cybernetic leg were complete. Lopez was gone forever.

"Landing rights have been denied, Commander. They're threatening to defend themselves from intrusion."

Viljoen cracked his knuckles. "Good. We can take that as a threat. It's always more fun going in the hard way. Bring us in as close to the building as you can, and we'll jump down. Kruger, you know the drill. Get a gun on that door and cover our drop."

Thandie leaned out the shuttle door with her rifle on her shoulder. One by one, the rest of her team leapt the five-foot drop to the ground. Doctor Matthews landed like a cat, without a sound. The others followed her with less grace. Thandie unclipped her safety line and made the drop last. Her feet hit the pavement with a thud.

They made it within ten yards of the front door when two automated laser rifles rose from stanchions on the property. Abernathy shouldered his heavy gun and fired, reducing one to smoldering bits with a well-placed explosive shell. A bright blue light on the remaining gun indicated it had been armed, and then Viljoen stumbled back from a sniper shot to the chest.

It didn't penetrate his armor.

"Davis, forward shields!"

"Aye, sir." The medic activated her kinetic shield, and all other shots deflected off it like pebbles against glass.

Thandie took aim, released her held breath, and fired. The sniper on the roof jerked once, then fell out of sight. Viljoen gave her a thumbs-up. He darted out from their cover and rushed the final distance to the door. Thandie brought up the rear.

"Masks on, everyone."

Their commander pulled a sphere from his belt and activated the small device. After a silent count to three, he opened the facility's front door and rolled it inside. Trailing wisps of smoke immediately began to leak out. Viljoen waited five more seconds before bursting through the door.

"Get down! Anyone who remains standing after this warning will be put down," Viljoen roared into the smoking office. "Keep your hands where we can see them, arms out in front of you, palms up. Chang and Williams, secure them all."

"On it, sir!"

The squad stormed the room and spread out, while the two marines bound and secured the harmless civilians. They proceeded forward with caution.

"Located a map detailing the fire escape route. Data uploaded to our links," Creswell said. "Building is three floors with two sublevels.

"Which way to the server?"

Creswell tapped a button on his forearm, and a readout

appeared in computer language—beeps, lines, 1's and 0's. "There is a signal inbound to the *Jemison* originating below us, sir."

Davis grunted. "You know, for once, I'd like to find all the bad crap on the top floor. Or in the pretty courtyard."

"Agreed." Viljoen tapped his communicator. "Assault team to *Jemison*. We've breached the building and are requesting backup. We've encountered hostiles in the facility and automated laser turrets on the perimeter."

"Bravo team en route, Commander."

The floor immediately beneath them contained empty equipment labs. Shiny new prosthetic parts lined shelves and racks in neat rows. They cleared each space then took the stairs down to the bottom level.

A lone guard stood watch in front of a door at the end of a long hallway. Viljoen offered him the chance to surrender. He wasted it by raising his firearm and catching a single bullet between his brows.

Davis plucked the fallen gun from the floor before they proceeded into the basement laboratory. Its expansive floor spread for several yards in either direction, filled with sleek, silver, waist-high towers. The impeccable server room housed at least a dozen machines.

"What the hell... Whoa! Whoa!" A man in a white lab coat threw up his arms and stumbled back from a wide desk near the entrance.

"Down on the floor," Thandie ordered, training her gun on the man.

Creswell holstered his weapon and moved to the impressive computer banks. The touch panels lit up beneath his hands. "Ask him for his password."

"You heard the man." Thandie finished patting down

the technician, securing his wrists behind his back. "What's your login?"

"I don't have one, I swear."

"You work here and you don't have codes?"

"Look, I don't have the access codes. I'm just a junior technician. I come down every hour to check the temps."

"Creswell, see if you can get in the system. Matthews, get this egghead out of here."

"I'll take him up with the others." The doctor grabbed the technician up from the floor and pushed him toward the door. He went without any resistance.

"This is gonna take a few," Creswell called over from the terminal.

"Do what you can. I don't want to be here any longer than we need to be," Viljoen said. "The rest of you, secure—"

"*Jemison* to all teams. We have a situation." The commodore's voice came over the comm line with intermittent static.

"What's going on, sir?" Viljoen asked.

"Kaiden is going crazy. They activated some sort of programming, and he hauled ass out of Medical. He knocked Jem offline, hell if I know how, and shorted out our engines. Everything is going to shit but it's worse than anything DuPrie did to us. It's like... we're under a cyberattack," Gareth filled them in. "I'm trying to regain control of the *Jemison*."

Viljoen swore. "Damnit, Creswell, we need to be in that system."

"Almost... Got it!" Creswell shouted. "Holy shit. Gareth, you *are* under cyberattack. I'm in their system now, but the only code originating from here isn't attacking the ship. My best guess? He's hacking Jem by thought."

"But there's gotta be something controlling him," Gareth argued. "We need to find the control signal and sever it. He's going to vent the entire ship if you don't do something! Our sedatives aren't working. Hart and Vargas shot him with over a thousand CCs of the good shit."

Viljoen paced the room anxiously. For the first time since her arrival to the *Jemison*, Thandie saw fear in his eyes.

"Okay... Download in progress. Hot damn, that's a lot of info!" Creswell exclaimed.

"I'm looking through your video link now, Creswell. These are 250 zettabyte servers," Gareth said. "Standard for cyberware corps. It'll take you fifteen minutes to nab that much data on your equipment. We don't have that kind of time."

"Abandon your work on retaking the *Jemison* and join me in this system. If we work together to sever the signal to your brother, the rest will fall in place."

Three tense minutes passed, the two hackers growing increasingly desperate. Creswell's fingers flew over holographic displays and several lines of glowing green and yellow data glittered in the air.

"No good, Lockhart. Signal is rerouting."

"I'm on it. Shit. It moved again."

Thandie's palms grew damp as she listened to the back and forth between the techies. Hacking and computer software were beyond her knowledge, but she understood the stakes if they failed. Her friends, her crewmates—everyone aboard the *Jemison* was in danger. Including Xander. The thought tore her up inside.

"I can't get anywhere close to the command signal," Creswell called over, sweat soaking his blonde hair. No matter what he tried, the screen flashed red. "It's beyond the scope of my ability."

"If you can't shut it down, we won't have any choice but to kill him." Commodore Bishop's grim voice took over the line. Killing Kaiden was the very last thing that any of them wanted.

Gareth became very quiet. At first, it seemed he had left the communications line entirely. "Pull the power. It's a long shot, but it's the only thing left that may work. Knocking out the facility's power will kill the interlink with the satellite. If there's someone there controlling my brother, they may lose access for a brief period while reconnecting to the next signal relay."

"Over here." Leaping up, Creswell moved to a large power generator on the opposite wall. With Abernathy's help, they managed to open the front paneling and began work on the inner lining.

"What if there's a backup?" Viljoen asked into the line.

"Let's hope there isn't," Xander replied. The sound of his voice, strong and even, flooded Thandie with relief.

"Last connection and... got it. Right, let's see what we have here." Creswell pulled the shielding panel off. The inner core glowed with pristine white light. Thandie turned her face aside and squinted. "Damn it all! That's a Valkyrie conduit." Creswell threw the panel aside in frustration. "I don't know how to deactivate one of these without causing some serious damage, lads. We'll be better off blowin' the entire building. It'll save the *Jemison* but lose everything here."

"We need that data for our fellow marine," Thandie said.

Commodore Bishop growled. "There isn't enough time to evacuate the lot of you from the facility, Creswell. Find another way to do it. Lockhart, can you walk him through a safe method for powering down the... whatever the hell he called it. We're on borrowed time. Kaiden depressurized the cargo bay."

"It's a Valkyrie conduit. They're overpriced cubes of white matter," Gareth said. "They become unstable energy when disrupted. The only safe method for powering it down is to hit the deactivation switch. It's going to take half an hour to go cold. Minimum."

Thirty minutes they no longer had at their disposal. Twenty-five minutes after the *Jemison* depressurized and its 447 inhabitants became cold corpses.

"I'm sorry, Gareth."

A single gunshot echoed over the line. The report of a hand cannon silenced the communication link of all chatter.

Viljoen sighed, dropping his head. "Shit."

"Oh no." Fairchild's hands flew over her mouth. Davis moved over and squeezed her shoulder.

Like everyone else in the room, Thandie waited in strained silence, willing the sick sense of dread to go away. They were too late and now a good man was dead. A man who counted on them all.

"Shit! He's not down." The communications link became filled with panicked shouts and cries of warning from Xander and Gareth.

Three successive shots followed. Hart screamed for Ethan to run.

"Take it down, now!" Gareth yelled. The comm line died to static.

Viljoen took aim at the power panel with his gun.

"Are you feckin' crazy?" O'Malley yelled. "You shoot that and you blow us all up!"

"My family is up there!" Abernathy exclaimed. "I

can't... we need to do what we can. I've got a little boy up there, and he's only four. Four bleedin' years old. I'll die before I let anything happen to those people."

"He's right. We have to get that power source out somehow," Viljoen argued. "We knew what we were getting into when we came down here, and the way I see it, none of you have a better idea."

"That's true," Davis agreed. "It's us or the ship. We have civilians. Our fellow service members have their families on the *Jemison* on our residential deck. It has to be us."

Two options loomed before them, losing the ship or giving their own lives. To Thandie, the solution seemed simple. "Commander, tell him I'm sorry. Tell him I love him. So much."

"Tell who—Kruger, what are you doing?" Viljoen tried to snag her by the wrist but Thandie's cybernetic arm was stronger, allowing her to jerk from his hold. She didn't stop to think or reevaluate her plan.

Thandie plunged her right hand into the open power box and closed her fingers around the miniature star. White heat encompassed her fist, but her mechanical strength dislodged the power source from its setting. The optimistic side of her expected to feel no pain, believing it would scorch through the synthetic nerve endings too quickly for her to feel it.

She was wrong.

Her fist combusted and the fire spread, a flash of lightning traveling her synthetic skin and melting the metal skeleton beneath. The remains of her hand resembled an aged candle left in the sun. The acrid odor of cooking flesh and hair filled her nostrils.

It was a hundred times worse than the accident that mangled her flesh and blood arm years ago. An inhuman shriek tore from Thandie's throat, but her uncooperative bionic limb refused to release the conduit.

Somewhere to her right, a marine screamed, "Do something! Get it off her!"

It sounded like Elizabeth, but she couldn't be sure, unable to hear much over the sound of her own agonized wailing.

"No! Get away from her," Creswell shouted. "Everyone down, now!"

The disrupted Valkyrie conduit pulsed, dimming and flashing multiple times. It stuck fast to Thandie's disfigured hand and white exploded before her eyes.

CHAPTER TWENTY-FOUR

Gareth dropped into the chair beside Xander's workstation. "Need to talk?"

Xander shook his head. "I'm fine, mate. Keep your concern for your brother, where it belongs."

"You're also my friend. The funny thing about concern is that it can focus on many different things, aye? Are you worried about Kruger?"

Chuckling quietly, Xander nodded. "A bit. It feels silly to worry when your brother requires 100% of my attention, and yet, here I am, thoroughly distracted."

"I wouldn't want you working on my brother if you were an unfeeling asshole. You're an amazing doctor because you've got your heart and you feel," Gareth said gently.

"Enough about me. How are *you* holding up?"

Gareth gazed at his twin through the observation panel. "It's... weird. Since he returned, I can sense things more clearly. It's not how I felt during our childhood, but... It's like he's almost here again."

"He's in there. Nisrine is certain of it, so you aren't alone, and you're not imagining it. We're going to free him from their control and punish everyone responsible for this."

Gareth nodded. "And Kruger is going to come away from this safely, too. You love her, you know. I can feel it whenever the two of you move beside one another. It's like an arrow straight into my senses. I used to envy you."

"Gareth..."

"You have a good thing here. You know... I thought I'd never want another woman after Tara pulled her bullshit. Used to think that little tart was as good as it gets. Our child dies and she mourns Rosie by sleeping around. Didn't think I'd ever move on. Maybe that's why the only dating I've done happens to be with an anonymous avatar in an online videogame."

"I've seen you with Flidais. Perhaps you're not together in person, but whatever you have is real," Xander cut in.

"Maybe. Maybe I'm using it as a crutch to avoid taking my life forward. Who could say for sure? I don't even know her real name. She could be married, for all I know."

"Have you tried asking?"

"No." Gareth chuckled and rubbed his neck. "My big brother... he'd be laughing at me right this moment. Asking why I'm so afraid. When Rosie died, he burned all of his leave time to get me on my feet again. Had been saving it, but he used it for me. Didn't think twice about it. Doesn't matter what I needed, he was always there for me. All my life." Gareth rubbed his face.

Xander passed him a nearby tissue box. "Sounds like a good brother."

"The best."

"I've got a pair of trays for the two of you from the officer's galley," Kathleen called from the doorway. "Come sit with me and eat. It's lonely out here," she claimed, infusing a hint of light-hearted warmth to her voice.

"Come on. Let's get some food into you before you pass out. You'll be no good to him when I have him awake if you're passed out in the next cot, mate."

Gareth resisted at first, but with Xander's insistence, he left his seat. The human brain required food as fuel to thrive, and as a psychic, Gareth needed a larger quantity than most others. Missing a meal could be the difference between a crippling migraine that landed him in his bunk for a couple of days and staying coherent to help his twin.

Both men settled at the medical station's counter alongside Kathleen. To Xander's left, a floating monitor detailed Kaiden's vitals, assuring he was stable. Two identical trays awaited them, some sort of creamy casserole with a heavy serving of noodles, two palm-sized meatballs, steamed veggies, and slices of cheesecake.

Xander picked at his plate, but Gareth shoveled his meal down like he was creating a new galactic record. "Feel better?" Xander asked, shoving his cheesecake over after watching Gareth scrape the remaining crumbs of his together.

Gareth laughed quietly and dipped his head. "A little, yeah. It's just... I can't lose him again. I want to tell Mum we found him and that he's gonna be all right."

"We're going to do everything we—"

The translucent glass holographically presenting Kaiden's vitals lit up like a holiday display, casting hues of green, red, and yellow from its surface. The numbers changed to indicate his racing heart rhythm and rising blood pressure.

Xander pushed his tray aside and dragged the terminal display closer.

"What's happening?" Gareth demanded.

By appearances alone, Kaiden seemed normal and no different than any other man in his early thirties. He rested peacefully with his eyes closed, but his chest barely moved.

"I don't know. Everything is within normal limits here. Let's have a look then," Xander muttered, glancing through the observation window.

Kaiden bolted to a sitting position and climbed out of the bed, crashing equipment to the floor. Lines snagged and tore from his body, sending a trickle of blood down his medical gown.

"Oh shit!" Gareth stared through the glass. "What the hell's he doing?"

"Jem!" Kathleen cried. "Seal Observation Room One."

The magnetic locks activated and secured Kaiden in the room, but then he beat the door with both fists until he dented the metal.

"Kaiden, stop." Gareth attempted to reason with his brother over the intercom. "You're safe now on the *Jemison*, just like I promised."

Another loud bang on the door was the only reply. Kaiden's stony features never changed.

"I don't think he hears you," Xander said in a low voice. "Look at him."

Kaiden struck the door again, but the barrier held and kept him contained.

They released collective sighs of relief. "Thank God," Kathleen said.

Kaiden crossed to the observation window and thrust

his fist against the glass, his unnerving stare sending chills down Xander's spine.

"Oh shit." If Xander could shatter unbreakable glass, what could a souped-up cyborg do?

The second punch splintered the thick pane's interior layer, creating a network of fine cracks spread out across the buckling glass.

"Jem, evacuate Medical!" Xander's cry sent up the alarm. "Send additional security personnel to Medical!"

The window shattered with the third punch.

"No one here wants to hurt you." Xander raised his hands up, palms out, and placed himself between his patient and the door. They had to keep him from leaving the medical wing.

Kaiden grabbed the doctor and swung him around, launching him halfway across the room and into Kathleen, who crumpled beneath his weight with a startled cry.

"Are you okay?" Xander asked in a groaned breath. Pain registered, sending twinges of agony across his back, but he didn't have the time to acknowledge it and mope on the floor. Fire spread throughout his shoulder and pulsed down his arm. It had to be dislocated.

"I'm fine. But what the hell! I thought you said he was turned off."

"He *was*. Get the tranq gun. Quick!" Needing both arms at full working capacity, he gritted his teeth against the pain then wrenched his arm into the socket again.

Kathleen slammed a case on the desk and unsnapped it to reveal their stash dedicated to hostile patients. He loaded a cartridge into a gun while she did the same. For a noncombatant, her aim was good; the dart sank into the meaty portion of Kaiden's posterior where he lacked metal augmentation.

"Nice shot," Xander commented. His dart nailed the cyborg in the throat.

Nothing happened.

"Bridge to Medical. What the hell is going on down there?" Ethan's voice cut through over the comm system.

"Kaiden Lockhart awakened from his hibernation. He's no longer responding to sedatives," Kathleen reported back.

"Security is on the way and so am I."

"Copy that, sir. We'll follow his movements." Kathleen grabbed two field kits and followed Xander out into the hall. Kaiden strode with purposeful steps ahead of them, making his way unhindered through the ship's corridors.

"Shit, he's getting in the lift." Gareth shoved a hand through his hair. "Jem, can you hold him in there?"

"Negative, Chief Lockhart. He has overridden my lockout commands. Destination: Engineering Deck. I have issued evacuation protocols."

"He can cause all sorts of trouble down there." Gareth muttered.

"Jem, can you slow the lift down?" Kathleen asked. The A.I. provided no response.

Gareth swore.

"What? What now?" Xander asked.

"I don't know what the fuck just happened, but he deactivated her somehow."

A thousand scenarios floated around in Xander's head, none of them good.

They took the lift down to Engineering and stepped out in time to witness the end of Kaidan's brutal assault on a five-man security team. Four guards groaned from the floor. The last man flew over the cyborg's shoulder, slammed mercilessly to the hard deck with a technique that wrenched his shoulder from the socket and snapped the bone. His shock baton rolled uselessly away from his limp fingers.

Oblivious to his pursuers, Kaiden stepped over his victim without batting an eyelash, intent on reaching his destination.

"Mum taught us judo," Gareth said in a rush, "but I've never seen him move that fast before."

"It's the upgrades." Xander said, equally shocked.

"Go on, I'll oversee all of this." Kathleen knelt down to assist the nearest security officer. Xander crouched nearby and retrieved his baton.

The two men trailed Kaiden to the main engine room. He pried the doors open, forcing the magnetic locks apart as if they were nothing more than Velcro. Then he stepped into the abandoned space and set his palms flat against the computer console on the main terminal. His expression remained as impassive now as it had when he first awakened in medical, like a wandering sleepwalker unaware of his actions.

"What's he doing?" Xander asked. He and Gareth remained in the passageway outside.

"Best guess? He's jacking into our propulsion systems. Give me a minute, there should be a panel out here I can hook up to."

They both crouched down in an alcove off the corridor, thirty feet from their target. So far, Kaidan hadn't shown any hostility without provocation. Xander kept an eye on him while Gareth crouched down and hooked his tools into the ship's diagnostic network.

"What the bloody hell is happening on my ship?" Ethan's furious voice echoed down the passageway. Kaidan's head turned, so Xander grabbed his friend and pulled him out of sight.

"I believe he's interfaced with all the *Jemison*'s systems, sir," Gareth answered. Streams of data flowed across the open space above them. To Xander it all looked like gibberish. "Shit. He's burrowed in there like a tick."

"Unacceptable." Ethan scowled and drew his firearm. "We go in there and we get him out."

"If we go in there, he'll attack," Xander argued.

"If we don't go in there, we risk the safety of everyone on this ship." Ethan replied, as grim as Xander had ever seen him. "He's done something to Jem and is mucking about in *my* ship's systems. I want to know why."

"What if we shoot the console? Destroy it?" Xander understood the stakes, and he was certain Ethan didn't want to take extreme measures against Kaiden, but he would if he needed to. As the commanding officer, the ship came first before a single man's life.

"He'll just go to another and you risk causing an explosion in the drive systems. He picked his spot well." Gareth's fingers flew across the holographic interface. "God, he's fast. By the time I manage to block him he's opened two more pathways. He has an advantage over me I can't overcome—he's doing it by *thought*."

Ethan frowned, shook his head, and opened a line to their surface squads. "*Jemison* to all teams. We have a situation."

"What's going on, sir?" Viljoen asked

Ethan gestured for Gareth to pass on the details regarding Kaiden's damage to the ship and systems. While the systems tech worked with the planetside team, Xander fell back a step and lowered his voice.

"This didn't happen until our team went planetside. That means the enemy is afraid, and the ground squad is too close to reaching them. Whoever is controlling Lockhart has to be in that facility."

"I hope you're right about that, Xander. If the team can't end that signal, we'll be left with only one option."

Take out Kaiden, by any means necessary. The unspoken words hung between them.

Gareth pulled up another screen on the panel and Xander shifted aside to grant Ethan more space to oversee what was happening. A gritty image from Creswell's helmet occupied the upper left corner of the feed.

"I'm looking through your video link now, Creswell. These are 250 zettabyte servers. Standard for cyberware corps. It'll take you fifteen minutes to nab that much data on your equipment. We don't have that kind of time."

"Abandon your work on retaking the *Jemison* and join me in this system. If we work together to sever the signal to your brother, the rest will fall in place."

The two techies put their best ideas out and tried several different methods to hack the planetside systems. Most of the jargon between them flew right over Xander's head so he didn't even attempt to make suggestions. Their bleak tones and colorful swears were more than enough to convey their failed attempts.

"If you can't shut it down, we won't have any choice but to kill him," Ethan told the ground team.

"Pull the power," Gareth said after a long moment of silence. He continued, detailing out his idea to Creswell while Xander and Ethan peered down the corridor to see if Kaidan had moved. He remained at the terminal, still as a statue.

"You think that'll be enough to do it?" Ethan asked in a low voice.

"We better hope so," he muttered.

The footage wavered as Creswell moved positions. Xander's throat constricted when he caught a too-brief glance of Thandie in the video while her team discussed shutting down the facility's power, thus severing the signal to whoever controlled their fellow marine.

Another alarm tone blared through the ship.

"No! No, no, no." Gareth slammed his hand against the wall. "Kaiden started the depressurization process in the cargo bay."

They had five minutes before the *Jemison* became a floating tomb.

An entire string of swear words left Ethan's mouth. Over the comms, Xander listened as the team debated blowing the facility. His heart sped. If they blew it, the ground squad wouldn't have the time to clear the building. His last words in the hangar would be the final thing he'd ever said to her—too few, too little. He should have told her he loved her, but hindsight was always a thousand times clearer than the present.

Gareth's face went chalk white as he finished discussing options with Ethan. "The only safe method for powering it down is to hit the deactivation switch. It's going to take half an hour to go cold. Minimum."

Time they didn't have.

Ethan leaned out into the passageway and took aim. "I'm sorry, Gareth."

A second after his somber apology, Ethan squeezed the trigger. The bullet snapped Kaiden's head back, then he tumbled to the deck and lay on the floor.

The first sob from Gareth broke Xander's heart.

"I'm sorry, mate... we did everything we could." Sighing in defeat, he lowered one arm around his friend's shaking shoulders, while Ethan crouched beside the body. Then something tugged at his subconscious. Something wasn't right. Why wasn't there any blood? "Ethan, get away from him!"

A split second later, Kaiden's fist shot up, but Ethan staggered back, narrowly avoiding a blow to his chin. "Shit! He's not down."

Kaiden moved too quickly for Xander's mind to register what happened. A fist hit Ethan's ribs, and then he was airborne. The back of the man's head struck the deck, but he never lost control of his pistol.

"Ethan, no! Get out of there!" Xander called to him.

Ethan fired three more point-blank rounds at Kaiden's chest. One missed outright, the second clipped him in a metal-enhanced rib, but the third entered between the bones into actual biological matter. Despite the blood spilling from the circular bullet wound, Kaiden never uttered a single sound. Nothing changed.

"Take it down now!" Gareth yelled to the surface team before hurling his own body at his brother. Kaidan batted him aside.

Xander activated the shock baton in his hand, igniting a sizzling arc of electrical current at its tip. Against cyborgs with older, unshielded equipment, the baton could be devastating. He wasn't counting on it to knock Kaiden's electrical systems offline, but he did hold on to the hope that it would knock him out, or at least slow him down.

Before he could maneuver into place, Kaiden swung around with a punch aimed for Xander's face. He ducked aside, and touched the live end of his baton to his attacker's elbow, but Kaiden shrugged it off without any reaction.

Kaiden landed a glancing blow across Xander's shoulder, which almost made him lose his grip on the baton. He gritted his teeth, fingers tingling with pins and needles, and drove his weapon against Kaiden's thigh. The cyborg's knee buckled, then an invisible force thrust Kaiden away into the wall where his big body left a person-shaped dent. It had to be Gareth.

"Gareth, catch!" Kathleen called.

Another shock baton arced toward them. Gareth caught it out of the air and lunged back into the fight.

Kaiden avoided one strike after the other, weaving in and out despite Xander and Gareth's joint effort to take him down. They narrowly blocked his attacks with their weapons, but Xander lacked Gareth's agility, balance, and telekinetic ability. Kaiden's fist came dangerously close to splitting open his head until Gareth spun a roundhouse kick that knocked his brother off the mark.

Damn, they were both so quick. Xander had never trained with Gareth before to see him in a combat situation, but it quickly became evident he could have never stood against Kaiden on his own, despite the advantage of his Lexar traits. He rolled his shoulder, glad the minor damage had already mended.

Gareth's baton struck Kaiden in the lower spine. He arched his back but inevitably recovered seconds later to sweep Gareth's feet out from beneath him. With murderous intent, he crouched above his twin and raised Gareth's head by a handful of hair.

Seeing his chance, Xander leapt forward and extended his baton toward the back of Kaiden's head, touching the arcing prongs to the base of his skull.

All of Kaiden's muscles seized then he collapsed. This time, Xander was positive he would remain that way. At least for a little while.

Kathleen beat Xander to the punch, producing a set of medical restraints from her field pack. "See to the big boss. I've got this."

"Good timing, you showing up when you did. Thank you." He clapped Kathleen on her shoulder and moved over to Ethan. "Still breathing?"

Ethan groaned from the floor. "Lockhart, get in the system and shut down what he did or we won't be around to save his life."

"He's already on it." Xander assured him. "Be still, mate. You won't be breathing easily for long if you try to trot back to the bridge with fractured ribs."

"Who's trotting?" Ethan's chuckle swiftly turned into a pained wheeze.

Kathleen kept guard over Kaiden, out of his reach. After everything they'd witnessed, they didn't trust the wrist restraints to slow him down if he regained consciousness.

"Decompression sequence aborted," Gareth relayed. "Communications are up. I'll get Jem back online in a few minutes."

"Are we back in contact with our teams?"

"Not yet, sir. Scanners show there was an explosion in the facility. Looks like it was contained to the lower level."

Xander's fingers stilled against Ethan's chest. A chill crawled down his spine and his pulse quickened, a sudden sense of dread overcoming their recent triumph in subduing Kaiden.

"Hold on," Gareth spoke up suddenly. "Incoming message on the back-up channel." He switched through the frequencies until a familiar voice crackled to life over the static.

"*Jemison*, this is Creswell. Requesting immediate emergency trauma response. I repeat, immediate emergency response."

"Xander, I need you to stay here with Kaiden. Hart, get a full team together now and whatever extra marines you can fit on the shuttle. I'm not losing any more people. Not today."

CHAPTER TWENTY-FIVE

By the graces of adrenaline and stimulants, Xander remained on his feet for over seventeen more hours to provide the care Thandie needed. It wasn't the longest time he'd spent working above her on an operating table, but it was the most desperate. She coded twice during the surgery.

Losing Ylona had been beyond his power. He hadn't been there. He understood and relinquished his guilt the moment the trauma team wheeled Thandie in on the gurney. There'd been nothing he could do for his wife.

But he *could* save Thandie. Her mangled body needed his expertise, and he threw everything he had into resuscitating her, until Death surrendered the fight and decided the tough cyborg had more to do out in the galaxy.

He worked above her to the point of exhaustion, personally applying aerosolized replacement skin after removing damaged tissue. A sense of unnatural focus came over Xander that guided his hands with superhuman dexterity. By the end of it, he could barely tell anyone his name, let alone power-down his surgical laser.

Kathleen had to pry it from his fingers and deactivate the tool herself after he slumped onto a stool beside the operating table. The other doctors had been in and out, swapping as necessary to provide their unique specialty services.

"We will transfer her to a room," Lilibeth assured him gently. "Please. You are in our way." A tiny smile accompanied her words, smoothing away some of the grim mood.

Xander reluctantly stepped into the hallway while the two women applied nanogel and Bio-Tape to Thandie's numerous injuries, the latter a thin membrane designed to promote healing in fresh skin grafts. Oshiro waited for him, open concern etched into his tired features.

"You should shower and rest, Xander. Kathleen and I will take turns sitting with her," Oshiro promised, pressing a small cup of tea into his hands. The fragrant steam wafting upwards was familiar, a family remedy Oshiro had pressed on him a few occasions in his lifetime. He accepted the cup then shuffled down the hall without a word.

He didn't feel like arguing with Oshiro but already planned to clean up and sit with Thandie himself.

Xander washed his face, changed out of his scrubs in the locker room, and then settled behind the desk in his office for only a moment to enjoy the tepid cup of green tea. He was asleep before he set the empty mug on his desk.

He'd been too out of it to realize the damned man knew how to drug him.

Soothing notes from the strings of a cello gradually slithered into Xander's hazy consciousness. A few more minutes passed before the increasing volume pulled him completely from sleep to the dim interior of his office. The automatic desk chair had leaned back and tilted into a perfect incline. Someone had also sprawled a medical warming blanket over his chest. Cozy heat radiated from the double-insulated piece of material.

"The hell?"

"Good morning, Doctor Vargas," Jem greeted him. The office lights gradually brightened to their normal daylight settings.

Xander jerked upright in a panic, only to realize someone would have retrieved him if Thandie had taken a turn for the worse. "What time is it? How long was I out?"

"Ship time is 0216. We allowed you to sleep for eight hours."

Despite the protesting of his back and sore muscles, he rose from the chair and tossed the blanket behind him over its arms. "Status on Thandie Kruger?"

"Sergeant Kruger remains in stable condition. All vitals are within normal limits."

"Status on Daniel Viljoen?"

"Commander Viljoen has been released from medical."

"Did we have any other major injuries from that skirmish?"

"Negative, Doctor. All further injuries were minor and treated by medical technicians."

"What's the status on Kaiden Lockhart?"

Jem's silky voice took on a chilly edge. "Kaiden Lockhart is awake and requesting your presence. Commodore Bishop is with him now."

"I didn't go into his braincore yet."

"Commodore Bishop would not allow Doctor Oshiro to wait until you awakened," Jem informed him. "With the blueprint Lieutenant Creswell obtained from the laboratory, and my assistance, they were able to safely perform an emergency craniotomy to remove the guidance chip without causing further harm."

"How long did that take?"

"Less than one hour. Doctor Oshiro is an accomplished neurosurgeon. Kaiden awakened only an hour ago."

The fine hairs on the back of Xander's neck rose. Did Kaiden recall anything about their frantic efforts to bring him down?

Rested, but still emotionally exhausted, he shrugged into his lab coat and stepped into the hallway. His route took him past Thandie's room, where he peered in at her through the observation window. Floating vitals with large green numbers confirmed Jem's assurances, so he sucked in a relieved breath and watched her for a while.

Once completely satisfied with watching the rhythmic rise and fall of her chest and stabilized vitals, Xander drew up her chart for a quick look. Good. Oshiro kept his promise. Kathleen and Davis were the most recent to enter and leave, maintaining a steady supply of drugs to eliminate Thandie's pain—and also keep her heavily sedated. He reviewed everything else on the chart and estimated another two hours until she awakened.

Someone had set the glass observation panel to Kaiden's new room to *privacy*, transforming the clear glass to an opaque mirrored hue. By habit, Xander knocked first before entering.

"Finally awake, eh? You look a sight better, mate." Ethan offered him a steaming mug of coffee before the door even clicked shut. "By the way, you were drooling in your chair. Thought you should know."

The friendly taunting put Xander at immediate ease and diffused what he expected to be an awkward meeting.

Kaiden ducked his head shyly and focused on his hands, both of which were folded over his lap.

"Kaiden, this man is Doctor Vargas. We've got him to thank for having you back," Gareth said gently.

"Hello, Doctor," Kaiden said in a hoarse whisper. He barely made eye contact. His right hand raised briefly then lowered with a dull slap against his hospital-gown-covered thigh again. "Thank you."

Xander offered his hand. "Call me Xander, please."

Uncertain, Kaiden glanced at his brother first for approval. When Gareth nodded, the older twin shook with him, barely applying pressure.

"It's good to finally see you awake, Kaiden. How are you feeling?"

"Like shit, sir. I... Gareth told me I hurt a lot of people here."

"You hit like a Lexar dreadnought, but I'll live. So will the others that you injured," Ethan said cheerfully. "I assure you, it's nothing I haven't felt before, mate."

Kaiden didn't appear convinced or comforted by their assurances. "I'm guessing you all didn't come here to pat my hand and tell me it's all going to be okay. You have questions and military protocols directing you to hand me over to United Command. I'm not dumb. I know what happens next."

Xander glanced at Ethan. He looked too at ease, his expression too cordial, if he planned anything of the sort.

"The HMS *Bulwark* is en route with an ETA of about seven hours. I'm not going to lie to you, son. They have orders to take you back to Command for treatment," Ethan said.

"Ethan. You know as well as I do that they'll subject

him to weeks of questioning before he receives a bit of treatment," Xander said. "*If* he receives any at all."

"I know, but they think he's a risk," Ethan replied.

"He's dangerous, yes, but that doesn't excuse medical neglect. And turning him over without receiving help is exactly that—neglect."

"What if they lock him away again? Hide him?" Gareth's worry carried over in his voice and pinched features.

"Don't talk about me as if I'm not here," Kaiden spoke up. "I know what they plan to do, Gareth. It's all right."

"Kaiden—" Gareth began, only for his brother to swiftly cut him off.

"The doctor's right. I'm a weapon now, and that's all I'll ever be."

Xander growled. "No. You're more than a weapon. That isn't at all what I meant."

Ethan nodded. "Trust me, son, whatever they intended for you to be, they failed. The very fact that you are sitting here, apologizing and worrying about what happened under their control, proves that."

Growing angrier by the second, Xander slammed one fist into his other palm. "Then we need to protect him. We owe it to one of our own to keep him safe when he needs us."

"Yeah, about that. As I was planning to say before your passionate interruption... I've sort of tossed the rulebook aside and taken some pre-emptive measures to guarantee Kaiden's safety. Until we can ferret out this nonsense, I believe no one is to be trusted."

Xander bit back a sharp retort. "I'm guessing you have a plan. So are you going to clue us in or keep up the suspense?"

"Nisrine submitted an official report to the Royal Archives on Astreya. You know how they like to have everything in triplicate and stored on their tidy shelves." Ethan waved his hand. "The head archivist took it upon himself to personally message and send over a copy to Her Royal Majesty, the Queen. She has requested an audience."

"What?" Gareth's eyes practically bugged out of his head.

"Your brother is getting a royal reception home," Ethan clarified. His wide grin reached smug proportions. "I'd like to see them sweep that away into forgotten obscurity."

"Does the *Bulwark* know that?" Xander asked, floored.

"I imagine they will shortly." Ethan's amused laughter filled the room. "You're not going to the *Bulwark*, Kaiden. The *Jemison* will deliver you to Albion by royal decree."

"I can't believe it." Gareth sank back into his seat again and stared at Ethan in wonder. "Thanks."

"No need to thank me. I'm only doing what's right," Ethan said.

Kaiden's voice dropped to a slight whisper. "Is it going to be... public?"

Ethan's expression softened. "To a point, yes, but I think the queen is a wise enough woman not to make a spectacle out of you. The important thing is that too many people in the upper echelons will be aware of your situation for you to be easily hidden away again. The queen is big on pomp and ceremony, so the media has been notified that a lost hero has been found."

"I'm not a hero," Kaiden quickly spat out.

"You are," Xander gently said. "Thanks to your actions, over two dozen souls were spared from that laboratory. They're alive because of you."

"I don't know how I did it," Kaiden said. "They

routinely drugged me for ease of handling, but that day I was clear-headed for the first time in a long while."

"I think I know why," Xander said. "We also sedated you, but suddenly, all at once, most of the drugs were cleared from your system. Their own tool became their undoing. Perhaps it isn't fully functioning or wasn't properly deactivated in the lab after one of their tests, but it saved you."

"Were you aware at all during your jaunt through the ship?" Ethan asked.

Kaiden dropped his gaze to his lap again. "In a way. Imagine you're in a hovercraft set to autopilot, but you're unable to deactivate the program. It takes you wherever it chooses, and you're merely there, along for the ride."

"Trapped in your own mind." Gareth's voice shook.

"Yes," Kaiden whispered. "I don't know whether it'll help your investigation or not. I remember everything, but what I know may be useless to you."

"Any detail helps," Xander assured him. "No matter how minor it may seem to you."

"Okay. I'll tell you whatever I can before we reach Albion."

"We have a few days, Kaiden." Gareth sighed in relief.

"Your brother's right, mate, there's no need to rush it all out now."

"Doctor Vargas," Jem interrupted. "I thought you would like to be informed that Sergeant Kruger is exhibiting signs of premature awakening."

The coffee mug in his hands slipped and only quick fumbling saved it from shattering against the floor.

"Go, Xander," Ethan told him. "You should be there when she wakes up. Gareth, Kaiden, and I have this."

"Thanks, mate."

CHAPTER TWENTY-SIX

THANDIE AWAKENED TO THE VOICE OF THE MAN SHE loved most, his quiet murmurs the only sound in the room. Raising her eyelids seemed comparable to bench pressing an elephant, and when she did finally open them, a distorted view of the world greeted her, blurred beyond recognition.

Unable to focus, she closed her eyes once more.

"Thandie?"

God, she wanted to see him. It felt like ages had passed since she'd last looked into Xander's gray eyes. Fighting her heavy eyelids, Thandie tried again to bring the room into focus.

"Hey now, don't try to get up just yet." His hand pressed to her left shoulder and nudged her back against the bed, though she didn't even recall trying to sit up. Her desire to remain awake warred with her body's need to continue resting.

Xander's concerned face swam into her view, derailing her desire for more sleep. A strange sense of déjà vu crashed over her, like they'd been in the same position before. "What happened?"

"You almost died. You've been asleep for hours since the surgery. Are you in any pain? How do you feel?"

Surgery. The word penetrated the fog and grounded her back in reality. She remembered unrivaled agony, the scent of burning skin and circuitry, and the deafening bang of a shotgun preceding the blinding light of an explosion. Panic and fear seized her when she recognized the loss of pain.

"My arm. I can't... I can't move my arm." The realization struck her at once, a sobering truth that shook off the final vestiges of the sedative and replaced it with panic. Her pulse quickened on account of the adrenaline fueling her new sense of coherence. It took her back to memories she had tried desperately to forget.

"Thandie, breathe." Xander's cool fingers swept over her brow. Soothing. Familiar. "Your replacement will be ready and waiting for us at the hospital on Albion. I already placed the order with your measurements."

"What did you do to me?"

Xander drew in a deep breath. "We reinforced your ribs after we dug out the scattershot from the round Viljoen fired at your arm. Lil synthesized new tissue for the second and third-degree burns to your anterior torso while I reconstructed your shoulder so you'd be a fit for the new arm. Other minor repairs, mostly cosmetic."

Memories resurfaced of the military doctor on her old vessel, especially his avoidance of her eyes and the way he'd patronized her with a pat on the remaining arm, telling her a cybernetic limb would become her new replacement *one day*. Thandie spoke the misdirecting language of military doctors fluently, and when she read between the lines, it all became clear.

She was hideous—a one-armed freak with a face

covered in burns. The insidious little thought slid through her mind and brought tears to her eyes.

"I want to see it."

"All right," Xander agreed quietly.

He reached up to grasp the holographic screen and redirected it toward her. It was meant for real time video conferencing from the sick bed, but since it wasn't connected to another screen, it merely displayed Thandie's own face back at her. A shiny dressing covered the skin on her right cheek and jaw, fitted perfectly to the shape of her face. Another protective dressing curved down her neck toward her shoulder, where the remnants of Xander's surgical work revealed her bandage-wrapped stump. Due to the nature of her injuries, she wore no hospital gown, only a sheet for modesty and strategic application of gauze.

It wasn't as bad as she expected. The pounding behind her ribs eased, and a full breath filled her lungs. "And the rest?" Her voice cracked.

Xander nodded. He peeled back the bedsheet tucked around her chest, and one by one he drew away the corner of the bandages. A dozen circular scars littered her torso from the waist to her right breast, joined by a crescent incision. "Lilibeth says it shouldn't scar. We applied the aerosol graft in time. How do you feel? Are you in any pain?"

She shook her head. "I barely feel anything. Did we save the ship?"

He smiled and smoothed her hair back from her face. "You're on it right now, sweetheart, and to tell you the truth, I've never been so angry with someone and proud of them at the same time in all my life."

She swallowed back the dry lump in her throat. "Everything was happening so fast but I just knew what I had to do."

"We're all still here because of you, Thandie. Every single person on this ship has you to thank for their lives. And... nearly losing you made me realize there's a lot unsaid between us."

Of all the places she'd expected to talk about their relationship, medical hadn't made the list. She'd envisioned something romantic—candles and moonlight, or even another seaside dinner.

"All I could think about down there was that you were on the ship and about to die. I couldn't let that happen."

Xander sat on the edge of the bed and took her hand. Each sweep of his thumb across her knuckles set off butterflies in her stomach.

"If you had died, I don't know what I would have done. After I lost Ylona, I never expected to find anyone else. Never thought I could experience love again or that I would even want to. Then you showed up in my life and everything has been better."

Her pulse sped up again. Love?

"I should have said so much to you in the hangar—shit, *before* the hangar, on Elora, and maybe even before that. I love you, and it has nothing to do with my genes or what I am. Only a fool *couldn't* fall in love with you, Thandie."

Hot tears welled in her eyes. Her chest felt too small to contain her swelling heart.

"Thandie, please say something."

"I love you, too." The words burst out of her and once she started crying, she couldn't stop. "I don't know when it happened, but it did. You're everything I've always wanted and the thought of losing you terrified me. I didn't know if I'd survive through it, but I knew I had to make sure you lived so you could go on helping people like Kaiden." And then the vague, nebulous sense of familiarity clarified at last and broke through the medical haze. "Like you helped me over two years ago. You were one of the doctors who saved my shoulder."

He squeezed her left hand. "Closer to three years now, I guess. You remember that, huh?"

She nodded. "Your eyes. I always knew I'd seen them before, but it never clicked. Why didn't you ever say anything?"

"Because I knew that was a painful time for you. One you didn't like to talk about."

"My doctor wanted to discharge me from the navy. He said my shoulder couldn't be salvaged for a prosthetic."

"I thought otherwise."

"So this is twice now you've saved me."

"I guess the universe was determined to get us together, one way or another. Which means I won't be letting you go anytime soon."

She reached up and caressed his cheek, staring into his silver eyes. How funny life was, leading her to Xander not once, but twice.

"What's going to happen to me?" Thandie finally managed to ask.

"We're going to keep you in medical until we reach Albion, where you'll get your new arm. After that, I'm not exactly sure." He turned his head to kiss her open palm. "I guess I'll just have to use some leave time to stick around the naval hospital throughout your recovery. I have weeks of it."

"You'd use your leave time for me?"

"There's nowhere else I'd want to be. No one I want more. You're my everything, Thandie, and I'd give you the stars if I could."

ABOUT THE AUTHOR

Vivienne Savage is the pen name of two best friends who write everything together. One works as a nurse in a rural healthcare home in Texas and the other is a U.S. Navy veteran. Both are mothers to two darling boys and two amazing girls.

All of their work varies in steam level, so pop by the VS website for details on which series is right for you!

For more information
www.viviennesavage.com
vivi@viviennesavage.com

Printed in Great Britain
by Amazon